SCARY STORIES WITH B.B. HALLOWEEN COLLECTION

A FULL MINI SERIES COLLECTION BY

BORIS BACIC

TABLE OF CONTENTS

SHORT INTRODUCTION

No introduction! Who reads those anyway?

Start reading and I hope you enjoy my stories!

EMERGENCY BROADCAST

CHAPTER 1

This all started a few hours ago. It was supposed to be my day off and I had already planned to lay around in my house and eat junk food all day long. I hauled a bunch of snacks and drinks to the living room, not feeling even a little bit of regret over the few pounds I was about to put on.

I turned on the TV and jumped on the couch, scrolling through facebook while a movie played in the background on the screen.

It must've been about 5pm when I got bored and decided to stretch my legs a little. When I returned from my excuse for a healthy smoke break, I saw that the movie on the TV was gone and was instead replaced with one of those emergency broadcast screens with colorful rectangles.

A male voice resounded from the TV:

"REPEAT. DO NOT LEAVE YOUR HOMES UNDER ANY CIRCUMSTANCES. THIS IS NOT A DRILL. REPEAT. THIS IS NOT A DRILL."

5 seconds pause.

"ATTENTION CITIZENS. THIS IS AN EMERGENCY BROADCAST. FOR YOUR OWN SAFETY, PLEASE LOCK YOUR DOORS AND WINDOWS IMEDIATELLY AND DO NOT LEAVE YOUR HOME UNDER ANY CIRCUMSTANCES. REPEAT. DO NOT LEAVE YOUR HOME UNDER ANY CIRCUMSTANCES. THIS IS NOT A DRILL. REPEAT. THIS IS NOT A DRILL."

The message kept replaying.

I flicked through some channels, only to be met with static. At first I laughed at the absurdity of the situation. This can't be real, can it? And then it hit me – maybe we were under attack. North Korea or maybe another terrorist attack?

In any case I turned off the TV and decided to lock my doors and shut all the windows, covering them with blinds along the way. Before I did though, I peered out the window, only to be greeted with an empty street and nothing suspicious.

I sat back on my couch and messaged my friend on facebook, asking him if he saw the same broadcast.

He didn't respond though and messenger said he was online 10 minutes ago. As I scrolled through the rest of the feed I saw nothing out of the ordinary on my friends' feeds. I googled the news, looking up my town, but there was nothing.

I started to relax a little, beginning to think this was indeed all either a prank or a technical error. But then I heard something outside.

It sounded like someone cackling, but it only lasted for about a second before it stopped. I held my breath and listened, hearing another cackle in the process, equally short and disturbing.

And then a feminine scream that was suddenly cut off. It was as if whoever was screaming was suddenly muted with a pause button.

I approached the door carefully, looking through the peephole, but I saw nothing out of the ordinary.

And then another very short and barely audible scream.

I decided to go to the window, thinking I might see more. I slowly pulled the blinds aside just enough to see a portion of the street and my heart almost exploded.

Standing right in front of me, with her face to the glass was a woman, staring right at me. Her eyes were bloodshot and open so widely they looked like they would pop out. She was snarling, showing teeth that were stained with dark red liquid and causing the window to fog up every second or so.

Her hair was messy and dirty and her nails caked with dirt.

I screamed and backed away, knocking down my table lamp in the process. I stood there for a while, staring at the blinds, knowing the woman was just behind them, since I could occasionally hear a faint tap and scratch on the glass from her nails.

And then she spoke.

"Open the door! Please! Please! They'll find me!"

I stood there, dumbfounded.

"Please, I know you're in there! Just open the door please!"

I reached for my phone and dialed 911 with trembling hands, but was met with a dead line. I tried a few times, but there was no service.

"Please! Let me in!"

"Let us in!" – a male voice joined the woman at the window.

And then another one at the door. And another and another until my entire house was surrounded by a reverberating cacophony of pleading voices, some desperate sounding, and others impatient and aggressive.

I retreated to the stairs, waiting for them to go away. After what seemed like an eternity, they started shutting up one by one until I was left with a deafening silence I was grateful for. Did they get bored and decided to leave me alone?

I decided to peer out of my peephole to see if it was safe. When I did I barely stopped myself from gasping loudly. Through the peephole, I could see a middle-aged man's face with bloodshot eyes, just standing there, not moving, staring at my door. Around him were more people, just staring blankly at the walls and windows.

I backed away and would approach the door every few minutes since then.

They've been standing in front of my house for five hours now.

I waited. And waited. I foolishly kept glancing outside to see if they had left. It was almost dark and I felt like I was losing my mind.

I even contemplated opening the door, thinking they might not want to harm me. And as a last resort I held my kitchen knife close, so that I can try to fight them off or in the worst case scenario, slit my wrists. Thoughts raced through my head about them breaking in and ripping me apart limb by limb with their bare hands, so I did not want to find out what they planned to do to me and how creative they were.

As I sat there, trying not to make any noise I decided to peer outside one last time. Looking outside I was faced with the same people, standing in the same position, still staring at my house.

But then there was a sound. Something that sounded like three deliberate gunshots a few blocks away.

Almost instantly, the people jerked their heads towards the sound and without any hesitation started sprinting towards the source, some of them screaming along the way or making animalistic sounds.

I thought there may have been like ten or twenty of them surrounding my house, but I was wrong. As I was looking through the peephole to see them leaving, more and more of them just kept running past my house, almost for a whole minute, which made me think for a moment the horde would never end. But eventually all went still and there was no person or sound remaining anywhere in the vicinity of my house.

That's it. I'm safe, I thought. I put my back against the door and breathed a sigh of relief.

And then I heard another voice. I looked back through the peephole and saw someone across the street. A black woman and a middle-aged man were moving cautiously towards my house in a crouched position. The woman had an axe and the man seemed to be carrying a baseball bat.

"Come on, they'll be back soon." – the woman gestured for the man to follow her and they stopped right in front of my house.

"Hey, you there." – she tried to speak quietly, but loud enough for me to hear.

"Hey!" – she knocked on the door – "You need to come with us now. Those lunatics will be back soon."

I clutched the knife harder and held my breath.

"Look, we're not one of them. Now come on, open the door."

"He's not gonna open." – the man shook his head – "Come on, let's go."

Maybe it was the fact that I desperately wanted not to be alone anymore in that moment, but I quickly unlocked the door and opened it slightly.

"Hey." – I called out to them from behind the door, concealing the knife.

"Finally." – the lady said – "Come on, they'll be back soon. We need to evacuate."

"Wait, the broadcast said we should stay inside." – I argued.

"Fuck that. There's no help coming. Now come on or we're leaving to the evac site without you."

I knew there was no time to argue and much less time to prepare supplies to bring before those freaks returned, so I just locked my house and left the keys in the nearby bushes.

"I'm Angela, by the way. And this is Travis." – the lady said – "It should be safe to leave the neighborhood this way."

I introduced myself and asked what was going on.

"Don't know exactly. People just started acting crazy. The town's been quarantined, but there's one checkpoint where we can get out."

"They got soldiers there." – Travis said with his raspy voice – "Should be safe to wait for this to blow over outside town."

"How do you know?" – I asked.

"I don't for sure. But it's our best bet."

"First we gotta find our guy." – Angela said – "He insisted on firing a few shots to distract them and save your ass. He'll meet us at the gas station."

The walk to the gas station was uneventful. The streets were empty, but we did see crashed cars and a few dead bodies from a distance. I had never seen a corpse before, let alone mangled and butchered ones like these, so I tried to look away and not think how these people died.

No crazy people were on the street, though. Or anyone alive, for that matter.

When we got to the station, there was a young man waiting there. He couldn't have been more than 18.

"Ricky, nice work back there." – Angela greeted him – "Here's the guy you were risking your ass for."

"I owe you, man." – I shook his hand and waited for the group to give further instructions.

"Hey Travis, you okay?" – Angela asked him and when I glanced at him, I saw that he was pale.

"Yeah, just tired is all. I'm gonna use the restroom." – he replied and disappeared inside the gas station.

Ricky suggested we scavenge the remaining food in the station so we went inside. The inside of the gas station looked like it was left in a panicked hurry. Some of the items were knocked over, the floor stained with liquid from broken bottles and the majority of the shelves left pillaged.

Ricky assured us he had already scouted the place and that it was safe, but I still felt uneasy, as if one of those people would jump me from around the corner.

I gathered whatever I deemed necessary, like chocolate bars, chips, water and of course, cigs. You never know when you might need them.

I went into the restroom to take a leak when I heard a loud crash from inside.

"Travis, you okay?" – I called out to him.

I heard his voice, but he didn't respond. It sounded like he was having a heated discussion with someone.

"Travis?" – I heard him from inside one of the stalls so I called out his name.

He was whispering loudly, murmurs that I couldn't make out. I carefully approached the stall and stopped, listening to him. I was able to grab only a few phrases in his indistinct chatter, like 'can't get away', 'out, out, out' and 'feed them to'-something.

"Hey, Travis? Are you okay in there?" – I asked and against my better judgment decided to slowly open the door.

Before I even realized what was going on, Travis burst out of the stall and jumped on top of me, knocking me on my back.

I held him back as he thrashed against me. His face was all red and his eyes bloodshot, veins bulging from his neck and forehead so violently that they looked like they would explode in any moment.

"OUTSIDE! NO CONTROL! FIND THE HOST!" – he screamed, the gibberish, his spit flying all over me.

"Get off me!" – I tried to pull him off, but he was too strong.

The door of the bathroom burst open and Angela and Ricky ran in, shouting at Travis to stop it. A few moments of frenetic screaming, shouting and struggling and then Travis went completely limp.

I pushed him off, only then realizing that there was a fire axe embedded in his forehead. His eyes were wide open, still bloodshot and a pool of blood was forming on the floor around his head.

I backed away to the wall, breathing heavily. And as the adrenaline subsided, I started to feel a burning sensation all over my arms. I had deep scratches and spit from Travis all over me.

"Oh no. No no no no." – I stared at the scratches, my hands trembling uncontrollably.

This is it, I thought. All those zombie movies I watched and this is how it ends.

"Dammit, Travis." – I barely heard Angela say while standing over his body.

She and Ricky discussed something, but I was in my own world then.

"Hey, you okay?" – Angela shook me out of my trance.

"He... he infected me." – I said with a trembling voice.

"You're fine." – she responded.

"But the virus? He scratched me and I think I got some of his spit in my mouth and on my wounds."

"This isn't a virus." – Angela shook her head – "It's a parasite. And we all have it inside us."

"Parasite?" – I was still in shock from everything that had just happened – "I thought you said you didn't know what was going on?"

Angela sighed:

"I work for the town's pharmaceutical company as a secretary. When this all started today, I got a message on the company phone from my coworker Daniel. He was very vague, but he told me not to go to work today, that it's not safe in town. He said there's a people-killing parasite which is immune to medication and that we all have it, so we should take antibiotics to suppress its growth. That's all I know."

"What?" – Ricky interjected – "That's crazy!"

"I know how it sounds." – Angela continued – "Look, Daniel is a researcher at the lab, so I'm sure he knows something more than we do and he is not one to exaggerate."

"Where is he now?" – I asked.

"He hasn't responded to any of my messages. For all we know he could already be dead. And the last thing he sent me was that we should evacuate via the bridge. He said army will be there. Our best bet right now is to reach that evac point."

"But if we're all infected, there's no way we can leave town." - I said.

"I know." - Angela responded - "Look, the government is organizing an evacuation for a reason. They might have a cure for this, or at least a temporary solution."

Ricky and I agreed. I asked about finding some guns, but they disagreed, stating it would be suicide. Those freaks were very, very perceptive and firing even a single bullet could swarm hundreds of them on us in a matter of seconds. That meant cars were out of the question, too.

They also told me that they also seem to work as a beehive, cooperating really well with each other and not attacking their own. On top of all that they seemed to retain some form of intelligent thinking, which explained their behavior in front of my house.

By the time we stocked up with food and water it was already dark, but Angela suggested we move now for better cover. The checkpoint was supposedly not far away, so it wouldn't take longer than an hour to reach it. We each took one antibiotic pill which Angela had on her, hoping against hope it would slow down the parasite until we reached the checkpoint.

I expected the town to be filled with screams and other inhuman sounds made by those things... and I was right.

The sounds were distant, but always present all around us. A scream here, a crash there, putting all three of us on edge, carefully taking every step and frantically looking behind and around us.

At one point there was a loud scream right behind us and as we turned around we saw a naked man running one block away and disappearing around the corner. We wait, not sure if he was toying with us. A few seconds later, another scream was heard from the adjacent street where the man had just vanished. The next few seconds were a mixture of two screams, one violent and blood curdling and the other pleading, along with the sound of loud pummeling, until the latter was the only sound that remained.

I wanted to help whoever was in trouble there, but Angela stopped me and silently shook her head.

All three of us just moved on without a single word to each other. As we neared the bridge, the horrid sounds around us slowly started fading away, until the only sound remaining was our own footsteps echoing throughout the street.

After an excruciating hour of sneaking and praying that we don't run into one of those people who would attract others, we finally made it to the bridge. There was a makeshift barricade made from barbed wire and cement bags.

There were dozens of corpses strewn about the road in front of and on the bridge itself, one even slumped across the barricade, making the entire scene look like a war massacre.

We ducked behind a wall and observed the bridge. On the other side of it at the end of the street was a tall wall, which hadn't been there before. I remember asking myself how the fuck they managed to cordon off the entire city so quickly.

"Do you see anybody there?" – Angela asked.

"It looks deserted." – I squinted my eyes, trying to detect any signs of movement across the bridge.

"Army guys must be ahead. Let's check it out." – Ricky said.

"Wait. We have to be careful here." – Angela interjected – "What if there's no checkpoint at all? Or if they mistake us for one of those lunatics?"

"What choice do we have? We're running out of time here. I'll go first. Stay behind me and watch our backs." – Ricky stood up and started towards the bridge before Angela or I could argue any further.

We watched as Ricky jumped over the barricade with great finesse and we followed, carefully stepping around the dead bodies and pools of dried blood. Looking at the corpses made me feel uneasy. There were women and children here, mothers embracing their children in their final moments. Angela mumbled 'oh my god' to herself next to me and said:

"Were all these people trying to evacuate, but didn't make it?"

"I don't know." - I shook my head - "But these people were definitely not the freaks."

I inadvertently started to think about what could have happened here and how these people felt in those last moments. Just as I was about to entertain that morbid thought, Ricky called out to us from across the bridge.

"Uh, guys?" – he was kneeling over one of the dead bodies on the road – "I don't think there's gonna be an evac."

"What do you mean?" – I asked.

He pointed to the body he was inspecting and then stood up, putting his arms on his hips.

"These bodies all have bullet holes in them." – he gestured to us – "I think this was the army's doing."

What happened next was too fast for my brain to process. There was a glint on top of the wall, Angela screaming Ricky's name, a loud bang that echoed through the street and Ricky's head kicking forward from the bullet's impact as he went limp and fell down without a sound, the poor kid probably never even realizing what hit him.

"CONTACT!" – we heard someone yell from the wall as a hail of bullets starting being fired in our direction, barely missing us by a thread.

Angela and I quickly stumbled backwards, running for our lives frantically, while the sound of bullets persisted. We ran for what felt like miles until the gunshots faded and then finally stopped completely. We stopped in the middle of a street, breathing heavily and trying to process what the fuck just happened.

But the silence didn't last for long, because the sound of bullets was quickly replaced with a different, equally ominous one. The screams of the freaks which froze your bones to the marrow, bringing along with them impending doom.

Their death cries were all around us now. And they were drawing closer by the second.

CHAPTER 4

I frantically looked around for some desperate way out of this situation. The screams were so loud now that I expected the freaks to appear from around the corner any second and swarm us.

I noticed a small store with an 'open' sign on the door, so I tried it with all my strength, hoping to god it's unlocked. To my surprise, the door easily gave way, making me stumble headfirst inside.

"Angela, come on!" – I called out to my surviving partner, who seemed to be preoccupied frantically looking around, clutching her axe.

"Angela!" – I yelled again and she snapped her head to me and practically jumped inside.

I shut the door and ducked behind the counter just in time to see a dozen freaks run past us on the street, all screaming along the way and muttering some gibberish, just like Travis did. Angela and I silently stared at each other breathing heavily and probably thinking the same thing - what the fuck just happened?

The gunshots started again, but were very distant this time. The screamers all seemed to be flocking to the sound of gunfire, which was good for us.

A few more minutes passed as we listened to the cacophony of bullets and screaming with an occasional freak running past the store. Eventually, Angela and I started to regain our composure when all the outside noise died down.

"They shot Ricky." – she said, looking down – "They shot him…"

"Listen, we need to keep moving." – I approached her, glancing at the street every couple of seconds – "We're not safe here and evacuation obviously isn't happening. Do you know of any other safe places?"

She thought for a second with her eyes closed, as if she had trouble recalling.

"Uh… the only other place I know is my company." – she finally responded – "It's got pretty good security and… but I don't know how safe it is there now. Other staff members could be infected there."

"It's our only option now. The pharmaceutical company is not far from here, right?"

"Yeah, we should be there in no time. I have an access card." – she seemed to finally snap out of her trance and focus.

"Alright, here's what we do. We go to your company, we wait it out a few days. If it has good security, maybe your coworker Daniel and some other people could be working on a cure, right?"

"I don't know. It's a long shot. They could all be dead or gone by now and the building overrun."

"Look, your coworker is the one who told you this was a parasite and that we can slow it down with antibiotics. He might, just might know something more. And since the government doesn't plan to let us out, we might as well see if we can get treated first and then look for another way out."

"Okay, okay." – she nodded – "Let's go check it out. If there's even the slightest chance of survivors being there, we need to get there. And if it's deserted, we can still stay there for a bit, until we figure our next move out. And if the freaks are there…"

"We'll cross that bridge when we get to it. Right, let's go."

I clutched Travis' baseball bat and peeked outside through the glass door. It looked safe enough, so we slowly exited the store and started making our way to the destination.

"The pharmaceutical company is at an intersection, so we gotta be real careful." – Angela said.

Sure enough, as soon as we exited the alleys and reached the main street, we saw a bunch of freaks scattered on the road, aimlessly walking around between abandoned car and dead bodies. Their footsteps looked unnatural, almost as if they forgot how to walk and were now learning it from scratch. From time to time they would scream, shout some gibberish or even violently cough and retch.

"We can use the garage to get to the entrance." – Angela said and pointed to a security barrier which opened to an underground garage.

Carefully, we descended down, making sure we made as little noise as possible. The outside noises faded once we reached the bottom, which greatly improved our morale.

A lot of the cars over here seemed untouched. Only a couple vehicles were crashed and left like that, so whoever had parked here never had a chance to escape.

We stuck to the walls and it's a good thing too, because soon we heard another discontinued scream. We froze in our tracks, trying to identify where it was coming from, but it was difficult due to the echo and the size of the garage.

Another scream echoed. Have they found us? We waited for what seemed like ages, but nothing happened. I decided to take a peek and realized there was one man in a business suit standing in the middle of the garage.

He was facing away from us, just standing and his head twitching every now and then in an uncontrolled motion.

"The door is right there." – Angela whispered, pointing to the left of the freak.

I thought about sneaking past him and there was a good chance we could have made it, but it was a gamble.

"Give me your axe." – I told her and she hesitantly gave it to me, asking what I was doing.

I looked around again to see if there was anyone else in the garage, but it seemed clear.

"Stay here until I take care of him and if he sees me, don't try to help me. We're both just gonna get killed."

I inhaled deeply and started taking very slow steps toward the freak. I held my breath, afraid that even the slightest noise would alert him.

The freak shrieked and then went silent. He hadn't seen me yet. Step by step, I got closer and as I did, I was able to hear him more clearly. The freak was muttering something between moans and head jerks.

"N-no… can't do it… b-break free…" – he said among other things.

I was only a few feet away from him now. He screamed louder, which made me stop dead in my tracks. My heart was pounding a million miles per hour. This is it, I thought. He's gonna turn around and in a matter of seconds his friends will join in and rip me apart.

But he just went silent again and continued doing what he was doing before. I gripped the axe as tightly as I could, exhaling silently and bracing myself.

Before I could give myself the chance to chicken out, I raised the axe above my head and brought it down with full force. The freak jerked his head in my direction one last time, just in time to see me, but it was too late. The axe connected with his collar bone, bringing him down to his knees, with blood spurting everywhere.

He tried to open his mouth to utter something, but only a soft gasp came out before he fell sideways, his eyes still open as the pool of blood started to form around him.

"Oh shit." – I gasped at the sudden realization of what I had just done.

I felt sick all of a sudden and had I eaten prior to that I would've emptied the contents of my stomach.

I just killed a human being. I stared at the dead body for what seemed like ages, thinking about whether this man had a family and what his name was, until I felt a tap on my shoulder.

"Hey, we gotta go." – Angela reminded me and I nodded, unable to say a word.

She snatched her axe from the dead body and said:

"You had to do it. If you hadn't killed him, you can bet your ass he would've done it to you." - she approached the door and swiped her card on the reader, which made a loud beeping sound.

The sturdy door unlocked. I took one final look at the man in the suit and his empty gaze, before Angela reminded me that we had to go.

"Thank fuck." – she sighed as the door closed behind us – "Let's-"

A male voice suddenly resounded on the loudspeakers:

"Angela, is that you?"

"Daniel?" – she responded, looking around for the source.

A moment of silence and the voice crackled back to life:

"Come on up to the second floor. I have something important to show you."

CHAPTER 5

"Well come on up, it's safe." – the voice repeated – "I'm in the security room."

Angela and I looked at it each other in bewilderment. She led us upstairs to the second floor through the once pristine hallways that were now decorated with knocked over garbage bins, broken vending machines and from what I could see, some staff members.

We rounded the corner and reached the door with the 'SECURITY' sign. Angela was about to open the door, but I stopped her, recalling how they surrounded my house and tried to trick me into letting them in. For all we knew Daniel was already dead, or worse. But before we could consider our next move, the door swung open and in front of us appeared a man in a lab coat, staring us down.

"Took you long enough." – he said in a matter-of-factly tone and went back inside the room.

We followed. Inside were a dozen monitors which were tracking movement via surveillance cameras throughout the building. I noticed movement on some of the feeds from those freaks, walking aimlessly about certain sections of the building and outside. Just like the ones on the street we saw earlier.

Daniel sat in the security guard's chair and faced us. I only then noticed the gun next to him on the desk.

"Dan, I thought you were dead." – Angela said.

"My thought exactly. I heard the army's killing our own, so when I told you to go there..." – he shook his head – "I tried contacting you again to prevent you from going there, but I couldn't reach you. I'm sorry, I should've known."

Angela shrugged after a moment of silence.

"Dan, you said that this was some sort of parasite. Is there a cure for it?" – she asked.

"There's no cure." – he responded with hesitation and my heart dropped – "You can slow it down with antibiotics, but even then it's just a matter of time before the parasite develops resistance. We tried finding a cure, but we failed."

"What is this parasite?" – I asked.

Dan sighed and nodded.

"Ever heard of toxoplasma gondi?" – he asked.

I didn't respond.

"Toxoplasma gondi." – Dan repeated – "A parasite which can only thrive in the intestines of cats. It infects a rat and takes over its mind. It then allows the rat to become easy prey and be eaten by the cat, which ingests the parasite and voila! It lives a happy life. Now, the parasite itself doesn't harm humans. It causes some minor behavioral changes, yes, but people can live with it without ever knowing they have it."

"This wasn't all just an accident, was it?" – Angela and I listened carefully, holding our breaths.

No." – Dan sighed, looking embarrassed - "No it wasn't."

He continued after a short pause.

"The government was highly intrigued by the psychological changes t. gondi caused in humans, so they thought 'what if we could control the parasite and use it to our advantage?'. So they established a fake pharmaceutical company in this town and moved us to conduct the project here. They hired some citizens like Angela to retain the image of a normal company, but behind the scenes we were experimenting with t. gondi."

"But why?" – I asked – "Why use it?"

"Lots of reasons, but the main one was creating an obedient and compliant nation. That was the initial goal, at least. After the initial success of manipulating t. gondi and making sure the behavioral changes it caused in humans would be the ones they desired, the guys in command gave orders to start infecting citizens."

"What?!" – Angela was appalled.

He took off his glasses and rubbed his eyes.

"We administered the parasite via throat swabs and tongue depressors. You probably remember the 'precaution' the town had in order to prevent a possible Ebola outbreak five months ago. All citizens had to complete a mandatory throat culture and were therefore infected without even knowing it. The ones who moved out of the city in the meantime were tracked carefully. They've probably been neutralized or arrested by now."

I thought about all this for a second.

"I never took the throat culture." – I replied.

"How?" – Dan asked.

"I hadn't moved here by then."

"Well, then unless you ingested some feces which contained this specific parasite, you're safe."

I felt a surge of new hope. I felt as if I could run for miles. Dan continued:

"Anyway. Everything was fine at first. Town's crime rates started dropping, more stability in the city and so on. In fact it was going so well that the top guys planned on running another experiment in which they could engineer the parasite into causing different behavioral changes and use it as a weapon of mass destruction."

"But then things got out of hand?" – Angela asked.

"Yes. People started complaining about feeling sick and then there were reports of violent attacks and... well, you know the rest. I've observed some of the infected and apparently what happens is exactly like with the rats. The parasite takes control over the host. I don't know if the host is still aware, but my guess is he is. Probably like some other parasites, the host just can't control his actions."

"So why would the parasite cause this kind of violent behavior?" – I asked.

"My guess is they want full control. They probably control most of the neurons in the host, but not all of them."

My mind went back to all the things I had heard the freaks say since this all began – find the host, no control, out...

"See this?" – Dan pointed to the camera feed on which we saw a freak at the front entrance twitching and holding his head, as if he was in pain – "Whatever human is left in that body is fighting for control, but the parasite is too strong."

He turned back to us:

"After the outbreak, the government announced evac at a few checkpoints in the city, but they changed their plans when they realized the severity of the situation. Our research team was to be extracted in case of an outbreak, but they never showed up, leaving us here to die. All those years working for them and this is how they repay us."

He stood up and paced around. He raised his index finger and continued:

"But the government doesn't know one thing. When they moved their research here, the team was aware of a potential outbreak and the head of the research built a secret exit unbeknownst to his superiors. That's how most of the staff escaped from here. They're outside the city already, no doubt."

"Wait, they got out?" – Angela interrupted.

Daniel reached into his coat pocket and pulled out a key.

"This key was given only to the research team." – he gave it to Angela – "Inside the storage on the 2nd floor basement is a fenced off area which you can open with this key. From there it's a straight shot from the sewers to freedom. The superiors were always told it's a waste dump, so they never suspected anything."

"Wait, what about you?" – she asked.

He smiled vaguely and sat back down.

"There's no escape from what I've done. This is my purgatory. You better go. It's only a matter of time before the government purges the city."

Just then, a loud crash was heard downstairs. All three of us glanced at the camera feed only to see the freaks crashing through the glass doors at the entrance.

"Shit, looks like we're out of time." – Dan said and shoved his gun to Angela.

"Dan..." – Angela started but he raised his hand and silenced her.

"Go!" – he said impatiently – "I'll distract them for you!"

Without hesitation, Angela and I sprinted down the corridor which already had screams reverberating throughout it and called the elevator. We waited, hoping it would arrive before the freaks did and when it finally did, we jumped in and hit the B2 button.

The last thing we heard before the door closed was Dan's voice shouting "OVER HERE YOU INFECTED FUCKS!" and the screams becoming even more violent, if that was even possible.

The sound of their footsteps and screams echoed through the pipes all around the elevator as we descended and we prayed it would not stop before reaching the basement.

The screams grew weaker and a few seconds later, the doors opened and we stood in a dark hallway. Another very loud shriek echoed as one freak came right at us, but before he could reach us, Angela put a bullet in his forehead, silencing him permanently.

We sprinted through the dark basement until we reached a sturdy-looking door. She used the key to open it and ushered me inside the dark, cluttered room which was the storage.

On the other side of the room was a gated fence which led to a dark passage. Angela unlocked it and motioned for me to go first.

I rushed inside and as I did, I heard the sound of door closing and key turning in the hole. I turned around and saw Angela standing behind the gate, a look of defeat on her face.

"Angela, what are you doing?" – I asked.

She shook her head:

"This is the end of the line for me."

"Angela wait, maybe you're okay. We can-"

"I can already feel myself changing." – she cried – "You have to go without me."

I was at a loss for words. I knew she was right, but my brain was looking for an alternate solution. Angela wiped her tears and reached into her pocket, pulling out a picture.

She glanced at it and let out a loud sob. She then handed it to me and upon inspecting, I saw it was a picture of a little girl in a school uniform, smiling widely.

"That's my daughter Helena." – she said – "Her address is on the back. Please, find her and give it to her."

"Angela, come on, you can give it to her yourself once we're out." – the screams in the distance were starting to grow louder again.

She shook her head and sniffled, wiping away her newly formed tears.

"Promise me." – she grabbed my hand through the fence firmly – "Promise me you'll find her."

I nodded and uttered the words with a trembling voice:

"I promise."

"Good. I'm gonna give these bastards a memorable farewell." – she dropped her backpack on the ground and readied her gun.

The screams which we had heard on the upper floors prior to this were now permeating the basement in full force.

"Angela." – I called out to her and she looked back at me.

"Thank you." – I said.

She nodded and disappeared out of the room.

The next few seconds were a mixture of screams and gunshots, until all that remained were just the screams. I closed my eyes and wiped the tears. I barely had the motivation to move, but I knew I had to go. I had to get out and find Helena.

The next few hours were a blur, trudging through smelly water in the sewers with barely navigable corridors until I finally saw the rays of sunlight coming between bars of another fenced gate.

It was unlocked luckily and I stepped outside into a canal filled with mud and probably shit. I heard the whirring of a helicopter and looked above in time to see it fly under the morning sun in the direction of the city.

I glanced back, seeing the city which was now cordoned off by huge walls and military vehicles around it.

They were far away from me though, so I was safe. I pulled out Angela's picture to make sure it was still in my pocket and looked at the back of it. Below the address was Angela's personal message scrawled in a hurry. It said:

Mommy will always be proud of you, even if it means I can't always be there for you. I love you more than anything, baby.

Mom

P.S. Listen to your dad while I'm not around!

I suppressed the tears which I felt welling up in my eyes and put the picture back in my pocket.

I changed my identity after that. News of the outbreak spread quickly and the media showed the death toll, with the names of all the people who had died – including my own. The CBDC explained the incident to the media as 'an unfortunate outbreak of an unknown virus'. They further mentioned that the city had to be completely sterilized and the situation was now under control.

According to the news, there were no survivors.

INFECTED CITY

CHAPTER 1

"We're almost at the LZ!" – the chopper pilot said to us.

"Roger that." – captain Reynolds responded and turned to the rest of us – "Safety off and get ready to go."

All six of us readied our weapons and waited for the chopper to land. When it did, we got out to the grey cloudy skies above and a cacophony of military orders being shouted all around us. I observed the gigantic wall which cordoned off the infected city. It stood there insurmountably, not letting anyone in and more importantly, preventing anyone from getting out.

"Captain Reynolds, follow me." – one of the soldiers said and we went after him to the giant metallic entrance.

A high-ranking elderly officer was shouting at a timid soldier in front of the gate.

"Colonel, they're here." – the soldier who escorted us saluted the colonel, grabbing his attention.

He looked like he hadn't slept in days due to the dark bags under his eyes. The officer nodded at the soldier, dismissing him. He gave Reynolds a stern look:

"You're here early. Were you briefed?" – he asked with a scruffy voice.

"Just the basics." – Reynolds responded calmly – "Our orders are to rescue doctor Kidman, secure his research and escort him out of the city."

The general nodded and took us to a tent which had a map of the city on the table in the middle.

"Kidman was last located at the pharmaceutical company here." – he pointed to a location on the map – "Reports indicate the place was overrun a few days ago when a couple of civilians went inside, but the horde has dispersed since then. You may run into a few stragglers though. If Kidman is dead, secure his research and get out."

"What's the report on survivors?" – Reynolds inquired.

"That's not your concern. Chances are most survivors are already dead and those who aren't are infected with t. gondii. If you encounter any survivors and deem them a threat to the mission, use lethal force. If they are not in the vicinity to become a direct threat, ignore them and move on. Rescuing doctor Kidman and securing his data is the priority."

"With all due respect colonel, but we don't answer to you." – I interjected, somewhat annoyed – "We're not military and the reason we were sent here in the first place was to fix what your guys couldn't."

He jerked his head to me, but seemed unfazed by my statement.

"That's enough, Pierce." – the captain shot me a stern glance and then turned back to the colonel – "What kind of behavior do the people infected with t. gondii exhibit?"

"Ever seen a zombie movie?" – the colonel asked, his gaze still fixated on me before looking back at Reynolds.

"Rabid behavior?" – Bracken, the explosives expert asked.

The colonel nodded.

"Well they basically tend to attack violently, regardless of the disadvantage they might be in. They mostly come in groups though, so be careful not to draw too much attention since they can swarm you. Another thing you need to keep in mind is they tend to show intelligent behavior, so they might try to act human sometimes before actually engaging. That's why we can't risk rescuing survivors." – he looked back at me.

"Understood. Anything else we should know?" – Reynolds asked.

"That's it. We'll keep in touch via radio. Once you find the doc, radio HQ for evac."

"Come on already, we're wasting time, dammit!" – Daniels, the loudmouth of the team shouted.

"Daylight's burning. Alpha, move out." – Reynolds ordered and the colonel gestured to the gate guards to let us through.

One of the two soldiers swiped a card on a reader next to the gate and it started opening slowly, as if to give us enough time to change our minds before it was too late. As soon as it opened by a crack, I was able to see a street littered with mutilated dead bodies and blood stains on the ground.

"Road ahead's infested with those freaks, so you'll have to go around to reach the doc's location." – one of the soldiers said.

Reynolds nodded and walked past the threshold. The rest of us followed. As soon as all six of us were inside, the gate closed behind us. The noises of the military behind us got muffled, but was still audible, giving a false sense of security. None of us looked back, although I'm sure everyone on the team contemplated whether we had just sealed our own fates.

"Weapons ready and keep quiet. That means you, Daniels." – Reynolds said.

"Whatever." – Daniels mumbled under his breath.

"The doc shouldn't be far from here. We can take this route." – Burton, the team scout said.

As we rounded the corner, all noises from outside the city died down, leaving us with deafening silence. The number of corpses on the streets decreased in comparison to the front of the gate, but it was still a gruesome sight for eyes.

"Geez, look at this mess." – Daniels said quietly – "This parasite the government's been experimenting on is quite something, huh?"

"Well let's not stick around to end up like them." – I responded, shooting a glance at a young woman who had her entrails hanging out of her belly – "Let's find the doc and get out."

"What's so special about this doctor?" – Jackson, the team's quietest member asked.

"He's got a cure for all this." – Reynolds said – "If we find him, some of these people can still be saved. And in case the infection spreads he'll be able to stop it."

"Wait, you hear that?" – Lincoln interrupted and the whole team stopped.

There was a distant high-pitched scream, followed by regurgitating sounds.

"Came from over there" – Lincoln pointed to the East.

"Let's turn here just to be sure." – Reynolds pointed to the adjacent street and we followed him.

We walked for a few minutes in silence, listening as the screams intermittently permeated the air all around us, always distant, but close enough to put as on edge.

"Hey, you guys see that?" – Daniels looked across the street into an antique shop with a broken glass.

There was a little girl standing in the shop, staring at us, motionless.

"We gotta help her." – he said, striding towards the girl, ignoring the captain's orders to get back.

We quickly followed trying to stop him, but he was already inside the shop, kneeling in front of the little girl. She stared at him with a blank expression, not responding to whatever he was trying to communicate with her. The rest of us pointed our guns at her as a precaution.

"Whoa whoa, put the guns down." – he turned to us, raising his hand.

"Daniels, move the fuck away from her!" – Reynolds ordered.

"She's just a little girl, captain. She's not gonna do us any ha-"

Before he even finished the sentence, the little girl's blank expression turned into one of pure anger and she lunged at Daniels, knocking him on his back. There were a few seconds of wrestling, Daniels holding her at bay while she flailed her arms and legs, spitting and screaming. Burton used the butt of his weapon to knock the girl out, instantly muting her screams.

"Jesus!" – Daniels shoved her off himself and stood up, backing away.

Burton approached the girl and leaned in to make sure she was unconscious. He then turned back to Daniels and said:

"What the fuck were you thinking?! This is exactly what HQ told us to avoid you moron!"

Everyone stared at Daniels, who held his head down. In retrospect, we should have been a lot more cautious, because the next moment, there was a loud thumping sound and when we all looked at Burton, he had a large glass shard sticking out of his neck. He grabbed at the shard and pulled it out, making blood spurt out of his neck and then fell down, knocking over the few remaining antiques from the shelves. The little girl stood over his body, staring down at him with bemusement. Reynolds fired a few shots at the girl, instantly making her fall limply and then he ran to Burton, who was coughing up blood and gasping for air.

"Burton, stay with me!" – he shouted in panic, pressing down on his bleeding neck.

After just one second his gloves were soaked in Burton's blood and the pool that formed around him on the floor kept growing bigger. Burton stopped coughing and went completely still, his eyes still open in shock. The captain stood there motionless for a while and then stood up and strode to Daniels, grabbing him by the collar and pushing him against the wall. The rest of us were about to intervene when the radio crackled to life and a voice resounded on the other end:

"Alpha, they're onto you! You have a horde inbound from the North!"

Just then, the air was filled with the most horrifying, blood-curdling screams I had ever heard before.

CHAPTER 2

"Let's move!" – Reynolds shouted as the sounds of violent screams that were distant just before drew closer by the second.

We ran outside, leaving Burton's body behind and as soon as we set foot on the street again, the screams became even louder and more rabid. A few people sprinted in our direction, flailing their arms aggressively. They had bloodshot eyes and the same look of pure hatred which the little girl had. Some of them had blood on their clothes and I was certain that it wasn't their own.

We fired a few shots and stopped them in their tracks but just then a big group of them appeared right around the corner. There must have been at least a hundred of them, all sprinting at us with such visible hate in their eyes that I knew they couldn't wait to get their hands on us to rip us apart.

"Move your fucking asses, Alpha!" – Reynolds shouted between shots and we started to retreat down the street.

More of the freaks intercepted our path, so we turned left into an alley and ran for it, shooting the occasional zombie that would be in our way. The horde was right at our heels, which I heard from the snarling and shrieking behind. Some of them were shouting something, but I couldn't make out what they were saying.

"There! Go!" – Bracken pointed to a school at the end of the street and we started sprinting towards it in unison.

The doors were open and we jumped inside. I turned around and fired a few shots at the horde, making a few of them tumble down and the ones behind them stumble over the dead ones and lose balance.

"Close the door! Now!" – I shouted while the others shut the door, holding it as firmly as they could with their backs.

Daniels tossed a metal pipe to them and they barred the door with it, backing away just in time for the horde behind us to bump into the door, making it rattle violently. For a second I thought it would give way at the hinges, so I held my gun at the ready, as did the others. But after a few failed attempts at breaking in, the violent crashing turned to simple banging on the door, after which that stopped completely as well and we were left with only the sound of our heavy breathing. We breathed a sigh of relief, but only for a second.

The sound of something loud crashing to the ground came from the floor above, followed by a set of frantic footsteps echoing from one end to the other and then stopping entirely.

"Alright. Here's what we do." – Reynolds said, pointing his gun at the ominously dark hallway in front of us – "We go to the back entrance of the school. It'll lead us right where we're supposed to go. From there it's a straight shot to the doc."

We nodded in agreement and started moving through the school very slowly. Since most of the windows were barricaded in a hurry, it was pretty dark even with the light coming in through the cracks and we had to turn our lights on to navigate the hallway. It quickly became apparent that the school teachers and students tried to hide inside, but didn't make it. The hallway and classrooms had dozens of corpses in them, teenage students and school staff alike, all killed brutally, some massacred beyond recognition. As we passed by one of the classrooms, we saw through the open door a student inside, sitting at his desk, clutching patches of the hair on his head so tightly it looked like he would rip them off, rocking back and forth, mumbling something. We snuck past him as quietly as we could, keeping an eye on him along the way.

"Dammit, hallway's blocked." – Reynolds remarked when we reached a bunch of chairs and tables stacked up highly, blocking us from going through.

The exit was right there beyond the barricade, too. Double doors barred with a metal pipe, just like we did at the entrance.

"There's a staircase on the other side." – Bracken pointed beyond the barricade – "We can probably use the stairs from the second floor to reach the exit."

We agreed and turned back to look for the stairs. When we passed by the classroom from earlier, the student was gone. I didn't want to peek inside and risk being seen, so we just decided to use extra caution. After a couple of grueling minutes of walking through the dark, corpse-infested corridors we reached the stairwell which led to the second floor.

Just as we got to the bottom of the stairs, there was a sound of something heavy being dragged across the ground on the floor above, followed by a barely audible grunt.

"Eyes open." – Reynolds ordered and took point, climbing the stairs slowly.

The second floor was even darker than the first one, with no visible light coming from any cracks between barricaded windows. There were almost no corpses there either, just a few blood stains here and there, knocked over lockers, etc. I wasn't sure if I should be alarmed or relieved at the lack of dead bodies. As we proceeded, another set of footsteps resounded somewhere in the distance behind us. We quickly turned around but no one was there. Then another one from the direction we were just facing before. We turned just in time for our beams of flashlights to catch a figure disappear behind the corner.

We held our breaths, trying to detect the faintest noise. Reynolds gestured for me to watch the team's six, so I moved to the back and pointed the gun into the corridor behind us. As we started moving slowly, I walked backwards while keeping an eye on anything that could surprise us. Slowly but steadily, the staircase we had ascended upon was moving further out of my view and we were close to the other set of stairs which would take us down to the exit. And then I heard a voice in the distance. It sounded like someone pleading or crying. I stopped to focus on it. It wasn't far away, coming maybe from the classroom on the right.

Looking back now, I know I should've ignored it, but my conscience couldn't shake the feeling that it might be someone innocent in distress. I slowly inched closer, trying to decipher what the sound was. I opened the classroom door and it became a lot clearer then. It was definitely a female voice pleading, but also faintly banging and scratching on the door at the back of the classroom. I couldn't make out any words aside from 'please', though.

I felt myself moving inevitably towards the noise, each step making the voice clearer. The woman kept repeating phrases like 'please', 'I'm locked in here' and 'I need help'. As I reached the front of the door, in addition to the meager banging and scratching I could see the door rattling slightly. I stood there for what felt like an eternity before finally grabbing the doorknob, ever so slowly. As soon as I did, all sounds from the other end stopped, as did the rattling itself. I braced myself to unlock the door and then...

I felt a hand on my shoulder. I turned around quickly, pointing my gun at Lincoln, who simply shook his head and said:

"Don't."

I looked back at the door and then nodded to Lincoln. As we started towards the exit, the pleading and banging started again, this time more hysterical than last time. We ignored it and went to catch up with the team. We saw them at the end of the hallway, pointing guns around corner, not moving and as Lincoln and I turned there, we froze as well.

In the hallway in front of the stairs stood dozens of infected people. They all faced in our direction motionless, but had their heads down and eyes closed. It looked like they were sleeping while standing. It was surreal, as if someone had just unplugged their batteries. They didn't even react to the flashlight beams. Reynolds slowly approached the one in front and bent down, cautiously shining the light directly into his face.

"Captain, what are you doing?" – Bracken asked.

"They're unresponsive. I think we can get past them." – Reynolds whispered, straightening his back and lowering his gun.

"You willing to bet your life on it?" – Bracken replied.

"Come on, follow me." – Reynolds ignored him and squeezed his way between the freaks. The rest of us shot each other a suspicious glance and then followed the captain. We moved slowly between the freaks, doing our best not to touch them, carefully observing each one we passed by. After a minute or so of grueling maneuvering, not knowing if any of them would attack us at any moment, we were in the clear and the staircase was in front of us.

"Holy fuck." – Lincoln said coming out last from between them – "That was intense."

He was barely able to finish that sentence before the next thing that happened. All freaks in the hallway suddenly lifted their heads in unison.

"Lincoln, run!" – I shouted and we opened fire, but it was too late.

Lincoln was swarmed by them and they were biting, scratching and mauling him. We tried to get them off him, but they were coming at us as well. Lincoln's screams were drowned out by the shrieks of those lunatics pretty soon and we found ourselves running down the stairs with rabid voices at our heels once again. When we reached the first floor, Bracken removed the pipe from the door and kicked it open, allowing us to get inside the school gym. There was a door at the far end and we ran to it, out footsteps echoing throughout the whole room and the screams following closely behind.

"We can't let them follow us!" – Reynolds shouted and faced the incoming horde.

He started to unload into those fuckers and we followed his lead, mowing them down one after another. There were dozens of them, but we managed to put enough distance between ourselves and them to shoot them all down before they got close.

Even when only a few of them remained, they ran right at us, never retreating. The gym that was pristine and untarnished when we walked in a minute ago was now littered with countless dead zombies. Reynolds reloaded his gun, visibly tired and furious. Beads of sweat were hanging from his temples and he stared at the pile of dead bodies in disgust.

"Dammit. Poor Linc." – Daniels shook his head.

"Let's move on." – the captain coldly said and turned to the door – "The doc's close now."

CHAPTER 3

The air outside felt welcoming, despite the smell of rot and death in it. We barred the school door behind us to prevent any stragglers from ambushing us. When we returned to the street, the coast seemed clear. There were dead people everywhere, crashed signs, cars and broken objects, but nothing was moving.

"Alpha, give me a sit-rep." – the radio voice resounded.

"HQ, this is captain Reynolds. We lost two men, but we're close to the target location."

"Copy that. From what we can tell here, nothing's moving near the pharma company, but you can expect some resistance inside."

"Roger that. Alright people, let's move it." – Reynolds ordered, stepping up his pace.

When we rounded the corner, Reynolds pointed to a big building near the intersection. He said:

"That's our target. We need to be quiet, so get your knives out and in case we're overwhelmed, open fire."

The building's entrance was completely obliterated. Glass shards which were once part of the entrance door littered the floor of both the interior and exterior of the company. As soon as we stepped on the glass and made a crunching sound, a very short, but violent gasp was heard from the inside. Then, frantic, uneven footsteps that got louder by the second until one lady showed up in front of us. She had blood around her mouth and bloodshot eyes.

She stared at us, snarling and hissing. Her head twitched and I wondered if the person she was before was still aware of anything or the parasite took over control completely. Reynolds stepped forward, clutching the handle of his knife firmly.

"Come on, gorgeous." – he taunted the lady.

That was more than enough for her. She screamed and ran to the captain, but he stopped her by grabbing her by the neck. She flailed her arms, trying to reach him, still having a bloodthirsty expression on her face. Reynolds held her like that for a few seconds and then with a swift move stuck the knife into the woman's eye. She immediately went limp and fell to the floor. The rest of us secured all other entrances and waited to see if the woman's screams attracted more of them. No one came, so we were safe for the time being. Reynolds picked up his knife and used the radio:

"HQ, we're in."

"Doctor Kidman and his research should be in the lab on the 4th floor." – HQ responded.

We proceeded through the ransacked facility. It was surprisingly empty. A few dead scientists here and there, garbage bins and vending machines knocked over, but nothing else in particular. When we finally reached the 4th floor, we followed the signs to the lab section. The laboratory had glass walls, which I assumed were heavy-duty and not easily breakable. The inside of the lab itself looked like a mess, with various broken vials and spilled liquids on the floor. From what I could tell, no one was inside. There was a vending machine on the inside leaning against the door as a barricade.

"Anybody see anything?" – Reynolds asked.

"Nothing." – I said – "The doc could've left by now. Or died."

"Let's check the lab. Daniels."- Reynolds gestured to the team member.

Daniels slid the door aside with his free hand and carefully pushed the vending machine to stand upwards.

"Weapons out." – Reynolds commanded, sheathing his knife.

We did so and went inside, scanning the room.

"Doctor Kidman?" – Reynolds called out with his gun raised – "We're here to rescue you. Are you here?"

A few seconds of pause ensued. Then, out of a corner a person in a lab coat jumped out, rushing with scissors in hands at Reynolds, who was turned away. Just as he was about to stab the captain, I opened fire on the attacker, knocking him backwards on the floor.

"HOLD YOUR FIRE!" – Reynolds shouted.

He looked at the attacker, who was holding his bleeding wound, writhing on the floor.

"Goddammit, Pierce! We needed him alive!" – Reynolds got in my face.

"Nice seeing you again, captain." – the attacker spoke in pain, scooting away and leaning against the nearby wall – "The government sent you to salvage what they fucked up?"

"Captain, you know him?" – I asked.

Reynolds turned to the doc.

"Kidman. I was hoping you'd be more reasonable." – he said – "Give us what we came for and we'll provide you with first aid."

The doctor chuckled, but his expression quickly turned into agony. He said:

"You know as well as me I'm a dead man. And there's no way I'll cooperate with those fuckers. I won't let them have the sample. Or my research."

"Captain, what's he talking about?" – Bracken asked.

The captain didn't respond. To this, the doctor let out a short laughter and said:

"Oh, you poor bastards. They didn't even tell you."

"Tell us what?" – I asked impatiently.

"You're not here to rescue me or to find a cure." – he responded – "Your real objective was to secure a sample of t. gondii and steal my research so that the government can continue to weaponize the parasite."

"Shut up!" – Reynolds yelled at Kidman.

The doctor continued:

"But you're too late. I already destroyed everything... research... samples... all gone..."

"You destroyed them?" – Reynolds was furious.

The doc chuckled painfully again:

"Look around you... this is the future that the government wants for the entire nation... they're not interested in a cure. And why would they be? The whole purpose of the parasite is to control the people... it's too valuable for them to just let it go..."

"Is this true, captain?" – I asked.

Reynolds kept quiet, to which the doctor laughed again. He started wheezing loudly.

"Just like me... you were used..." – he said before closing his eyes and sliding sideways on the wall, going completely limp.

"Captain!" – I called out again.

"We have our orders." – Reynolds responded – "What the government does with this is for the greater good of the nation."

"Greater good?! Have you not seen the thousands of innocent dead people by now?! Women, children?! How is this for the greater good, captain?!"

"I won't argue with you, Pierce. You can follow your orders or you can die here. Your choice."

By this moment, white hot rage was boiling inside me and I simply pointed my gun at the captain, which he did right back at me.

"I can't allow you to do this captain." – I said, my hands shaking.

"I'm warning you Pierce, stand down." – he said, looking impatient, but in control of emotions.

We had a stare off for what felt like hours. I expected the captain to simply shoot me, since to him the mission always came first. I had completely even forgotten about my team mates. And then another gun was pointed to the side of Reynold's head.

"Drop the weapon, captain." – Bracken said.

Daniels went to the other side and pointed his own weapon. Reynolds eyed each of us, as if he was weighing his options.

"Don't do this, captain." – I said when I saw the indecisiveness in his eyes.

He stared at me, his weapon gripped harder than before, veins bulging on his temple. And then he just lowered the gun, allowing Bracken to confiscate his gun. Just then, the radio crackled to life.

"Alpha, what's going on over there?"

Reynolds stared at me coldly and said:

"If we don't secure the sample, there's no evac. Let's find a sample and go home."

"Alpha, respond." – HQ said again.

I ripped the radio away from Reynolds and threw it on the ground, stomping on it.

"You stupid motherfucker." – Reynolds shook his head.

"Face the wall over there." – I gestured with my gun.

"Are you joking?"

"Face the fucking wall!" – I shouted.

Reynolds obeyed, placing his hands on the opposite wall.

"Daniels, cuff him." – I said.

Daniels cuffed Reynolds to the radiator and stepped back.

"You're making a big mistake!" – the captain jerked his cuffed hand effortlessly, making a clanking metallic sound – "There's no way out of the city you dumb fucks!"

"When we're out, we'll radio HQ to rescue you." – I said – "We'll leave you with enough food and water until then."

We dragged the vending machine close enough to him so that he can reach it with his free hand. The remaining three of us turned around, ready to leave.

"Don't leave me here, you sons of bitches!" – Reynolds scoffed – "I'll find you and I'll kill you all! You hear me?! I'LL KILL YOU!"

We ignored him and waltzed out of the building while his cursing and yelling followed behind. When we were finally out, rain had started.

"So what the fuck do we do now?" – Bracken asked, stepping into the rain and turning to us.

"There's gotta be a way out somewhere. A place they're not observing." – I responded, not believing my own words.

Just then, a voice came over the radio. But it wasn't HQ.

CHAPTER 4

"This is Adrian Taylors. I'm in the clock tower and I have survivors with me. We'll be leaving the city in four hours. If anyone's alive out there, get to the tower ASAP. Repeat. We'll be leaving in a few hours. After that, you're on your own." – we listened to the voice over the radio carefully, hanging on every word.

"Well goddamn. This couldn't have come at a better fucking time." – Daniels grinned.

"Hold on, this could be a trap." – Bracken shook his head.

"Well trap or not, we really have no choice right now." – I told them and leaned in to my radio – "Adrian, do you copy?"

No response.

"Adrian. Do you copy?" – I repeated.

"Maybe it's a one-way radio." – Daniels shrugged.

"Well either way, let's go and check it out." – I said – "It's either that or we die in the city. HQ won't help us."

The drizzle outside quickly turned into a downpour, which worked to our advantage, since we could move faster without alerting the infected to our presence. The clock tower was on the other side of town, so we had a long way to go. Night fell soon and the rain showed no signs of subsiding, but we pushed on. There were a few stragglers here and there, but they were either wandering the streets aimlessly or just standing and twitching. We were able to get past them without being noticed, so the only problem we encountered up until then was when we reached the main street leading to the clock tower.

We were on an elevation above the street and were able to overlook our path to the tower. The clock tower rose high from the distance, its giant handles stopped on 9 hours and 25 minutes. The road between us and the tower was littered with hundreds of zombies just standing there, with no particular reason. The radio resounded again:

"This is Adrian. We're at the clock tower and will be leaving in 3 hours. If anyone's alive out there, try to make it here before then. After that, you're own your own."

"Adrian, do you copy?" – I tried again, but no response.

"We need to go around these guys." – Daniels said – "What's the best route to take?"

"Let's slide down this hill and then we can take a detour." – Bracken responded.

I observed the slope in front of us. It looked a little risky, but doable. The bottom had a muddy pond, so the landing looked safe. I nodded. Without any hesitation, Bracken stood up and approached the muddy slope. With careful footing, he started to slide down. Daniels and I watched as Bracken balanced himself perfectly all the way down until reaching the bottom, falling waist-deep into the pond of mud. He then gestured for us to follow.

"You go first." – I told Daniels and he slid down a little less graciously than Bracken, but still reached the bottom safely.

It was then my turn. I took position on the slippery slope and slid down, gaining speed as I went further down. Then I fell into the muddy pond, managing not to dive under.

"Alright, let's-" – I started and then stopped.

I felt something grip my boot in the pond and before I even had a chance to shake it off, a figure jumped out of the mud, and tackled me, causing the both of us to fall into the mud. Before we dove under I saw a hairless face with an open mouth and bloodshot eyes trying to produce a dry screech. I felt the dirty water filling my mouth and bony fingers being wrapped around my throat. And then just as quickly as the fingers grabbed me, they went loose and I jolted up, spitting mud. I wiped my eyes just in time to see Bracken pulling his knife out of the skull of the assailant.

"Move, Pierce!" – he yanked me up, wiping the mud off his own face.

Daniels was already across the street behind a house, out of sight of the horde and waving for us to get our asses there right away. We looked at the horde and saw one zombie staring suspiciously in our direction, so we bolted out of the mud and joined Daniels. The zombie approached the pond of mud we were in just before, sniffed, hissed, looked around and then turned and left. I spit the remaining mud which was in my mouth and cursed.

"That was too damn close." – Bracken scoffed.

We took a detour, which was relatively safe, save from a handful of freaks here and there which we managed to sneak past. In about 20 minutes or so, we had finally emerged from an alleyway and reached the clock tower. There was a massive wooden door at the bottom, with a couple of zombies walking around. The three of us split up and took care of the zombies with knives before they could hear or see us.

I knocked on the door loudly. No response. I knocked again.

"Hey, we heard your broadcast!" – Daniels shouted – "We're just looking for a way out!"

We waited some more, with only the sound of rain accompanying us. And then the sound of the door unlocking came from the other side. The door opened a crack and a teenager stood there, timidly observing us behind the door.

"Hey." – I said softly – "We're not gonna hurt you. We heard your broadcast. We're looking for a way out."

He didn't respond, but instead looked at my teammates.

"We're not government." – I said, suddenly realizing armed soldiers didn't really make a good first impression.

The boy hesitated for a few seconds before swinging the door wide open and motioning for us with his head to come inside.

"Alright, alright. Get on." - he shut the door, muffling the rain outside.

The place inside was ransacked and the salvaged items were used for a barricade on the windows. Inside were two more teenagers, boy and girl.

"I'm Adrian." – the boy who let us in introduced himself – "This is Clara and Tom. Hey, can you put those guns down? You're making me real nervous."

"Adrian, we heard you over the radio. You said that you were leaving the city. You know the borders are guarded, right?" – Bracken said.

"We do." – Clara nodded – "Adrian has a friend who's gonna pick us up with a chopper."

"Chopper?" – Daniels frowned – "That's a rich friend you got there."

"Guess you could say that." – Adrian said – "We need to be on the rooftop of a nearby building soon. Having connections is pretty useful, huh?"

"The city's surrounded by military. The chopper won't be able to enter the city. Not to mention getting out." – I shook my head.

"My guy IS the military. Relax, all's good. We'll be out of here in no time." – Adrian smiled.

I sighed, suspicious of the whole situation. How is it that a guy who's no older than 18 had connections with someone who pilots a chopper in the army and is able to get them out of a quarantine zone? But I decided to go along, since we had no other choice right now.

"So how long until your guy gets here?" – Bracken sat on a nearby bench.

"He'll radio us when he's close. Shouldn't be long now." – Adrian responded.

We spent the next couple of hours waiting, talking to each other and trying to make the time go by faster. I contemplated everything we had been through so far and wondered what captain Reynolds was doing at this moment and if he was still handcuffed in the pharma company.

And then suddenly a voice came over the radio, jolting me back to reality:

"Adrian, you there?" – the voice said.

Adrian rushed to the radio and picked it up:

"Yeah, still here. You coming?"

"Yeah. Be there in a few. Get to the landing zone."

"Let's go." – I stood up and went to the door.

"You guys stay behind us." – Daniels said to the teens.

I opened the door and we went out. The rain almost completely stopped.

"Over there." – Tom pointed to a building across the street.

We climbed the fire escape and made it to the rooftop and soon we heard the whirring of a helicopter in the distance. In a matter of minutes the bird was above us and it slowly landed on the building, making all papers and other trash on the roof scatter. The pilot turned off the engine and the chopper doors opened.

Then, all of a sudden, a group of soldiers emerged, pointing their guns at us:

"DROP YOUR WEAPONS! ON THE GROUND, NOW!" - they shouted commands at us and before we could explain anything we were forced on our knees and our guns confiscated.

"So you actually got 'em, Adrian. Nice work." – one of the soldiers chuckled and I was confused.

"Hey, what's going on Adrian?" – I asked, but the soldier shut me up.

Just then, another soldier stepped out of the chopper, stretching his back and cracking his neck.

It was captain Reynolds.

"Captain?" – Daniels tried to stand up, but was knocked back down by a soldier

"Surprise, assholes." – he said, focusing on me – "Told you I'd find you."

Adrian interjected:

"Listen, this little family reunion is nice, but let's talk business. We upheld our end of the deal. Now it's your turn. Pay up."

"Yeah. Yeah, sure. Men, give them their reward." – Reynolds responded.

The soldiers raised their guns and opened fire. There was a loud scream and a 'please god no' before it was silenced forever.

"Fuckin' brats."- Reynolds shook his head and continued – "Thought you'd just leave me behind and abandon the mission, huh? Well no matter, we managed to secure one sample the doc didn't destroy, so the mission is accomplished. But we can't just let you go home, no no. Not after what you pulled at the pharma company. So, now, let's see which one of you pricks will be lucky. If it were up to me, I'd kill you all right here. But HQ has other plans."

He pulled out a device that looked like a scanner and pointed it at me, pressing a button on it. It started producing a synchronized beeping sound.

"This device will tell us if any of you are infected."

He held the device trained on me for what seemed like forever and my heart felt like it would jump out of my chest in anticipation of what was going to happen. And then the scanner started to beep violently and a red light on the front started glowing. Reynolds lowered it and smiled.

"Well then." – he said – "Looks like we got ourselves an infected one."

I stared at the captain in disbelief. I'm infected? How? How did I contract the parasite?

"No that can't be right." – I shook my head – "I'm not infected."

"Well, let's check it again then." – Reynolds pointed the scanning device at me again and pressed the button.

The beeping started and after just a few seconds the red light turned on and the beeping became even more violent.

"Nope, still infected." – Reynolds shrugged.

He approached Bracken and scanned him. Just like with me, the device turned red.

"Shit!" – Bracken cursed.

Reynolds approached Daniels and scanned him as well. After a few seconds of beeping, the light turned green and the beeping stopped.

"Well, lucky you, Daniels." – Reynolds said – "You never did like to get your hands dirty, did you?"

Daniels sighed in relief and then glanced at us with a look of guilt on his face. Before I could fully comprehend what he was thinking, Reynolds pulled his gun out and blew Daniels' brains out.

"No!" – Bracken tried to stand up, but was knocked down and beaten by the soldiers.

Reynolds knelt down in front of me:

"You guys are the lucky ones. You get to go home alive."

He stood up and gave a command to one of the soldiers, entering the helicopter. One of the armed men approached me and swung his gun. Everything went black after that.

After god knows how long, I woke up in a brightly lit room. I adjusted to the light and observed my surroundings. I was in white clothes that resembled that of hospital patients' gown and was located in a tiny room with a bed, sink and toilet inside. In front of me was a huge pane of glass with a door in the center and on the other side pristine white walls and a perfectly clean ceiling and floor. An exit door was on the other side, as white as the walls, barely distinguishable from the walls. The glass was blocking me from exiting and I started to understand in my half-conscious mind that I was a prisoner here.

"Hey. Hey!" – I shouted and then started to ram the glass door with my shoulder.

After about ten rams, I saw that there wasn't a single mark there and my shoulder was throbbing. I shouted some more, knocking on the glass, but there was no response from anyone. I sat down, defeated and thought about everything.

The last thing I remembered was me being scanned for infection, Daniels being killed by the captain and me getting knocked out. How the hell did I get infected? Was it the muddy water? I wondered where Bracken was. I looked around and saw a surveillance camera in the upper corner of the room, so I started to shout at it.

"Hey! I know you can see me! Tell me what the fuck is going on here!"

I wanted to reach for the camera to rip it off, but it was way beyond reach. I cursed, pacing around the room for what felt like hours until I just gave up and lay on the bed, falling asleep.

I woke up to the sound of door slamming shut. I raised my head and saw Reynolds with two armed men in the room outside, striding towards me.

"Rise and shine, pretty boy!" – Reynolds shouted and I approached the glass door.

"Reynolds, what are you doing?" – I asked, furious and desperate.

"You're infected. Therefore you're valuable to the government. You're going to stay here and be used as a test subject so the researchers can continue to improve the parasite."

"What?!"

"Who knows? One day, when the parasite is under control, you might even walk free. But only if we're certain you'll be obedient. This is a very noble cause you're volunteering for, Pierce."

"The parasite takes over sooner. Your experiments won't give results if the parasite has already killed the host."

"You're right. And that's why one of the scientists in the facility has concocted an antidote or whatever which freezes the parasite for a long time." – he smiled maliciously.

"Where's Bracken?" – I asked.

"Oh, don't worry about him." – Reynolds dismissed my question – "You just do what we say and you won't get into trouble."

He placed his keycard on the door and it opened.

"Turn around and put your hands behind your head." – one of the soldiers ordered and I obeyed.

They handcuffed me and dragged me to a laboratory, where I was placed in a chair while the doctor gave me a shot. A soldier stood in the room the whole time, observing me.

"This will freeze the parasite." – he said – "For at least one month. After that we'll give you another one, but if you start to notice any changes, let me know."

He turned around and asked the soldier to help him with something at the shelf with vials. The soldier approached the doc and they were turned away from me. I looked around to see if there was anything that could help me escape. There was a scalpel right next to me. All I need to do is grab it and stab the soldier before he turns around.

I glanced at the soldier and then at the scalpel again. It was now or never. I braced myself to get up and grab the weapon. And just as I was about to do that, another soldier walked in through the front door.

"Doc, HQ wants a report on the blood tests." – he said, glancing at me and then back at the doc.

"Yes, right away." – the doctor responded – "Please escort the subject back to his confinement."

The moment was over and I was too late. I was taken back to my cell, being mocked by the soldiers along the way for being in the predicament that I was in. From there, being tested was a regular occurrence on a daily basis. It must have been about a week of living in that cell when one day no one simply came to bring me food or take me to the lab. I thought it might have been a day off or something, so I simply continued sleeping. But then, a few hours later, a power outage occurred, enveloping the room in complete darkness. I heard gunshots and screams echoing in the distance and instantly stood up, squinting in the dark and trying to make out what the sounds were.

EMERGENCY POWER RESTORED

A voice echoed throughout the facility and red lights turned on in the room, giving me some form of visibility. Then, the glass door in front of me suddenly opened and I stared at it in disbelief. I was free. Just then, the entrance door swung open and a soldier barged in with his gun trained on me and his flashlight blinding me.

"Freeze!" – he yelled.

"Don't shoot!" – I raised my hands.

The beam of light searched my face, forcing me to close my eyes. The soldier then lowered his gun, allowing me to see his face illuminated by the emergency light.

"Come on Pierce, we're getting the fuck out of there." – Bracken said.

CHAPTER 6

"Bracken? You made it!" – I could hardly contain my smile.

"There's no time for bromance dammit, we gotta move. The facility's been compromised. There's an outbreak."

He handed me a handgun and led me through the door.

"Listen." – he said – "Zombies or not, you can't hesitate. If they catch us, they'll put us back in the cell and continue their research."

"So how do we get out? I have no idea where the fuck we are." – I shrugged.

"We're in one of their underground research facilities. We're on floor B21. We can take the elevator out, but…"

"But what?"

"We can't let this thing spread. We can't let the government kickstart this program again, either."

"So how do we stop them?"

Bracken pulled out a C4 explosive and said:

"The main generator is on floor B31. If we blow it up, it will initiate a chain reaction and this whole facility will go to hell."

"Wait a second, soldiers are probably everywhere, we'll never make it.

"Soldiers are busy trying to contain the outbreak, there's only gonna be a few of them down there. Come on, let's go!"

Before I could say anything he turned around and proceeded down the hallway, forcing me to follow him.

"Hold on." – he stopped me when we reached the corner.

I heard voices and when I peeked, I saw soldiers frantically yelling orders and pointing their guns at something. They started shooting and screams suddenly filled the air, echoing throughout the facility. In seconds, the soldiers were overwhelmed by those rabid freaks.

"Now's our chance, let's move!" – Bracken ordered and I followed him.

"The elevator on this floor has guards in front, so we gotta use the stairs." – he said, jumping over a dead scientist.

I saw through the glass military and research personnel being attacked in the lab next to the corridor, but we used that diversion to move along without attracting anyone. Soon, we got to a fire escape and entered a flight of stairs leading both up and down. When I looked down, I couldn't see the bottom due to the dark and the fact that the stairs stretched far down. As we descended down the stairs, I suddenly felt dizzy and my legs becoming heavy as if they were made of lead. My stomach burned like someone stuck a fire poker here.

"No time Pierce, move it!" – Bracken helped me up, his boots echoing throughout the room.

"The parasite…" – I muttered – "I think it's starting to get to me. I thought they scientists froze it."

Bracken shook his head:

"No. They sped it up. The parasite can remain dormant for years inside the host. They wanted to speed it up."

I felt my heart sinking and with it all my hopes.

"There's no cure, Pierce. There's no way out for us. But we can give the people another chance. We have to do this. Got it? Do you got it?!" – he shook me by the shoulder.

I gave him a weak 'yeah' and he urged me to get back on my feet and continue. I couldn't despair now. We had a mission to complete. My strength returned and the pain in my stomach subsided, so we continued. About halfway through, I asked:

"How the fuck did you get out? And get that gear?"

"There was a subject who got taken over by the parasite." – he responded while continuing down the stairs – "He attacked one of the guards and I took down the other one and then killed the infected. I took the guard's weapon and uniform, I fuckin' hate those patient clothes they gave us."

I chuckled. Even here at the end of the world, he was nonchalant about everything. Just as we reached floor B27, the door swung open and three soldiers barged in. They spotted us, but before they had time to react Bracken and I shot all of them. As they fell dead, the unmistakable screams of the infected resounded throughout the facility, too close for comfort. I grabbed one of the dead soldiers' assault rifles and continued to run down the stairs with Bracken. I turned around to see how far behind he was, seeing he was only a few feet away. Another door burst open and a zombie ran in between Bracken and I, sprinting at my teammate. Bracken shot him and then three more ran in, practically sliding into the room. We eliminated them as well. Bracken rammed the door before the others could join and held it with his back, as it rattled violently.

"Go! I'll hold them!" – Bracken shouted, throwing me the C4 – "Set the charges!"

I picked it up and when he saw my hesitation, he yelled for me to go once again and I listened, telling him to hold on. I descended as fast as I could, hearing screams and gunshots on the upper levels. When I finally reached B31, I opened the door and ran towards the main generator room. Two soldiers pointed their guns at me, commanding me to freeze, but I shot one and ran for cover. The other one opened fire, but missed. I shot from around the corner and managed to hit him in the shoulder, knocking him down. I ran to him quickly, kicking his gun away from him and shot him in the face as he begged for his life.

The main generator room was much larger than I expected and the generator itself occupied most of the space. I secured the area and pulled out the C4. I set the timer to 10 minutes and placed it on the generator, from a side where it wasn't so visible. I then ran outside the room and sprinted across the corridor towards the elevator. Before I could reach it though, someone jumped on me from behind the corner, tackling me to the ground and making me drop my gun.

"Not so fast, Pierce!" – Reynolds shouted, pointing his gun at me.

I kicked his shin, knocking him down and jumped on top of him. As we wrestled on the ground I punched him, but he managed to knock me off of him. I got up just in time to see him swing his knife at me. I dodged and used the momentum to slam his head onto the wall. I grabbed his hand and slammed it against the wall over and over until he dropped the knife. As we struggled like that, he managed to wriggle out of my grasp and charge at me, knocking me on my back. He was on top of me now and started punching me violently.

"You're not gonna stop this, Pierce!" – he shouted, swinging violently as my face exploded with pain from each punch.

He then put his hands around my throat and squeezed. I looked to my left with my darkened vision and saw the knife on the floor. With all my remaining strength, I reached for the knife with the tips of my fingers and swung with all my might. I felt it connect to something and captain's weight was off me. Reynolds pulled the knife out of his shoulder and looked at me with pure anger in his eyes. I turned onto my stomach ready to crawl away, my vision blurry and my breathing painful. In front of me on the floor was the gun I dropped when Reynolds tackled me. I crawled towards it, hearing Reynolds' cry while he charged me again. I grabbed the gun and turned around. Reynolds was running towards me with the knife raised and I pulled the trigger.

Nothing happened. I did it again and again, with him drawing ever closer. Just as he was about to bring down the knife on me, three loud bangs resounded in the hallway.

Reynolds staggered and his look of anger changed to one of surprise as he dropped the knife and fell to his knees, coughing up blood. I looked to where the shots came from in time to see Bracken limping towards me.

"Well done, boys." – Reynolds chuckled painfully and looked up at me as I stood up– "You did it. But you're already dead men. You know that, right?" – he fell on his side, clutching the part of chest where Bracken shot him.

"Either way this ends, we stopped this thing from spreading. That's all that matters, captain. I hope getting killed over nothing was worth it." – I stepped around him and called the elevator.

"You didn't stop shit."

I turned around to face him. He continued:

"This thing will spread. Millions will die. And it'll be all your fault."

I felt more anger boiling up in me, but I controlled myself. Bracken however pointed his gun at Reynolds, completely red in the face. Just then more screams of those zombies resounded throughout the facility, drawing closer by the second. The elevator door opened.

"Bracken. Leave him. He's dead either way." – I said.

"He killed Daniels." - Bracken said.

"And I'd do it again." - Reynolds laughed - "I gotta just say. Blowing his brains out like that and silencing his loud mouth forever... priceless."

Bracken seemed even angrier, veins throbbing on his forehead.

"Bracken, don't do it. It's what he wants." - I implored.

The air was filled with those screams which got louder and louder.

"My only regret was not being able to kill each one of you that way." - Reynolds continued - "But that's why I brought you here. So you can continue to serve as playthings for the government. Until the parasite is ready. And then it can be released again. And you Bracken, would be the national hero who caused all that." - he laughed again.

Bracken looked like he was going to explode.

"Do it!" - Reynolds shouted, while I screamed the opposite.

The screams were very close now. And then Bracken just lowered his gun.

"You're going to die a slow death down here. I'm going to let those freaks tear you piece by piece." - Bracken said and entered the elevator.

"Goodbye, captain." – I said and pushed the ground floor button.

Dozens of zombies were coming down the hallway in our direction now. The captain reached out to us with his free hand and said:

"Pierce, don't leave me like this. Don't let them get me! Finish me off!"

I watched as the creatures started tearing Reynolds apart and his screams mixing in with that of the zombies before elevator the door closed. Bracken and I were quiet for the duration of the ride, listening to the echoing cacophony of screams, shots and moaning. We hoped the elevator would not stop anywhere along the way and luckily, it didn't. When the door finally opened, we sprinted out and through the empty lobby into the dark woods. I helped carry Bracken due to his leg injury and we ran for what felt like hours even though in reality it was just minutes. We stopped to catch our breaths, looking around for any potential dangers. Just then, the ground beneath us started shaking slightly and soon after we heard a very faint explosion in the direction of the facility.

"We did it, Bracken." – I gave him a pat on the shoulder, exhausted more than I've ever been in in my life – "Now let's get out of here before backup arrives."

He nodded. We managed to escape there and are currently in hiding. I can feel myself changing gradually day by day and I'm losing control of my body, so I know I don't have much time left. I'll have to end it myself before I'm completely lost to the parasite. I'm okay with that, since we managed to stop the government's experiment from spreading again.

At least, that's what I thought. There are more and more reports coming in on the news of people committing acts of violent attacks on others citizens, all over the country. There seems to be no connection between any of the attacks, except for one tiny details that they all share in common.

The attackers all have bloodshot eyes.

THE DEPRESSION PROJECT

What I'm about to tell you has haunted me for the past three years and I never told anybody about it, until now.

I work as security for a big medical research company. I started a few years ago and it was a pretty normal day-to-day job, for the most part. I'd spend most of my working hours staring at camera feeds and patrolling around the perimeter, with no incidents ever occurring.

Then one day, I was called into the office for a talk with the big shots in the company. Some of the higher-ups which I'd never even seen before were there, so I expected them to either fire me over something I screwed up or even worse - a lawsuit or whatever.

Their reason for calling me in caught me by surprise:

"You've been with us for a while now and you've proven yourself to be a valuable asset to the company. But I can tell you're made for bigger things. How would you like to undertake a more... momentous project?" – one of the bosses grinned widely.

He went on to explain that the company was going through an experimental project which, if done correctly, could cure depression. They all seemed especially excited about it, stating it would go down in history.

The catch was, I would need to take a 2 months long trip to one of the company's compounds where the experiment was to be conducted. I would have to stay there for the entirety of the experiment and would be briefed on the details upon arrival.

I was about to politely decline, but when they mentioned the compensation, my jaw dropped. Before I knew it I was on a plane to the compound where I would meet the rest of the staff.

Upon landing I was escorted to a remote mountain area where the facility was located. I wouldn't have even seen the facility had it not been for a bulkhead door leading underground. I noticed that the company didn't cut any corners with the construction of the facility. The facility itself was divided into two sections – East, where the patients would be and West for the staff. The middle was designed as a control room. The whole compound was very ostentatious in regards of high-tech equipment, electronic doors, rooms and amenities provided to the participants, etc.

There were a dozen other team members onboard, including three other security members, a medic, specialists in psychology and psychiatry and the team lead, doctor Miller.

Five volunteers who were diagnosed with depression were with us, who were familiar with the project. Our escorts reminded us that we are not allowed to leave the compound from the start of the experiment until the end, so as to not disrupt the project due its sensitivity. The subjects were not even allowed to exit their rooms for 2 months. We were told we can simply send a message via the master computer in case of an emergency and their escorts would be there within minutes.

Once inside, doctor Miller briefed us on our duties. As security, mine was to simply patrol the area, monitor the live feed on the cameras and restrain the subjects in case they acted up. Miller explained that every night at exactly 21:43pm, the subjects would be exposed to a certain radio frequency over the course of 4 seconds, which would affect their brain and eventually successfully eliminate depression completely. He didn't go into details about how exactly it's supposed to work.

All the staff would be wearing noise-canceling headphones to avoid exposure to the signal, due to possible adverse effects.

We settled in and prepared for the first day of work. The research team was conducting surveys and tests on the subjects, while I did exactly what I did back at the company – watched the live feed.

At 21:30, Miller assembled all the staff in the control room for the radio signal. He spoke to the patients through the loudspeakers, asking them to be as quiet as possible, since it was almost time for the radio signal to be played through the loudspeakers.

Miller gave all of us a pair of sound-proof headphones and personally made sure they were adequately set on each member. All outside noises were instantly silenced when I put on my own set. Once that was done, the doc put a pair on his own ears and pressed a button on the desk.

A bright red light appeared above our heads, which indicated that the headphones are to be kept on until it was over. Miller observed us one more time and after he made sure we were strapped in, he pressed another button.

After a few seconds, he pressed the same button again and the red light turned into a green one. He took off his headphones and the rest of us followed.

"Subjects, please raise your hands as I call on you." – Miller said over the loudspeakers and proceeded to call their names.

"Subject 1. Subject 2. Subject 3. Subject 3, please raise your hand. Subject 3, do you hear my voice?"

The first two subjects responded, but the third one just sat, motionless, staring blankly in front of himself.

"SUBJECT 3!" – Miller became impatient – "Dammit. Security, please go and make sure all subjects are alright. Research team, proceed with the survey. And please use caution."

I went along with one of the security members and two of the doctors to the East section where the subjects were detained. I looked through the thick glass door in Subject 1's room and he seemed okay. Subject 2 was fine as well.

With each subject I checked, I'd swipe my cards on the door to unlock it and the research team would proceed to examine the subjects.

When I approached the door for Subject 3, he still sat on his bed with his gaze fixed to the wall in front.

"Hey, buddy!" – I knocked on the door loudly – "You okay in there?"

No response.

"Hey? Can you hear me?" – not even a blink.

I stared at the subject through the thick pane of glass and I couldn't make it out from the noise of the other staff members, but it looked like the subject's lips were moving.

I swiped the keycard on the door and it slid open. I carefully stepped inside, observing the subject and his surroundings. His room seemed pristine, just as the day when we arrived, his half-unpacked bags in the corner of the room. I looked at him carefully, focusing on the movement of his lips. He was indeed saying something, but I couldn't make it out.

"Sir?" – I called him again – "Are you okay?"

He turned his head towards me very slowly while still sitting in the same position.

"I'm fine." – he grinned widely, not blinking.

I can't explain why, but when he looked at me I felt the hairs on the back of my neck stand straight. Something was off here, something in that unrelenting gaze that made every fiber of my being want to bolt out of there, but I just couldn't put my finger on it.

Luckily one of the doctors stepped in and as he did, the subject seemed to return to normal, grin gone and all. I got out of there as fast as I could without arousing any attention. Subjects 4 and 5 were responsive, so I was dismissed for the rest of the evening.

The following day I had guard duty, so I spent most of the time staring at the camera feeds. The subjects were doing their normal everyday activities and having examinations by the medical staff, but other than that nothing in particular happened. I observed Subject 3 carefully, but nothing seemed out of the ordinary.

Night came and it was time for the signal to be played once again. The subjects were told to stand facing the door this time while the signal was played and to be ready for inspection. We all repeated the routine – headphones on, red light on.

Something was different this time though. Although I couldn't hear the signal, I felt something when Miller pressed the button. It's hard to explain, but it felt as if for those four seconds I was standing naked in the dark in front of god knows what. I had never felt so vulnerable in my entire life like I did during those four seconds.

I heard one of my coworkers whisper my name, but when I looked to them, they were focused on Miller. There was no way I heard anything through these headphones, so had my brain played a trick on me from the deafening silence?

I became increasingly agitated for some reason and wanted to just throw these headphones on the ground. This effect seems to have been mutual with everyone, because they looked restless, shifting their weight from one leg to another, looking around at seemingly nothing in particular, etc.

One of the staff members ignored Miller's warning and took the headphones off while the light was still red, but Miller hadn't noticed it because he was transfixed on the cameras.

The light finally turned green and I felt a wave of relief wash over me as I took off my headset. Miller spoke over the loudspeakers to the subjects again.

"Subject 1, raise your hand."

It was then that I glanced at the cameras and noticed that all five subjects were still standing motionless. I would've thought the cameras froze, had it not been for the timer in the corner.

"Subject 1, raise your hand." – Miller repeated, but to no avail – "Security, please check up on them."

This time, two other security guards took the role of securing the subjects. I watched on the feed as they approached the doors and tried to get a response from them, but they just stared blankly. One of the guards opened the door to Subject 1's room and entered and then...

All of a sudden the power went out and the entire room was enveloped in darkness and total silence. And then I heard what sounded like a cacophony of gunshots and the most blood-curdling, demonic scream I'd ever heard in my life coming from the East section.

Seconds later, a frantic set of footsteps resounded in the corridor next to the control room and one of the guards barged in, breathing heavily and with a look of pure terror on his face.

"Lock the East section, now!" – he shouted between breaths.

"Why, what happened?" – Miller asked.

"JUST DO IT!" – the guard ordered.

The power came back on Miller slammed a button which beeped loudly. The guard holstered his gun and entered the room, exhaling loudly.

"Oh my god." – I heard one of the staff members mumble.

Even Miller was pale as a sheet of paper.

"Whatever those patients were before,"– he said as we stared in horror at what was on the camera feed – "they're no longer human.

To this day I cannot describe what I saw on those cameras in words which would do justice to the terror I felt, but I'll do my best to transcribe it here.

Subject 1 was standing in his room facing the door, still motionless, but on the floor in front of him was the body of a security guard. I couldn't tell what happened to him, but whatever it was must have been gruesome, because his side was cut open and blood was smeared on the floor and walls in a way that indicated that he died a quick death from a sharp slice.

Subject 2 was lying dead on the floor, dried up blood caking his mouth, eyes, nose and ears.

Subject 3 sat on his bed and stared at the wall in front blankly, just like the previous night. He was whispering something, but none of us knew nor wanted to know what, so when one of the staff members suggested turning up the volume, his idea was quickly shut down and the camera feed muted.

Subject 4 was the one who froze my bone to the marrow, because at first we couldn't see him anywhere in the feed. And then someone pointed to the slight movement of something in the upper corner of the camera.

Miller used a button to move the camera upward and when it reached the ceiling, some of the staff members gasped. Subject 4 was standing on the ceiling on all fours like a spider, his head twisted at an unnatural angle.

At the movement of the camera, the subject jerked his head towards it and scurried on all fours across the ceiling towards the camera at an impossible speed until the entire camera feed was covered with his face and bloodshot eye.

The eye rapidly darted in all directions, never blinking. I had to look away because I felt so uncomfortable.

Subject 5 was slamming the door with his head, leaving a bloody stain on the glass. The head thumps were changing intermittently, sometimes weak and other times loud enough for us to hear them all the way to the control room. It was an unsettling sound, to say the least.

"Miller, what the fuck just happened?" – one of the doctors asked and we all looked to the team lead, demanding an answer.

"I... I don't know." – Miller shook his head in bewilderment, still pale.

"Bullshit!" – one of the guards yelled – "You know something! You did something to them with that signal of yours, didn't you?!"

"You don't understand, this wasn't supposed to happen."

"Well what was?" – another member jumped in.

"Nothing!" – Miller became defensive – "Nothing was supposed to happen!"

"Then what did you play on the radio signal?!"

"THERE WAS NO RADIO SIGNAL!" – silence fell on the room as Miller shouted those words and for a brief moment

The sound of subject 5 thumping his head on the glass permeated the room.

"There never was a radio signal." – Miller continued – "This was all supposed to be a placebo effect."

"Then how the fuck do you explain this?!" – I pointed to the cameras.

"I don't know, maybe there was some kind of inaudible signal played on our headphones and it caused hallucinatory effects, that's-"

"Well what I saw back there seemed pretty fucking real!" – the guard shouted.

There were a few more minutes of people bickering before Miller shut them up.

"I think whatever is going on here cannot be explained by logic." – he looked at the cameras.

Subject 4 was now on the opposite wall, moving his head left and right in a jerky motion for no apparent reason. The knocking from Subject 5 never stopped and this seemed to agitate everyone, especially because we couldn't predict when the next knock would come and how loud it would be, causing some people to be startled.

"We need to get the fuck out of here." – I said – "Contact our escort."

Miller sat at the master PC and opened a program which I wasn't familiar with. A chat window opened and Miller typed:

SEND HELP NOW

It said 'user is typing' below for a few seconds until a message came through.

What is your emergency, team?

Miller typed frantically, making typos along the way.

GUARD DEAD

PATIENT SGONE CRAZY

SRND HELP NOW!!!

The person on the other end was typing for a few more seconds until another message came through:

Proceed with the project, team.

"What the hell?" – some of us said in unison as Miller frantically sent more messages to the person on the other end.

Proceed with the project.

The message came again before the user disconnected. We sat there in silence, with nothing but our thoughts and the incessant thumping which grew louder by the second. I glanced at the camera feed and saw that the glass door of Subject 5's room had a significantly larger amount of blood on the door and the subject's head and face were mutilated beyond recognition. Still, he kept at it relentlessly.

"Okay, okay." – Miller thought for a second – "We can get out through the main door and then we should be able to walk back from there. Might take a while, but we can do it."

We all stared in silence as we shared the same feelings about Miller's suggestion. The main door was directly at the end of the corridor where the patients were being kept in the East section.

When some members voiced their disagreement about this, Miller explained that there's also a door in the West section, but that it couldn't be opened from the inside, since it had no card reader, being created only for the purpose of emergency teams coming in and to discourage project members from wandering outside and jeopardizing the project.

Eventually, we agreed that we needed to send someone through the main door, who would then close it behind themselves and open the door in the West section, while leaving the subjects safely locked. In retrospect it would've been easier to just go through the corridor and exit from the East section rather than wait for someone to come around the other side. But the problem was, no one wanted to go. Although the patients were locked up behind heavy doors, just the thought of passing through that place filled me (and apparently everyone else) with inexplicable dread. All of us knew the doors would hold and not let the subjects break through, but there was something holding us back. Something about going through that corridor that filled us with immobilizing fear.

"Fuck it, I'll go." – one of the staff members finally said.

"I'll come with you." – a guard jumped in, drawing his gun.

"We'll be monitoring you via the cameras." – Miller remarked with visible relief – "The subjects are locked behind heavy duty glass doors, so there's no way they can breach it, but still, be very careful."

In a matter of seconds, the two volunteers exited the control room and hesitantly entered the East section.

As if on cue, the head bashing from subject 5 abruptly stopped. All four subjects stopped doing whatever they were doing prior to that and stared at one same spot. It didn't take us long to realize that the subjects were staring in the direction of the two volunteers. It was as if they could see them through the walls even before they entered the East section.

"We're in." – the guard said via the radio and we all stared at the camera feed, holding our breaths.

It was unnaturally quiet even with the two members' footsteps echoing through the camera feed. As the two of them passed by each subject's room, the subjects followed them with their gaze in unison. And then the staff member stopped in front of the door of subject 1, unbeknownst to the guard who continued striding towards the door. Subject 1 and the staff member stared at each other in some sort of trance, with only the thick glass separating them.

The entire team held their breath in anticipation. And then a terrifying realization hit me like a ton of bricks. The research member who went with the guard was the same one who took his headphones off earlier during the radio signal.

"Fuck, the door's locked!" – the guard shouted and tried to open the bulkhead over and over, but it wouldn't budge.

I was transfixed on the research member in front of the door the entire time. With a robotic motion, he pulled out his keycard from the pocket and placed it to the door. I was about to shout, but it was too late.

The loud beeping noise already resounded in an alarmingly loud manner and the door slid open.

"Get the hell outta there!" – I yelled to the guard over the radio, who was already sprinting full-on the across the hallway.

The cameras started glitching and freezing at this point, so we couldn't see clearly what was going on, but from the frames where the image would recover, we saw that all subjects, as well as the research member were following the guard with their gaze, not moving from their spots.

The guard bumped into the door, violently trying to open it.

"Fuck! The door's locked!" – he yelled – "Miller! Open it up!"

By this moment the camera feed completely cut off and all we had to go by was the sound from the radio, which emanated the guard's panting.

"Miller, what are you doing? Open it!" – someone in the room yelled, as the guard's pleading voice got drowned out by the group's shouting.

"Do you wanna let those things out?!" – he gave me a stern look and deep inside, I knew he was right.

"PLEASE!" – the guard pleaded through the radio – "FOR THE LOVE OF GOD! THEY'RE COMING! OPEN THE DOOR PLEASE!"

We heard a few gunshots echoing through the entire facility and between them the guard's panicked breaths. And then silence. For a few seconds at least.

After a few seconds the radio crackled back to life and there was a soft humming noise coming from it. It sounded like a lullaby, but a very unpleasant one. No one said a word for a long time, listening to that humming noise which repeated the same irritating melody over and over. We tried turning it off, but the sound persisted. Even after smashing the radio on the ground, the humming continued.

And then one of the female staff members spoke up.

"We have another way out."

"Well, what is it?" – Miller asked.

"I can override the West door from the master computer by inputting it as an emergency, since all the doors are electronic, but…"

"But?" – I asked when I saw that she hesitated.

"It will open all the doors in the facility."

For a few seconds, the only sound that could be heard in the control room was the incessant humming from the radio.

"I think we should reconsider our options here." – one of the remaining staff members said.

"For all we know, the door in the West section might not even open." – I replied – "This could all be a setup. And what if they're waiting for us just outside? There's no way they'll let us just walk free."

"If we stay here, we'll die." – the remaining security guard said.

Eventually, everyone agreed on overriding the doors, even if it meant opening the locks in the East section. The female researcher sat at the master PC and typed and clicked vigorously.

"This may take a while." – she said.

"Hurry it up." – the guard responded, visibly agitated.

"You wanna sit and fucking try?" – she turned to him.

"Alright, everybody just shut up!" – Miller raised his hand – "Let's all just calm down and give the PC expert some space."

This was all starting to get to us all and it was visible from our hostility to each other. Even Miller himself had a hard time putting up a straight face.

Everyone went quiet for a while and that damned humming was the only sound which persisted. I tried to ignore it as much as I could, but the harder I tried, the more I seemed to be drawn in.

The humming was consistent and sounded like it was on a loop. Same intonation, same length of pause before starting again, etc. Literally like someone was just replaying it over and over.

"What did you just say?" – the guard asked Miller, breaking the silence.

"What? I didn't say anything." - Miller responded, baffled.

The guard stood up and clenched his fists.

"I just heard you say something!" – he repeated.

"It must have been your imagination." – Miller calmly responded and turned his head back to the member at the PC.

"Don't fucking lie to me, Miller!" – the guard got in his face – "You just said that we're all gonna die here, I heard you!"

Miller pushed him back.

"I didn't say a fucking word, you lunatic! Now back off!"

"You're the reason why we're here, this is all your fault!" – the guard hissed.

At this point everyone else tried calming the two of them down, shouting over each other.

"I told you already that I don't know anything!" – Miller yelled at the guard as the crowd finally settled down – "Maybe if you paid attention in school more than you do now, you'd be in my position and understand instead of being a good for nothing minimum wage guard with no future."

It all happened so fast. As Miller turned his back to the guard, the guard pulled his gun out and shot a bullet straight into the back of Miller's head.

There were screams and Miller's body fell limply to the floor, his eyes wide open in shock, blood collecting around his head on the floor. My ears were ringing from the gunshot. I pulled my own gun out and pointed it at the guard, who was in utter shock at what he just did.

"Oh my god." – he mumbled, wide-eyed – "I didn't mean to…"

"I'm gonna need you to lower your gun." – I demanded.

"I didn't…" – the guard started sobbing – "…fuck!"

"I understand, alright?" – I tried to be as reasonable as adrenaline allowed me to – "We all had reason to believe he was behind all this. But just lower the gun so we can talk."

"I'm sorry." – he shook his head, sobbing.

What happened next caught me by surprise as well. The guard put the gun to his temple and fired faster than I could react, causing another ear-splitting bang.

The wall next to him was smeared in red and he laid dead on the floor. The humming suddenly stopped and turned into sinister chuckling before that stopped as well, leaving us in complete silence.

"Jesus." – I mumbled in disbelief as the other team members gasped and cried.

"How close are you to opening the doors?" – I asked.

The PC lady wiped her tears and responded.

"Just a few more minutes."

She got back to work and the rest of us waited, trying not to look at the dead bodies.

"Almost ready!" – she said after a while.

The subjects could apparently sense this, because they started to rattle and bang on the door, causing us to recoil. We prayed that the door would hold at least until all the locks were disabled.

"When the doors open, just run. And if the exit is locked, hide somewhere in the rooms." – I said.

One of the members who knew how to use a gun picked up the one from the guard and we all got ready mentally. My heart was thumping a million miles per hour and I tried not to think about those things in the East section as their rattling became louder and more desperate.

"Okay, get ready." – the PC expert said – "Here it comes, let's go!"

There was a loud beep which signaled that the doors were unlocked and that was our cue. That was the cue for the subjects as well, because right after that beeping sound there was a scream so violent and demonic that I could instantly feel the blood draining from my face.

"Run!" – I screamed and we all bolted for the door and towards the West section.

As soon as we opened control room door the blood-curdling screams permeated the corridor, muffling the panicked panting of my coworkers. Before we even reached the West section door, a scream of one of our members was heard, but we had no time to turn around because we heard rabid breathing and loud, clumsy footsteps right at our heels.

The screams now echoed throughout the entire facility and it sounded like they were merely inches behind me, which made me run faster than I ever thought possible. I didn't dare look back out of fear of what I would see behind me, so I just kept running and praying those things were not faster. I tried not to think about them grabbing me as I heard a few gunshots behind followed by a loud cry of pain and vile crunching sounds.

The exit was so close now. I thought that at any moment I would feel a hand wrap around my arm or ankle and that I would be pulled back into that hellhole, but my adrenaline pushed me to run.

There was a flight of stairs leading up and on top of them – a door which opened to the cold, night sky. I tumbled over the threshold, practically rolling forward on the grass before coming to a stop. Never before has the cold wind felt more welcoming than in that moment, but I had no time for respite.

Another desperate scream ensued and I looked back just in time to see the PC lady get dragged down the stairs into the dark underground by a long, bony arm. And then all sounds stopped. I looked to my left where the only other surviving member was and we both stared at the dark entrance, unable to move our gazes from it.

And then the humming started again. It echoed from the stairway, even more unsettling than it was over the radio. A thin and tall figure with elongated extremities appeared at the top of the stairs. Whatever human as left in the subject when he was locked in the room was gone now entirely. The creature walked slowly, but deliberately, with a disfigured grin on its face.

I pointed my gun at the thing and fired. The creature barely even flinched and just kept coming right at me. I shot again and again until I was out of bullets and the subject just chuckled, just like it did over the radio when Miller and the guard died. It came dangerously close and I felt powerless to move. It grinned even more widely as it realized this.

"OPEN FIRE!" – someone shouted and before I knew it the creature was showered with a storm of bullets.

The force of such firepower caused it to stumble backwards and then screech in anger before it finally fell dead. The shooting didn't stop then either for a solid 10 seconds.

I turned around and was quickly faced with soldiers shouting and forcing me and the other staff member on our knees. A man in a business suit stepped forward and smiled. I recognized him as the guy who offered me this project back in the office.

"I'd like to thank you in the company's name for your selfless contribution." – he said calmly – "Our deadline was two months, but you guys managed to complete it in just two days! You guys are the MVPs of the show! Now I know you guys have a lot of questions, but these things are best left, you know, unanswered."

"You sick son of a bitch!" – the other survivor grunted – "When we get back I'm going to the police and the press! You're gonna rot in prison for what you've done!"

"Oh, now that's gonna be a problem." – the man said – "You signed an NDA in your contract, which strictly said you would not disclose any classified information to outside sources. You would've known if you, you know, read it."

He sighed and continued:

"You know it just seems to me that you need more time to think about all this. Boys, take him back in."

A couple of soldiers grabbed the researcher and hauled him to the entrance while he was begging and screaming. They threw him in and used a keycard to lock the door while the man continued to beg them to let him out, swearing he would never say a word to anyone. After only a few seconds, his screaming became much more violent and then quickly faded away.

The man in the suit shook his head in disappointment and looked at me.

"Now..." – he knelt squatted down in front of me – "We won't have to do the same thing to you, right? You'll keep all this a secret, yeah?"

I nodded timidly.

The man placed his hand behind his ear and turned it towards me.

"What's that? I can't quite hear you."

"I'll keep it a secret." – I said, avoiding eye contact.

"Good." – the man stood up – "Because in addition to the promised compensation, you just scored a huge extra bonus. And on top of that, you got promoted to chief of security!" – he said enthusiastically and smiled.

"If that doesn't sound appealing, perhaps you would prefer a, you know, more suitable reward? Like working in certain company projects, and such?"

I shook my head in defeat.

"Good." – the man in the suit remarked – "Now let's get out of here, it's getting kinda cold. And somebody get the client on the line, I want to congratulate him on a successful project."

THE OCEAN SHOULD
REMAIN UNEXPLORED

"The distress call came how long ago?" – I asked the commanding officer as I suited up.

"Twenty minutes ago. The crew was on a mission in the sub, when something went wrong and they sent a distress signal. They went radio silent since then." - the officer gave me a stern look which told me to hurry up.

"What depth?" - Jackson, my mission partner asked.

"Around 1500 m. The sub is a new type and was designed to go down to 2000 m, so even if they sank further down due to malfunction or exterior damage they should be okay, since the bottom is roughly 1800 m below surface. Your mission is to rescue any survivors. In case there are no survivors, assess the damage to the sub and secure the black box."

"Any idea on what caused them to send the distress signal?" – I asked.

"Not sure." – the commander responded – "This is what they sent."

He pulled out a small device and clicked a button. A panicked voice started speaking over the device:

"This is the S-158! We have a hull breach and are in need of immediate rescue! We are South-West of your position, distance unknown! Depth 1500 m! Send he-"

The voice cut out.

"You'll have a GPS tracker in your submersible, which should locate the sub." - he put away the device.

Jackson and I jumped inside the vessel. The Dolphin, as it was dubbed, was able to withstand a tremendous amount of pressure and go down to 6000 m. It was not originally designed for search and rescue, but due to the urgency of the situation HQ had no choice but to let us man this vehicle. The backside of the submersible had a depressurization chamber which could attach to any other submersible externally and transport staff in and out.

"We'll keep in touch via comms. Get moving!" – the commander said and we closed the hatch, muffling the outside noises.

Jackson and I sat in our seats and got ready to dive. His job was to pilot the vehicle and mine to operate the depressurization chamber. Jackson pressed some buttons on the machine and the submersible hummed to life. Various screens started glowing, showing depth, sonar activity and status of the vehicle. I felt a little uneasy suddenly. The deepest I've ever been was 800 m when looking for undetonated missiles, but the usual mission had us going no deeper than 200 m.

"Here we go." – Jackson announced and the submersible went underwater, leaving the rays of sun above us and engulfing the entire interior of the submersible in light blue.

"Gonna take us a little bit to reach them." – he said – "The descent is always slower."

I stared out the glass panel, seeing a school of fish scurry away from our position. As we descended, sunlight rapidly started to fade away and the light blue color which surrounded us was very quickly being replaced with a progressively darker one.

"Look on the bright side." – Jackson smiled – "At least we won't be going to the Abyssal Zone."

"Let's just hope the crew members made it. I'd hate to be in their position right now, stuck at the bottom of the ocean in complete darkness, not knowing if rescue is coming." – I shuddered at the thought.

Jackson shrugged:

"Well if they managed to put their deep diving suits on, they should be fine. Those can go even deeper than the sub."

That situation didn't seem any more appealing than the one I had just mentioned - being at the bottom of the ocean, with god-knows-what lurking around, tons of pressure that can crush you in a second and no way to get back up, being forced to wait for a rescue.

"Cheer up, maybe they managed to escape on their submersibles and we just missed them." - he said.

It was getting so dark so fast and Jackson pressed a button to turn on the headlights, which illuminated our interior and the area in front, showing particles dancing across the beams. I glanced at the depth modulator and noticed we were at 280 m. The dark blue color quickly became black and all we could see outside was the part of the ocean which was illuminated by the headlights. Any remaining sea life that was seen up until that point was long gone now and I thought about the creatures who lived in such eternal and consuming darkness, devoid of all light save for the ones produced by themselves.

570 m... 580 m...

The increasing numbers on the depth modulator painfully reminded me that we were putting ever-increasing distance between ourselves and the surface, descending deeper into the unexplored abyss with every passing second. The darkness surrounding us seemed thick and our lights barely penetrated enough to see in front of ourselves. The pressure at this depth would be enough to crush us within seconds and the only thing protecting us from that was the heavy glass on the submersible. I tried not to think about it as we descended deeper.

900 m...

Jackson was quiet. I wondered if he felt as uneasy as me, but if he did, he was hiding it pretty well. I saw a faint light from a deep sea creature bobbing up and down in the distance before it disappeared out of sight.

"Think it's an anglerfish?" – Jackson remarked – "I'd love to see an anglerfish in person. Did you know they actually grow up to be larger than the average human?"

"Yeah?" – I indulged him, even though I really just tried to stay focused on the mission.

"Yeah. And here I thought up until recently that it was like something you can keep in your aquarium home." – he chuckled.

1500 m...

"We're close now." – Jackson said – "The bottom can't be more than 400 m away, so chances are we'll find the sub there."

"Keep your eyes peeled then."

In a matter of minutes, we finally saw something else besides the dark water.

"Hold up, we're here." – I pointed through the glass to the flat, sandy ground illuminated in front of us by our headlights.

"Alright, sub should be around here." – Jackson steered the submersible in the direction of the little dot on the radar and we slowly started moving in that direction.

"No sonar activity." - he said - "That's not good."

We squinted our eyes, desperately trying to look past the short range of illuminated area of our headlights, trying to spot any signs of debris, but there was nothing but a desolate ground which seemed to stretch endlessly in front of us.

And then all of a sudden we saw it. It came out of nowhere so suddenly that we almost crashed into it. A huge military submarine, just sitting on the ground.

"That doesn't look good." – Jackson remarked – "Let's see the damage."

He steered around the sub and it became apparent that it sank due to some serious external damage. The hull looked like some animal had literally chewed its way in, making a gaping hole in it.

"Holy Christ. The fuck happened here?" – Jackson became serious – "A big animal or something? It looks like some of the submersibles ejected, so at least they made it that far."

He steered the submersible above and over to the other side of the sub and then abruptly stopped. We both stared at the sight in front of us in disbelief. The sub was sitting right at the edge of a cliff which dropped into more endless darkness below, stretching as far as our lights allowed us to see.

"I thought this was the bottom." – I looked at Jackson.

"Y-yeah." – he stared at the crater – "That's what the commander said."

Just then a loud beeping sound came from inside our submersible and I nearly crapped my pants, thinking we suffered some damage or had an incoming threat.

"What? That can't be right." – Jackson said.

"What?" – I impatiently asked.

"There's a distress signal coming from one of the submersibles from the sub."

Alright, let's go find him." - I started to relax a little bit, knowing we weren't in any immediate danger.

Jackson looked at me. His facial expression told me what he was about to say wasn't good news.

"It's coming from 800 m below us."

"What the fuck is he doing down there?" – I asked, baffled.

"Dunno." – Jackson shook his head – "But whatever it is, he's not safe down there. His submersible can go down some, but not that deep, so he must be in his suit down there."

"We gotta go help him." – as much as I hated myself for saying that, I knew we couldn't just leave him down there.

"We should contact HQ for backup first, at least." – my partner responded.

"There's no time. It could take us a while to find him and he's running out of oxygen with god knows what down there. We need to go down now."

"Alright fine. Let's go." – Jackson sighed and with brief hesitation started steering the submersible directly down.

To say I was scared shitless was an understatement. Here we were diving deeper into the Midnight Zone, where barely any creatures ventured, let alone humans. It all made me feel so small and vulnerable, being in such an inhospitable place to mankind. There's a good reason why we can't swim all the way down here without our technology, I thought to myself staring into the abyss before me.

"Check this out." – Jackson shook me back to reality.

He pointed to the sonar which showed no activity. On the one hand that put me at rest, but on the other hand made me worry about that missing person who sent the distress call.

"See this circle on the sonar?" – Jackson pointed to a ring in the outer layer – "that shows potential threats like walls and rocks we can run into."

"But it's circular. And it's all around us." – I replied.

"Precisely. And it appeared as soon as we descended below the cliff." – Jackson responded.

"Fuck me." – I gasped – "This isn't a cliff at all. It's a sinkhole."

"Yep."

"What the fuck was the S-158 doing here?" – I muttered to myself.

We were approaching the depth of 2300 m. Nothing changed visually compared to the previous 1000 m, but we still felt uneasy being so far below the surface.

"We should've seen some life by now." – Jackson spoke – "There's supposed to be all sorts of sea life detected on the sonar, but we saw nothing. Not even the tiny creatures. It's strange."

"Maybe this is predator territory, or used to be."

When we approached around 2500 m depth, we started to notice a very faint red light blinking in the distance below us.

"That's it, that's our guy for sure." – Jackson said and sped up the submersible.

The red light would flicker on and off intermittently every second and as we got closer, it grew in brightness. When we were close enough to the light to identify the source, we stopped.

"Holy Christ" – Jackson said as we stared at the busted submersible which unmistakably belonged to the crew from S-158.

It lay sideways on the floor. The glass was completely shattered and the command console broken. And then I caught something else at the corner of my eye. Every time the beacon would flicker, it would illuminate something on the ground close to the vehicle. Jackson steered our vehicle in that direction and then stopped again, audibly gasping.

"Dammit." – I grunted at the sight in front of us.

A body of a dead man in a deep diving suit lay before us. He was missing an arm and leg and his torso was half-eaten. The helmet was cracked open and his open eyes stared blankly in shock.

"Dammit, we were too late." – I shook my head.

"He has a camera on him. Let's see if it has any valuable info." – Jackson said and maneuvered the sub closer.

He pressed some buttons and used what we call "the hand" to extend a robotic hand from the bottom of the sub and controlled it clumsily until he managed to grab the camera off the soldier's chest and retract the hand inside.

Once the water drained, I opened the panel at the bottom and retrieved the device. I plugged it inside the console and a video started playing. The camera followed a man from first person perspective on a submarine which was breached, frantically running and panting while screams of his crew members were heard in the background. He jumped inside a submersible, closed the hatch and quickly ejected himself into the water, muffling the dying screams behind.

He steered his vehicle upward as a ferocious screech which could not be from anyone human followed behind. Then for a split second we saw something huge swim across his view in front of the submersible before disappearing out of sight. The soldier gasped loudly and his breathing became even shallower. He glanced at the depth modulator which was rapidly decreasing from 1400 m. He was reaching the surface.

But then there was a loud crash which shook his entire vehicle and almost knocked him off his seat. His sub stopped moving and instead started to sink slowly.

"No, come on! Not now!" – he frantically slammed buttons as multiple warning messages appeared on the console screens. The sub couldn't start.

"Fuck!" – he slammed his fist on the keyboard.

The depth modulator was rapidly increasing now. 1300… 1350… 1400… 1500… 1700…

More and more warning messages kept popping out and as a last resort, the soldier entered a command on the keyboard to send a distress call.

The creature which hunted him was practically toying with him, swimming around his vessel, growling and hissing. We couldn't see anything except an enormous fishtail which would pop in and out of view occasionally.

In seconds, the creature disappeared completely and could not be seen nor heard. The soldier stood up and peered out the window, looking for the creature. But then, something even worse happened. A crack appeared on the glass in front of him. The soldier recoiled as the depth modulator screamed warnings about being deeper than deemed safe, but before he even had time to react, more cracks appeared and then the entire glass burst open, filling the inside of the submersible with water.

There was tumbling upside down and before we realized what was going on, the soldier was out of the vehicle and dropping uncontrollably into his inevitable demise with nothing visible around him. The next few seconds were filled with footage of him staring down at the black nothingness under his feet as he forcibly sank deeper and deeper, panting and desperately flailing his arms and legs to slow down his fall.

My stomach turned into knots as I watched him fall for what seemed like hours. Soon though, his feet finally touched the lifeless ground and he collapsed softly to the floor. He looked at his surroundings, hyperventilating and desperately trying to find something other than the darkness surrounding him.

The submersible's beacon appeared in his view soon and with a loud crash it touched the ground, not too far from him. He started to inhale and exhale in a controlled manner, stabilizing his breathing, as he took slow steps towards the now useless submersible. He spoke finally in a somewhat calm manner:

"If anyone finds this, I'm captain Conley of the S-158. My entire crew is dead and I'm the only survivor. And probably not for long. We ventured down here for a mission, but instead found something much worse. We woke it up from this forsaken sinkhole and now it's after us. This is a warning to anyone who finds this recording. Seal the sinkhole and bury this creature in it. Tell all units and explorers to stay the fuck away from this place as far as possible. If this thing ever sees the light of day, we'll suffer far greater casualties than one crew."

A soft growl resounded from nearby and Conley spun around just in time to see… something, for a second before it lunged at him. I couldn't take a good look at it, but whatever I saw in that split second did not match the description of any deep sea life I had ever seen before. The remaining few seconds of the footage were a black screen filled with Conley's screams and the creature's rabid biting. And then everything went silent and still.

Jackson and I looked at each other in disbelief. I was about to tell him to get us the fuck out of there and back to topside, to which he agreed, but then he looked at the sonar and cursed. I jerked my head towards it and let out a 'sonuvabitch' myself.

There was one huge dot on the radar. And it was heading straight for us.

"Get us outta here Jackson, double time!" – I shouted.

"Are you crazy? There's no way we can outrun that thing, look at the speed it's moving at!" – Jackson pointed to the sonar.

The red dot was getting closer by the second.

"Fire the decoy!" – I yelled.

"Wait. We want it to get close enough for that."

He turned off the headlights, instantly engulfing us in total darkness, save for our cockpit which had the console buttons and screens glowing.

"What are you doing?" – I asked.

The red dot was no more than 300 m away and it was moving at an insane speed.

"We need to lure it away from us." – Jackson responded – "And having our lights on won't help with that."

200 m...

A vicious scream echoed all around us which without a doubt meant that the beast had sensed us and was coming after us, making the hairs on the back of my neck stand straight. It felt discouraging knowing that the only thing that protected us from the inhospitable waters and the deadly predator was the tiny cockpit we were confined to. Unlike Conley, we had no deep diving suits onboard, so if our submersible got breached, we'd die instantly. I remembered captain Conley falling helplessly into the abyss and being stuck in complete darkness without any help and I almost felt relief for a second at the thought of an instant death from pressure.

The shriek was so loud now that my ears hurt. Jackson slammed a button and instantly a flashing decoy was fired from the vehicle, moving at high speed while emitting a loud beeping sound. For a brief second before the decoy disappeared too far out of our line of sight, we saw a huge fishtail illuminated brightly before being devoured by darkness again. I glanced at the sonar and realized that the dot was now moving away from us.

"Alright, take us up, but very slowly." – I said to Jackson, squinting my eyes through the impregnable dark.

Jackson turned our sub around to avoid even the console lights from attracting that thing and very slowly started ascending. Even moving so slowly, the submersible's engine made an alarmingly loud noise. Still though, seeing the depth modulator's numbers decrease slowly lifted our spirits, despite knowing we were nowhere near safe grounds.

I grabbed the radio while Jackson operated the sub in pitch dark.

"HQ, come in." – I radioed and held my breath for a reply.

"This... H.... What.... position?" – the voice over the radio crackled to life, but kept cutting out.

"You cut out. Repeat, HQ."

Another sentence filled with static and no audible words ensued.

"HQ, repeat." – I said again, but all we got once more was static.

"Shit." – I shook my head – "Signal might be affected in the sinkhole. I'll try again when we're out of this hellhole."

We were at 1700 m and going up. In just a matter of minutes, we were out of the godforsaken sinkhole and way past the busted sub. We started to relax and Jackson even turned the lights back on. That was a huge mistake though, because the moment he did, there was an ear-piercing scream, coming from below us.

"Fuck, go go!" – I yelled and Jackson put the sub into full speed, practically sticking our backs onto the seats.

The dot appeared on the radar again and it was closing in fast. We were still a whole kilometer from the surface and there was no way we could outrun that thing. The screams stopped, but were replaced by the sounds of something massive ripping its way through the water. Something crashed on the side of our vehicle, knocking me out of my chair. A humanoid hand with clawed fingers appeared at the edge of the glass, making a scratch mark on it. And then the whole creature came into visibility right in front of us.

It was smaller than we anticipated, but far more terrifying than I could ever imagine. It almost looked human, with a head that resembled that of our own species, save for two tiny holes where the nose should have been. It had a humanoid neck, torso and even arms. Its entire body was pale, but muscular. Its eyes were completely black and despite not having pupils, I could tell it was looking straight at me, hissing and showing off sharp rows of teeth.

The thing shook our submersible violently, making Jackson and me tumble up and down in the cockpit. Warning messages started popping up on screens and I heard the distinctive sound of glass cracking. This is it, I thought. We're gonna end up like Conley. But in all that mess Jackson somehow managed to slam the decoy button which launched another distraction.

The creature shielded its face from the bright light of the decoy and then went after it, slapping our submersible's already damaged glass with its enormous fishtail along the way. Jackson sat at the sub and sped up again.

"That was our last decoy!" – Jackson said, gripping the controls so firmly that veins were bulging violently from his hands.

I glanced at the sonar and realized the creature was coming back for us again.

"Come on baby, come on!" – Jackson yelled at the vehicle.

Darkness dissipated and the water was gradually becoming blue, illuminating more and more in front of us and never in my life have I felt so relieved to be out of that goddamned darkness. Before we knew it, the vehicle popped out of the water so violently it practically jumped and then dove back into the water, making us slam our heads forward.

We looked at the sonar. No activity from the creature.

"Looks like it's gone." - Jackson said.

"Yeah, well we'd best not wait for it to return." - I replied.

We sped up back to HQ, glancing at the sonar every few seconds to make sure that thing wasn't following us. The next few hours were blur - explaining to HQ what he had witnessed and how the entire S-158 crew was dead, being questioned by higher ranking officers and even men in suits and eventually signing some papers about not speaking about what we saw to anyone. The sinkhole was apparently sealed with explosives, but that's all the info I managed to get from my commander.

Jackson and I were forced to take a short leave after that and were forbidden from asking any questions related to the S-158 mission and the creature we encountered down there. But then a few months later, I decided that I deserved some answers, so I barged into the commander's office, demanding information.

"I'm not leaving until you tell me what S-158 was looking for all the way down there and what the hell that thing was." - I said.

The commander sighed from his chair. After a long pause, he simply said:

"Mermaid."

"What?" - I frowned.

"That thing was a mermaid." - he repeated - "The mythical creatures which sailors have been sighting for centuries."

I chuckled, but then realized he was serious. He stood up and turned his back to me, looking outside the window.

"The S-158 had a mission to investigate the sinkhole and bring back any intel they could find. There were sounds coming from the hole. Crew members described it as singing, so they went down to investigate. But instead, it turned out to be the home to that creature. They usually stay down pretty deep, so it's strange that they came to the top of the sinkhole to attack the sub."

"They?" - my eyes widened in shock.

The commander turned to me.

"We've been studying them for a while now. And the higher-ups agree they're too dangerous to engage, so orders are to avoid them at all costs. That's all I know. Now if you'll excuse me, I got some work to do. You are dismissed."

"Commander, I-"

"Dismissed!" - he slammed his palm on the table and I knew there was no point arguing.

I often wake up at night thinking about that fateful moment when the mermaid creature decided to go after the decoy instead of finish us off. I see its black eyes and pale feature, with a facial expression that's so hateful it can rip through metal. I often wonder what would've happened had it decided that we were more interesting as prey instead of the decoy. Would we end up half eaten like Conley, rotting at the bottom of the ocean?

But something far more terrifying keeps me up at night and I can't help but wonder whenever I try to drift into sleep and whenever I'm supposed to go back to the waters - how many of them are there?

LOCKED DOOR

PROLOGUE

I moved into my new apartment a week ago. I'd been meaning to look for a new place for a while now, but just couldn't bring myself to do it due to the long working hours and laziness. But when the oven broke for the fifth time in two months and the landlord refused to pay for repairs, it gave me a boost to move out faster. I had been living there for about a year without a contract since it was cheaper and close to the center, but the apartment itself lacked a bunch.

It was hard finding any suitable place at first, location and price-wise, but after a couple of days of searching, I saw one ad for a two bedroom apartment not too far from my own. The price seemed like a really good deal too, so I wasted no time calling the agency.

After scheduling an appointment with an agent, I met him in front of the apartment building.

"Hi, I'm Nicholas." – he shook my hand with a bit grin.

The apartment itself looked pretty new, so I hoped what I saw on the pictures in the listing was not deceiving. The friendly agent led me inside and we took the elevator to the third floor.

"This whole place is new." – he said – "They just finished building it a year ago, so everything is top-notch."

"And what about the owner? When do I get to meet him?" – I said, staring in front at the elevator door.

"Yeah, you probably won't get to. He keeps to himself a lot. In fact no one from the agency ever saw him in person either. He's verified and all, just doesn't like people, I guess. All you gotta do is pay rent online and that's it."

I simply brushed this off as a good thing. I was tired of my previous landlord coming monthly for 'apartment inspections', so the thought of being able to live in a new apartment without even seeing the new landlord was appealing, to say the least.

"Right this way." – Nicholas unlocked the door to apartment 304.

When he opened the door, my jaw dropped to the floor. I had seen the pictures online and the apartment looked amazing, but those agencies usually polish the pics a little. What I was seeing in front of me was exactly what I saw in the pictures – no more, no less. A spotless apartment which looked so flawless it contrasted even the building itself, which was without blemishes itself.

"The living room is over here. And right here, connected to the living room is the kitchen." – the agent perkily showed me around, but I was barely able to focus on what he was saying, being mesmerized by my ostentatious surroundings. Everything in the apartment seemed brand new.

"So, the price we talked about, I just wanna clarify. That's the price the owner wants?" – I asked, confused as to why someone would be renting a place like this one so cheaply.

"Yep, that's the one." – Nicholas nodded – "I know, you think there's a catch."

"That's not what I was-"

"It's okay. I'd be suspicious, too. But I can assure you, everything is in order here. Let's check the bathroom."

The bathroom itself wasn't very spacious, but it did have a fancy shower, which more than compensated for it. The bedroom was neatly organized, with a big bed on one side and a desk on the opposite. Since I work as a freelancer, this kind of setup seemed perfect as my office and sleeping space.

"This is amazing. I can't believe it's so cheap." – I smiled in bewilderment – "When can I sign the contract?"

"Right away, if you like." - Nicholas led us back to the living room and we sat by the table, after which he pulled out a bunch of papers.

He explained about the bills and everything that was included in the apartment, after which he gave me the papers and asked for my ID in return.

"So, I'll just need you to sign all of these." – he pointed to the blanks on the papers, eagerly awaiting.

I signed quickly, afraid he would change his mind if I didn't do it quickly enough. I glanced up and realized there was still a door we hadn't opened, down the hallway, next to the bathroom.

"Hey, what's over there?" – I pointed tentatively.

"Oh, that." – Nicholas' tone suddenly dropped – "Probably a storage room."

"Probably?" – I chuckled.

"Yeah, it's been locked since the start. Owner said the room's lock is rusted and he hasn't been able to open it in ages and apparently it would cost a lot to take the door down and repair the frame. If you need a place for some extra things, you also get a storage in the basement for tools and bikes. Will that be a problem for you?"

"No, not at all." – I shook my head, not taking my eyes off the sturdy-looking door.

In the end, who cared about one tiny room in the apartment, which wasn't even mentioned in the listing. I signed all the papers and Nicholas gave me the keys. It was all done so quickly that I didn't even have time to form any suspicions. I was just happy to get such a fancy place at such a low price.

I wasted no time moving my stuff from the old apartment, much to the grumbling of my previous landlord, who felt that I should leave the deposit to him due to 'furniture damage' and the last minute notice. I happily agreed, telling him in return that I would call the IRS to inform them of taxes he avoided by not making a contract. He dropped the idea and returned the deposit money without any further issues.

I spent the first few days in my new place trying out the fancy kitchen utilities, washing machine, etc. I hadn't really focused on the locked storage room, but given my curiosity, despite what Nicholas told me, I tried the knob, pulling and pushing violently a couple of times before letting it go. After that I simply forgot about it.

The tenants mostly seemed to be either at work or inside their own apartments when I came in and out and I only saw one elderly lady about a week after I moved in. I was walking towards my apartment and she was unlocking the door to 307.

"Hi, my name's Nathan. I live in apartment 304. We haven't met yet because I just moved in." – I tried to introduce myself and immediately realized how stupid it must've been to try striking a conversation with an elderly stranger, despite being neighbors.

She glanced at me sideways with a frown and then rapidly went inside and shut the door behind her. Well that was rude, I thought to myself, but decided not to let it bother me.

Overall, everything was great in my new place despite the unpleasant neighbor. That is until about two weeks since I moved in. One day I was returning from visiting a friend and as I put the keys into the keyhole, I froze. As soon as the rattling of the keys started, there was a sound coming from the inside of my apartment. It sounded like someone was scurrying off in a panic with a quick and heavy bat of footsteps. And then it stopped. I paused, trying to figure what I was hearing. I put my ear against the door, trying to hold my breath as much as possible. Did that really come from inside?

There was silence. I stood like that for a whole minute and nothing happened. And then a loud thud resounded from inside. It sounded as if someone knocked something heavy on the floor. I was sure I heard it from my own apartment, so I decided the safest thing to do would be calling the police. I backed away from the door, pulling out my phone, not breaking my gaze from the door.

"911, what is your emergency?" – the operator asked.

"There's someone in my apartment right now. My address is-" – I proceeded to give them my address and the operator explained a patrol would be there soon.

Two police officers arrived a few minutes later and I pointed them to the apartment. They drew their guns and barged inside, shouting warnings to whoever was in. I waited in anticipation for a few minutes until they came back out, guns back in holsters. They asked me about the locked door and I explained that it was a storage and has always been locked.

They told me no one was inside and probably never was, either, claiming I must have heard the sound from elsewhere. When I assured them the sounds came from inside, they shook their heads, explaining there were no signs of forced entry and nothing seemed to be out of place. Windows were closed, too. I thanked them and they were on their way.

Not content with the information they gave me, I decided to double check the apartment myself. Nothing was off, though. No missing or broken items, no damage to furniture, floor or walls, nothing.

I approached the storage door and stared at it, not sure what I was even thinking. I felt mesmerized, unable to break my gaze from it. The apartment was empty and yet, this room was unchecked despite being tightly locked. It felt like that game when an item is hidden under three cups which are shuffled and you already lifted the two which were empty, so you just knew the item was in the remaining cup. I felt myself grabbing the doorknob and twisting it. No dice. I pulled and pushed a few times, rattling the door handle in the process, but it wouldn't even budge. It was as though it was welded shut to the frame. Eventually I figured the cops were probably right. I heard the noise from elsewhere and just misidentified the inside of my apartment as the source. Still though, I couldn't help but feel a little uneasy that night, so I double checked all the windows and made sure they were closed and locked the door with both the bolt and the key. I was determined not to let anyone invade my private space.

A few more days went by and nothing out of the ordinary happened. I had forgotten completely about the incident that happened a few days ago and I simply went by with my daily routines.

Then one night as I slept, I was suddenly jolted awake from bed. I was drenched in cold sweat and breathing heavily. A feeling of immense dread came over me, which made me dart around the dark bedroom with my eyes. It felt as though I had just woken up from a nightmare, but there were no dreams in my memory. Something was definitely off. And then I heard it. The faint sound of a door closing shut came from outside my room. I glanced at the closed door of my room, trying to calm my breathing down. No other sound was heard, just the deafening silence of anticipation. I slowly got out of my bed and tip-toed to the door, putting my ear against it. At first I thought I heard nothing, but as I listened closer, I heard it. A barely audible scratching sound. Something about it sounded off. It was as if it was too deliberate, too controlled. The scratching would last for one excruciatingly long moment, as if something was dragged across the wall very slowly. And then it would stop for a moment before continuing with the exact same longevity and force, over and over. It sounded like it wasn't close to me though, so I slowly opened the door, peeking out into the hallway.

The scratching became louder now. I identified its source from down the hallway so I followed it, carefully taking each step. Before I even got there, I knew where the sound was coming from – the damn storage room. As I went around the corner and neared the door with each step, the scratching became faster and more intense and the pauses shorter. By the time I reached the door, it was so loud that I expected the neighbors to come knocking on the door, complaining of the racket. I stared at the door for a moment, listening to the ear-splitting scratching noise which permeated my entire apartment. I approached and ever so slowly placed my ear against the door.

The moment I did that, the scratching stopped. Not like it was the last scratch and whoever was inside decided to stop, but more like I interrupted them and they heard me by the door and simply stopped their final scratch mid-way.

I heard myself exhaling a slow and trembling exhale. The silence which suddenly enveloped the room felt more threatening than the loud noise from just before. It was like the silence in horror films where you hold your breath during an intense scene and you're in anticipation of a jump-scare. I tried to steady my breathing and detect any faintest sounds coming from the storage room, but nothing came. Then, out of nowhere there was a bang on the door from the other side, so loud that it sent me flying backwards on my ass. I didn't try to hide my panting this time. I stared at the door, expecting something to happen, the door to open and someone or something to jump out.

Three loud knocks resounded so unexpectedly that I nearly jumped out of my skin. Then I realized the knocking was coming from the front door. I scrambled towards it, unlocking it as fast as I could, not caring who was on the other side. As I opened the door I pushed past an elderly man, who had a look of frustration on his face.

"Hey, what the hell!" – he shouted.

"There's someone in there!" – I pointed to the apartment, ignoring the man.

He peered inside my apartment and asked:

"Where? Who?"

"I don't know, but they're in the storage room right there, around the corner!" – I kept pointing, breathing heavily.

The man sighed and looked at me. His look was no longer one of anger, but rather pity.

"Ah, the storage room. They probably didn't tell you." – he said.

"Tell me what?" – I asked, confused.

"Mice." – he replied, letting himself inside.

He stared at the door and then looked back at me and said:

"The storage room is locked tightly, or rusted shut, but mice probably found their way in somehow, must've been a hole in there or something."

"Wait a minute, mice?"

"Oh, don't worry." – he smiled when he saw my concern – "They travel through walls in the building and sometimes make these scratching sounds. You probably heard that."

"No, wait. That couldn't have been a mouse. There was someone in there, they slammed the door-"

"Mice." – he interrupted me – "They can get really big. They can't get into your apartment since the walls are really good, but they do live in walls. If you're really afraid, you should get a cat."

"I'm not afraid of mice." – I remarked angrily.

He raised his hands in a giving up stance:

"Sorry, meant no offense. Anyway I came to see what was going on since I heard you pacing around the apartment. I live below and it's really loud, so could you maybe keep it down a little bit at this hour?"

I opened my mouth, ready to argue, but wanted to get the conversation over with as soon as possible. I apologized for waking him up and he left my apartment.

"I'm Vincent, by the way." – he said. "Nathan." – I replied.

"You have a good night, Nate." – he waved me off and left.

The following day, I called a door repair service, not caring about the potential damage that would need to be caused to the walls. Hell, I was even ready to pay for the whole thing myself, so long as the door just got taken off. The repair guy came shortly after, carrying a toolbox with him.

"Hi, you called about the stuck door?" – he asked formally.

"Yeah, right this way." – I let him in and showed him the way.

He put his toolbox down and tried the knob. He tried pushing the door a few times.

"Yeah, it won't budge." – I said.

"It might be stuck in one or more places. Let me check."

He pulled out a piece of paper out of the toolbox and stuck it between the door and frame, running it around.

"Alright, door doesn't seem to be stuck anywhere." – he said, putting the paper down – "I may have to pry it open."

"Whatever you need to do, man. Listen, I'll be working my room while you're doing that, but can I interest you in coffee or something?"

"Nah, I'm good. I'll let you know as soon as I'm done here." – the man replied, switching his gaze between the tools and the door and never looking at me.

I went into my room and spent some time there working on a project, listening to the sounds of clattering tools from the hallway. Soon those sounds grew a lot more intense, followed by a very loud buzzing. He was probably cutting the door down. Thirty minutes later, the sounds stopped and the man knocked on my door.

"So, about the door…" – he started.

"Yes? Did you manage to get it open?" – I asked.

"That's the thing. I've never seen anything like it. Everything I tried failed. Even the saw couldn't leave a scratch on it. Moreover, but the saw was damaged from contact with the door. It's like, a normal wooden door, but it must be reinforced with something, because nothing's getting through it."

"Well, what do I do then?" – I asked.

"Well you can try hiring some other door services, but I doubt they'd be able to give you a different answer. The more expensive solution would be tearing down the entire wall and taking the door down. I tried to access the hinges, but since the door opens to the inside, the hinges are on the other side, so you're out of luck."

I thanked the man for his time and paid him, frustrated beyond words. By then I just figured I'd have to have live with this door being locked. I decided the best course of action was to just ignore the door and go on with my life, hoping I would not be woken up again in the middle of the night.

That night I went to bed later than usually. I didn't want to admit it to myself, but I was postponing going to bed out of fear that I might be woken up again by some sounds. By the time I finally did go to bed, it was past 1 am. I fell asleep fairly quickly and started having some weird dreams.

In my dreams, I was standing in front of a giant door surrounded by darkness. I was to small to even reach the knob, but pretty soon, the gigantic knob turned with an echo and the door started opening slowly with a loud creak. I waited in front, in anticipation, unable to see anything in the dark crack which separated the door from the frame. And then, two boney hands emerged from the dark and grasped the edge of the door. I stood there petrified, unable to move a muscle as the door continued to open, the creaking sound never ceasing.

And then just as someone or something was about to peek out of the corner of the door, I woke up abruptly. I was drenched in cold sweat and just stared into nothingness, as I processed where I was and what I had just seen. I glanced at my phone. It was 3:20 am. Feeling like I was not in control of my own body, I got out of bed and walked over to the door. I opened it and went down the hallway, approaching the storage room.

What I saw made me stop in my tracks. The door was wide open, extending into a long, dark hallway.

CHAPTER 1

I squinted my eyes while staring at the dark corridor. This didn't make any sense. The corridor which was supposed to be the storage room extended to an irrationally long distance, which I could see even through the dark. Was it for some reason going through the adjacent apartment? I stood there transfixed, trying to process what I was looking at. I tried to look past the consuming darkness in front of me, but couldn't. The corridor instilled an irresistible urge in me to come closer, explore it. But I couldn't will my body to take another step.

As I stood there, I thought I heard creaks echoing in the distance, faintly, but enough for me to discern what it was. More doors in there, perhaps? The longer I stood there, the stronger the urge to go inside got, but my gut feeling was telling me it would be a bad idea. I glanced at my watch and realized it was 3:35 am. Realizing that I had been standing there for the past 15 minutes broke me out of my trance and I took a step forward, grabbing the door knob. I pulled, but to my surprise, the door remained firmly in place. I grabbed with both hands, yanking hard. It wouldn't budge.

I tried grabbing the edge of the door and yanking it back and forth to unstuck it, but again, it was firmly stuck in place. I stepped inside and around the door to try to ram it from the other side and immediately I was enveloped in cold. It wasn't like the corridor was slightly colder than my living room, it was like there was a very distinct barrier between the two rooms, preventing the heat from going from my apartment into this enigmatic place.

I tried pushing the door with all my force, but turning my back to the consuming darkness immediately put me at unease, so after a few shots, I returned to my room. I stared at the corridor again and then noticed something. The door was less open than when I first saw it. I sat down on my couch across the door, staring at the darkness, thinking I would start seeing a face any moment there. I wanted to test something. I sat there until 3:55 and by then, the door was more than halfway closed. I was right.

The door was closing on its own. I sat some more and at exactly 4:19 there was a distinct clicking noise of the door locking. I had almost drifted into sleep by then, so this noise jolted me out of my drowsiness. When I looked up, the door was closed and locked firmly again. Did this happen every night? I had to find out.

I worked from the living room the next day, carefully glancing at the 'storage' door every couple of minutes. Did the landlord know about this? I wanted to contact him, but I also didn't want to freak him out with something he didn't potentially know and close the apartment down. And on top of that I had no means of contacting him, there was no phone number or address, just a bank account and name. I figured that the previous tenant must have known something, so I contacted the real estate agency. I had Nicholas' number, so I contacted him.

"Hi Nicholas, I'm the guy who took the apartment at-" - I gave him the address of the apartment.

"Yeah, I remember. Nate, right?"

"Yeah."

"Everything okay with the apartment?"

"Yeah, everything is great." – I faked a smile despite Nicholas not being able to see my face – "I actually had a question about the previous tenant."

There was a short pause.

"Yeah? What about her?" – he asked.

"Is there a phone or address I can contact her on? I think she left something here and I want to give it back to her."

"Oh." – Nicholas stuttered – "Actually, we aren't really allowed to give clients' information. But if you want, I can send someone from the company to pick it up and have them bring it to her."

"I see. Um, you know what, it's actually not a big thing, I'm sure it's not important." – I put the sentence together barely.

"Alright, if you're sure. Well do let me know if you happen to need anything else, alright?"

"Yeah, thanks Nick. Have a good one."

Something about the way Nicholas spoke seemed off. Like someone who's caught in an uncomfortable situation they didn't want to be in and needs to think of an excuse quickly. I considered the possibility that the agency might know more than then let on, but figured there was not much I could do about it for now.

I finished work soon, did some chores and took a 2 hour long nap in the afternoon. I had no intention of sleeping tonight and wanted to be ready. I watched TV until late in the evening, glancing at the door every now and then and drank absurd amounts of coffee.

3 am. I turned off the TV and stared at the storage door. I remembered the first time I saw it and I was full of curiosity. Now I still had that curiosity, but it was mixed with fear.

3:15 am.

The door remained closed. My phone vibrated on the table loudly, startling me. I grabbed it and turned off the vibration, annoyed at the interruption.

3:18 am.

I put my phone down and rubbed my eyes, feeling the weight of sleeplessness on my eyelids. A few moments later a loud clicking noise resounded in the room. The door. I stood up, my heart thumping in my chest. I waited in anticipation, but nothing happened. I started to think I heard the click somewhere else instead, but my doubts were washed away when the loud creaking noise from my dream last night started again.

The door was opening. I watched as more and more of the darkness from the corridor got revealed, making me feel uneasy like yesterday. The painfully loud creaking of the door ended when it fully opened, leaving me to stand in silence in front of the unknowingly long corridor ahead of me. I took a step closer, trying to see through the darkness. I turned on my phone's torch and pointed it there, but it only illuminated enough for me to see the darkness stretching further. It was definitely extending farther than a typical storage room. I wanted to step inside, but fear and rational thinking prevented me from doing so. I didn't know where this thing took and how far it went. And not to mention the fact that I had no adequate light to go in. And if the door closed on me before I left, I could be stuck in there until tomorrow night. Or longer.

I had to make sure what I would be getting into. So I decided to wait instead. I sat on the couch and sure enough, at 4:19 am sharp, the loud click of the lock resounded and the door was locked once again. I had to know what was in there, I just had to. The following day I bought a torch and a very long rope. I didn't know how far that thing went and if it had any crossroads, so I wanted to be safe. I mean for all I knew, it ended only after a dozen feet, but something told me that that wasn't the case. I got back home and barely had the time to take the rope and flashlight out of the bag before I heard the doorbell ring.

It was my neighbor Vincent.

"Hi, neighbor." – he smiled – "Got a minute?"

"Sure, wanna come in?" – I asked, gesturing for him to come inside.

"Yeah, sure." – he said and walked in.

He glanced at the flashlight and rope on the table and asked:

"Going mountain climbing?" – he asked.

"Oh you know, just going hiking this weekend." – I made up an excuse quickly.

"Oh nice. Where will you be going?"

"The usual most likely, trail 3." – I quickly said.

"Trail 3? Hasn't that trail been closed for a while now?" – Vincent asked suspiciously.

"Has it?" – I made a surprised facial expression – "I thought it was open."

"Not as far as I can tell. Something happened there a while ago and they closed it down until further notice. You can take trail 5 though."

He seemed to buy what I was saying, so I relaxed a little bit:

"Thanks. So what can I do for you, Vincent?"

"Just wanted to introduce myself properly." – he said – "Was everything okay since that night with the mice?"

"Yeah, you were probably right, it was just mice." – I brushed it off and told him to sit down - "Would you like some coffee or something to drink?"

"No, it's okay. I have to get back soon anyway. My wife Margery is probably impatient already." – he sat down.

His phone buzzed, so he pulled it out and started typing a message.

"So, what do you do for a living, Nate?" – he asked while vigorously typing on his phone, the sound of tapping resounding in the room.

"I work as a freelancer, coding stuff, that kinda thing." – I replied, sitting on a chair across from him.

"That so? You work from home?" – he nodded, taking his gaze away from the phone for a second to look at me before continuing to type.

"Yeah. How about you? How long have you been in this apartment?"

"Oh, since the building was built. It was me, my wife and our 19-year old daughter Susan, but she moved out about six months ago." – he continued typing.

"That sounds great. Speaking of that, I wanted to ask you something."

I paused for a moment, while the sound of typing continued.

"Do you know anything about the previous tenant of this apartment?" – I asked.

Vincent stopped typing suddenly, but continued staring at his phone.

"The previous tenant?" – he asked and frowned for a moment, before shaking his head – "No, don't know the person. Why do you ask?"

He scratched his cheek, finally locking eyes with me.

"I was just curious, is all."

"I see. Well, I'd better get going." – he slapped his knees and stood up – "If you ever wanna drop by for a cup of coffee or lunch, Margery makes a hell of a casserole."

"Thanks." – I weakly smiled.

He turned around at the threshold, saying:

"Oh, and one more thing. You be careful while hiking, yeah? Don't go too far ahead, even with that flashlight. That route 5 can be a little tricky sometimes. You understand?" – he was very serious.

"Yeah. I got it." – I nodded.

I noticed that he was looking over my shoulder, at the storage door.

"Good." – he smiled and looked back at me after a moment of awkward pause – "Have a good one, Nate." – he waved and left, just like last time.

I closed the door, replaying the conversation in my head. Was Vincent hiding something? My thoughts were interrupted when I saw the flashlight and rope on the table and remembered my mission for tonight. I took a nap in order to stave off being sleepiness and woke up around 8 pm. I ordered some food and like the previous night, turned on the TV to pass the time. When it was 2 am, I took the flashlight and tested if it worked. I turned off the lights in my apartment and made sure it could illuminate a good distance. I also took some spare batteries despite the ones in the torch being fully charged. You never know.

I took the rope and tied it to the leg of the couch and I tied the other end to my left wrist. I then proceeded to sit down on my couch and continued watching TV. 3:19 am came and sure enough, the loud click of the door resounded in the room, followed by the loud creaking as the door opened widely, revealing the abyssal entrance in front. I stood up. It was time.

I grabbed the torch and turned it on, pointing it at the dark corridor. It illuminated a good distance, but at the end of the beam was just more darkness. Part of me had hoped that the corridor wasn't that long, but that hope had vanished now and part of me realized that what I was dealing with could not be explained logically. Without further thinking, I stepped across the threshold and was immediately overcome by cold. I had completely forgotten about that. I was determined not to let that stop me and I didn't want to go back to dig out a jacket, so I simply proceeded. The corridor was barely wide enough for one person to pass through. The ceiling was just inches above my head. The entire corridor seemed to be made out of plain concrete, walls, floor and ceiling.

Step by step, I went deeper into the gaping mouth of the darkness, leaving the solace of my apartment behind me and dragging the rope tied to my wrist. I glanced back at the open door every now and then, afraid it would close earlier than I expected. As I went further in, the light which emanated from my apartment through the crack gradually became smaller and smaller, until I could barely see it. I heard distant creaking from time to time, which enforced my theory that there were other doors on the other side and not just the one from my storage.

My brain was telling me to stop and go back, but I was just too curious. I had to know what was on the other end. I went on, glancing at the watch from time to time. I figured I should go forward no more than 25 minutes, so that I have time to get back before the door closes. The door from my apartment was now just a small dot and the creaking in the distance became more frequent. At moments in felt like it was coming from behind me, so I'd turn around, but would see nothing. I glanced at my watch. It was 3:45 am. Just 5 more minutes and then I'll turn back, I thought. I'll run back to make it in time.

I went on a little bit further and then saw something different from the repetitive pathway up until now – there was something white on the ground. I approached it and realized it was a piece of paper. I bent down and pointed my torch at it. There were two words scrawled on it. Two simple words:

GO BACK

I read the words aloud and stared at them in bewilderment. Who left this here? Either way, it was time for me to go back, since it was almost 4 am and the rope was probably almost at its end. I stood up and just then, I felt something which made my blood run cold.

The rope which held my hand was gently tugged. I hoped that it was my imagination, so I stood still and pointed the flashlight down. My hand was trembling, but not moving. And then I felt the rope tightening and saw my hand moving back and forth once. And then once more. And then again. I held my breath, listening to the creaking sound in the distance behind me which echoed.

Suddenly, my hand was tugged violently enough to almost make me lose my footing and I quickly wiggled out of the rope and watched as it fell limply and slid across the ground, disappearing in the dark beyond the flashlight beam. I trembled violently and not from the cold. The beam of my flashlight aggressively bounced up and down from my trembling hands as the sound of door creaking got louder and louder until it felt like whatever was making that sound would just jump into my line of sight any second. I stared like that, breathing heavily, and then the creaking suddenly came to a halt.

It was replaced by another sound, but I couldn't tell what it was. It sounded like something being dragged on the floor. And then I saw it. A hand appeared in the light, a pale, skinny hand, with dirty and ruined fingernails that looked like they had been clawing at something solid. Another hand appeared, trying to get a firm grip on the ground with bony fingers. Very slowly, the hands dragged into view a head – a head with a messy, black hair which fell unevenly on the floor, covering the face which was looking down.

I couldn't do anything but stare, as the head lifted up, revealing one bloodshot eye which was not obscured by the messy hair and a face as pale as the floor below it. The woman then opened her mouth and from it came a loud door creaking noise. That was enough to break me out of my trance.

I turned around and ran as fast as I could in the other direction, not caring where I would end up. The creaking noise followed closely behind, never growing louder or quieter, but being present just enough to muffle my own panicked breathing as I ran. I sprinted through the corridor like that until my lungs started burning and then in front of me I saw a small white dot. As I ran the dot got bigger and bigger, revealing a door-shaped hole and I knew that I had to reach it, for it was my only means of escaping.

The creaking persisted, right at my heels and I knew that if I slowed down or stopped to take a break, that woman would catch up with me. The exit was so close now. I pushed my unwilling legs to continue going, holding my flashlight unsteadily in my hand. The white light which emanated from the door offered salvation, I knew about that, so I had to reach it before that thing caught up with me.

Just as I was completely blinded by the bright light from the door, I crossed the threshold, practically stumbling over something and painfully falling to the ground. I turned around just in time to see the woman from before standing a few feet away from me. She produced a weak creaking sound before retreating back in the darkness. And then the door abruptly shut with a loud bang, leaving me in total silence. I took a moment to calm myself down and absorb what just happened. I stood up and as I was about to turn around, a voice behind me spoke:

"You fell for it, huh?" – I turned around just in time to see man standing in the room.

CHAPTER 2

I stared at the man under the dim light, who simply flashed me a smile. Although he couldn't have been older than thirty, he had heavy bags under his eyes, his hair was messy and his cheekbones visible.

"Who are you?" – I asked him and observed my surroundings, still breathing heavily from the ordeal just before.

I seemed to be located in an apartment, but it looked like it had been abandoned for a while. The walls were dilapidated, cracked and stained with various colors. A musty couch sat in the corner of the room and the coffee table next to it looked like it would collapse if you leaned on it with one finger. The kitchen was in no better shape either, with the oven and other surfaces being covered in rust. The rest of the apartment was empty, like someone had selectively taken things out.

"Where are we?" – I asked.

"My name's Martin." – the man responded – "And we are in room 102. The room isn't occupied yet since it still needs some cleaning done, but it should be ready soon."

"Ready soon? Are you kidding?" – I let out a chuckle at the absurdity of his response – "Seriously though, what's going on here?"

Martin frowned and put his hands behind his back:

"I'm not sure what you mean."

"Did you not just see that thing in there?!" – I pointed to the door, frustrated.

Martin stared at me with a neutral facial expression. It was as if he didn't comprehend what I was saying.

"Listen, I just came here to tell you that they're looking for you. So come on, you already kept them waiting a while." – he shrugged calmly.

Before I could process what he said, let alone respond to it, Martin opened the front door and waved for me to follow him.

"Wait a second!" – I reached out with my arm in futility, but he was already gone.

I glanced at the door which I dropped out of, which despite its decay looked very similar to my own storage door. I made sure it was still closed and then ran after Martin.

"Martin!" – I called out to him, stepping out into the corridor, but he was gone.

I muttered a what the fuck to myself when I saw what was in front of me. It was clear that I was in my apartment building, but it was as if it had completely changed. The walls out here were no better than inside room 102, having lost their original color probably ages ago and their outer layers crumbling.

There were various scratches and writings, which made me assume it was vandalism. Upon closer inspection I realized that they were incoherent, but enigmatic messages which grabbed my attention.

CAN'T FIND HIM

One of the walls said in crude letters, indicating it must have been carved with little to no care or skill. As I turned around I saw another message on the opposite wall.

WHERE IS HE

Despite my surreal predicament, I couldn't help but stare at the writings, trying to figure what they could all mean. Who wrote this and why? Can't find who? I proceeded down the hallway, seeing more and more messages on the walls, which became increasingly more desperate.

WHO IS HE?

TRICKED

HELP ME

CANT GET OUT

I suddenly felt a strong urge to go to my own apartment, like a moth drawn to light. Everything would be okay and I would have my answers, if only I could reach my room. I went down the hall carefully, glancing behind every few seconds. I half expected that lady from the corridor to appear behind me or that horrid creaking noise to start and all of that put me on edge.

I hadn't made it even halfway through when I heard voices around the corner. I stopped, listening intently. It sounded like a man and woman were having a casual conversation, but I couldn't make out what they were saying. I tip-toed my way to the corner and put my back against the wall, listening.

"So what's your name?" – the male voice asked.

"Michelle." – the female voice replied.

"Nice to meet you, Michelle. I'm Vincent."

I gasped, instinctively jerking my head towards the voices. Vincent? My neighbor Vincent?

"I live in 204." – the male voice continued – "If you ever hear any screaming coming from my apartment, don't be alarmed, that's probably my wife Margery shouting at me."

He and Michelle let out a chuckle. That was definitely the same Vincent. My curiosity got the better of me, so I peeked around the corner. Vincent was leaning on the wall to the left, facing away from me. He was standing in front of a woman, but I couldn't see her from here.

"Hey!" – I shouted.

They ignored me.

"You should stop by for lunch or dinner sometime." – Vincent continued talking to Michelle – "My wife makes a great casserole."

"Vincent!" – still no response.

Hey, do you hear me?!" – I shouted, but he didn't respond.

I violently grabbed him by his shoulder and almost fell down face first, since my hand simply went through him. I stared in bewilderment as it all started to dawn on me. Michelle and Vincent probably weren't here physically. Was this happening right now back in the 'real' apartment? Or was it a memory?

"Thanks, Vincent." – Michelle responded.

I looked at her for the first time now. A young woman with blonde hair and green eyes, probably in her early twenties.

"Hey listen." – she continued, suddenly looking uncomfortable – "Has anyone ever told you anything... weird about the building?"

"Weird? Don't think so." – Vincent shook his head with a frown – "I don't know the other tenants that much, though."

"I see."

"Why, is something wrong with the apartment?"

"Um..." – she paused for a moment and then shook her head – "No, it's nothing."

"Well, if anything needs fixing, you can contact the super, he's always around."

"Thanks." – she smiled.

Her smile remained frozen like that and I realized then that both of them ceased moving completely. Vincent's look of concern while leaning on the wall and Michelle's crossed arms while she smiled. I stepped around Vincent and leaned in closer to Michelle. I waved my hand to see if I could touch her and suddenly felt a strong grip on my wrist, as my hand was pinned in place.

When I looked down, I realized that Michelle was gripping me so tightly that her fingers turned white. In a fit of panic, I tried yanking my hand away, but her grip was like a vice. I tried to pry her fingers away, but to no avail. When I looked up, I saw that she was staring at me with a look of fear on her face. She spoke, with a trembling voice, while the rest of her body was as still as a statue:

"You have to help me. Please. Find me."

I continued trying to pull away, but she wouldn't let go. She suddenly looked over my shoulder and her eyes widened in terror.

"Oh no." – she said, fear palpable in her voice.

I felt the grip on my wrist loosen and myself falling backwards uncontrollably.

"Hide! Now!" – Michelle said and her entire figure, including face froze again.

And then I heard it. The sound which on a normal day wouldn't have me bat an eye, but now filled me with such terror that I felt my blood running cold. The unmistakable sound of a door slowly creaking.

I turned around to see an emaciated figure with long black hair down the hall, crawling on the ground. I knew that I had to run right away, so I scrambled up and frantically started running as fast as my already fatigued legs allowed me to. I heard the creaking behind me become louder and more violent, as if someone opened the door in a quick manner, but the motion of the door opening was endless. It was ear-splitting and enough to give me a boost to not stop.

The door at the end of the hallway to what I knew was apartment 109 was wide open and it was beckoning me to run inside. I ran and ran, but no matter how much I did, the door always seemed to be the same distance away. I made the mistake of looking behind me and nearly crapped my pants when I saw the creaking lady closing in at a ludicrous speed crawling with her bony arms. For the one second I glanced at her I saw that her messy hair fell over her face, making me wonder how she was even able to see me.

I ran faster than I thought possible, my lungs and entire body burning, while the door in front of me seemed to only get farther and farther. But then suddenly the door got closer at an enormous speed, until I finally reached it and ran inside, turning around and backhanding the door with my fist, effectively shutting it.

I was about to put all my weight against the door to prevent that woman from getting in, but before I could do it, she rammed the door, shaking it violently in the process. I stood there and watched as the door knob rattled aggressively, with the now muffled creaking on the other side. I thought she would get in, but after a few dread-filled moments all sounds stopped completely.

I leaned on my knees, breathing heavily and feeling like I was gonna throw up.

"Funny place to go jogging." – a voice spoke behind me.

I turned around to see Martin standing in the dilapidated room, calmly staring at me.

"What the hell are you?!" – I asked between breaths, too confused, tired and scared to demand more firmly.

He gave me a look of pity, glancing down at his shoes before looking back at me and saying:

"Michelle is expecting you. But I'm afraid she will have to wait until next time. Visiting hours are over."

"You know where Michelle is? I need to talk to her, take me to-" – I stepped towards Martin, but with a swift and elegant motion he raised one hand and pushed me gently.

I felt myself falling backwards to the floor. When I rose up, Martin was gone. And not just him. The entire apartment in the state I saw it was gone. I was back on the floor of my living room. I jerked my head towards the storage door, which was closed. When I glanced at my watch I realized it was 5:21 am. Did I fall asleep before the door opened and I just had a vivid dream?

As I propped myself with my hands to stand up, I noticed something which made me stop and my heart race fast. Something on my right wrist. There were distinctive finger-shaped marks on it.

One thing was for sure, though. I had more questions than answers.

CHAPTER 3

I knew I had to get out of there and find a new apartment to live in, but I just couldn't. Something was very wrong and there were people who were potentially in danger. I couldn't just let them go.

The question which plagued my mind constantly was - who was Michelle? If she was the previous tenant, then Vincent lied to me about not knowing other tenants. I had to talk to him. But I couldn't just barge in at 6 am, demanding to know who Michelle was, so instead I decided the best approach would be coming for lunch and starting a casual conversation with him. Maybe his wife would also shed some light on the whole situation.

But first I had to get some rest. I was beyond physically and mentally tired and needed a break. I fell into my bed, feeling like I was going to fall through the softness of it and stared at the ceiling. It couldn't have been more than a few minutes when I started to feel my eyelids become heavy.

For some reason however, I couldn't relax. There wasn't any particular reason why I couldn't, I just couldn't. I closed my eyes and then shot them open. I thought I heard someone calling my name, so I looked around the room. It must have been my imagination, though, since no one was there.

I closed my eyes again.

"Nathan…" – a soft whisper made me open my eyes again.

Despite feeling my heart start to race, I struggled to keep my eyes open. I hazily looked around the room, but no one was there. I relented and closed my eyes again.

"Nathan…" – the whisper resounded again, louder and clearer than last time.

I opened my eyes once more, still struggling to keep them open despite the clear presence of another person in my room. I wanted to get up, but I couldn't. It's as if my body was just too heavy to even move my head.

"Nathan…" – the whisper was directly in my ear now, but I couldn't look.

I should have been frightened shitless, but for a very strange reason, the voice seemed to have an opposite effect and I felt my eyes staying closed for longer periods of time.

And then I heard the sound which made jump out of bed. Creaking. My eyes shot open and stayed like that. I could move again, so I scrambled out of my bed, frantically looking around, only to find an empty bedroom. After calming down, I glanced at my watch. 13:25 pm. I had slept through the entire morning without even realizing it, but felt surprisingly refreshed. I grabbed a snack and decided it was finally time to visit my neighbor.

I got out my apartment and as I closed the door, I saw that the old lady from 307 heading towards her apartment.

"Ma'am, wait-" – I started, but she shot me an angry glance and interrupted me.

"Stay the hell away from me!" – she said as she pulled out her keys and turned to the door.

"Ma'am, please, I just want to know a few things. About my apartment. My life could be at stake here. And possibly the lives of other people." – I recited as quickly as possible, out of fear of having her lose interest or interrupt me again.

She put her keys in the lock and then froze, shaking her head.

"All I can tell you is, you need to get out of here if you value your life." – she looked at me with utter seriousness – "That apartment is dangerous."

She twisted the keys and unlocked the door with a loud metallic echo. She opened the door, ready to step in.

"Wait, why is it dangerous? What do you know about it?"

My demands fell on deaf ears as the lady went inside and shut the door in my face yet again. I wanted to call out to her, but ultimately decided not to bother her. Besides, I had to go and talk to Vincent. I ran down the flight of stairs and got to apartment 204. I raised my hand to knock on the door, when I saw a piece of paper taped to it.

GONE FISHING. BACK TOMORROW.

It said on the paper. I ignored the message, my brain refusing to believe what it was seeing. I knocked three times loudly and stepped back. A moment later, I knocked again. No one opened. Of course they didn't. I put my ear against the door, trying to detect any noise. I thought for a moment that I heard someone talking, but then realized the sound was coming from another apartment. Defeated, I went back to my room.

I slumped on the couch in the living room, staring at the ominous storage door in front of me. I kept replaying the event from the previous night in my mind. Who was Michelle? The previous tenant? And who the hell was that Martin guy? He seemed so relaxed, despite being in such a predicament. It was as if he couldn't see what I saw, as crazy as it sounded.

I glanced at the bruises on my wrist to make sure I wasn't imagining the whole thing. Michelle told me to find her. If I did, maybe she would give me some answers. I remembered feeling a strong urge to go to apartment 304 in that twisted alternate reality, so maybe that's where she was.

At some point I fell asleep again and woke up a few hours later. It was almost dark out, so I decided to pass the time by working until 3:19 am, when the door would open.

3:19 came and sure enough, right on cue, the loud creaking ensued and the door opened. I hadn't thought about it up until then, but when the door opened I suddenly remembered the creaking lady. I was scared, yeah, but I knew I had to help Michelle. I contemplated calling the cops, but something told me the door would not open if someone else showed up. Deep down I knew that chaining or walling up the door wouldn't work either.

I luckily still had my flashlight from last night, so I grabbed it and strode down the dark corridor without a moment of delay. I focused on where the beam ended in front of me and continued taking large steps, to get through the dark place as soon as possible.

Not even five minutes into my walk I saw the light at the end of the hallway. I ran towards it, expecting to hear that creaking sound any moment. It never came though and I passed through the bright threshold, stepping into the dilapidated room from before once again.

"Welcome back." – an voice devoid of any emotions said.

When I looked towards the source, I realized it was Martin.

"I see you found the place faster this time. Looks like you're making yourself at home." – he smiled and gestured to the door.

I didn't try talking to him. I knew I'd get no concrete answers, so I simply nodded and left the room. The apartment was exactly how I remembered it last night, looking like it had been abandoned for ages. I carefully proceeded down the hallway, still expecting the creaking lady to show up. My footsteps alarmingly echoed through the entire corridor, as I swiveled my head left and right to make sure no one else was around.

Soon I reached the stairs and pointed my beam at the top. I couldn't see anything, even with the flashlight. The beam should have illuminated the top easily, but it was like the light was just cut off at one point which acted as an invisible wall. I heard something heavy being dragged across the ground on the floor above and I instinctively pointed my flashlight to the ceiling. The dragging sounded as if someone was having a really hard time moving the object, so they would yank it and stop before the next yank. This lasted for about a dozen yanks, moving all the way from one end of the ceiling to the other, until it just stopped completely.

I held my breath in anticipation, but nothing happened. Then, a very faint creaking noise came from somewhere in the distance. I couldn't tell where from though, so I shot around, scanning the place. No creaking ladies. I suddenly felt uneasy standing here, like a sitting duck. It felt as though eyes were on my back, but I couldn't confirm my suspicions.

Unwillingly, I took a step towards the stairs, not taking my eyes off the darkness in front. Luckily, as I climbed each step, the darkness in front of me started dispersing and my light penetrated more, revealing steps further in front of me. The long flight of stairs extended much longer than it should have and it took me over a minute of straight climbing until I reached the top.

The second floor was far worse than the first one. The walls seemed to be covered with something strange and as I illuminated a portion of the wall with my torch, I thought I saw the walls moving. I came a step closer to see and when I realized what it was, I gasped loudly.

Maggots. Hundreds of thousands of them covering every inch of every wall, slithering across each other. I pointed my beam up and to my horror, they were on the ceiling as well. I turned around and bolted for the stairs, but almost ran into a wall full of maggots instead. Where the stairs had been just a moment ago was now a solid wall.

I started panicking, but when I pointed my beam to the floor, I realized that it was clear of all maggots. Not a single one was on the floor and instead they amassed on the walls and ceilings in unison. I breathed a sigh of partial relief and hurriedly strode through the hallway, making sure to keep my head down and swat away at any paranoid feeling I had of something creeping on my skin.

Then, a loud creaking noise resounded right in front of me. I widened my eyes and shot the beam around. When I looked to my left, I saw that the door to 204 was opening. Vincent's room. When the door was fully open and the creaking stopped, I heard voices from inside.

"We can't do that." – a female voice was heard.

I went inside the apartment and expected to find some more dilapidated walls and maggots. Instead I was baffled at the way it was clean and normal-looking. No worms, no worn-out walls and scratches. It was a solid apartment worth living in that didn't belong in this place anyhow and yet, it was here.

"We have no choice, Margery." – Vincent's voice was clearly heard from inside.

I followed it and saw him and who I guessed was his wife sitting at the kitchen table. They both seemed like they hadn't slept in days.

"The other tenants could become suspicious." – Margery said with a trembling voice.

It looked as if she was suppressing a sob.

"We have no other choice, Margery. We'll keep it a secret. And we'll ask others to keep quiet about it, too."

"But what if they don't, Vincent?"

"I'll make sure they do. No one will know about this. I promise."

Vincent put his hand on Margery's and they froze like that.

"It's time to go, Nathan." – I heard a voice behind me.

I turned around to see Martin standing there, as calm as ever.

"Who the hell are you?" – I suddenly felt a surge of anger – "What do you want from me?!"

He calmly shook his head before saying:

"You still don't understand. It's not about what you want. You still need time to understand."

"No, you liste-"

Like the night before, he pushed me and I fell to the ground, waking up in my own apartment.

"Dammit." – I cursed loudly.

I glanced at my watch and realized it was 4:20 am. Guess I'll have to try again tomorrow, I thought. I slumped into bed and fell asleep almost instantly. No voices or presences this time. When I awoke, it was 11 am. I felt groggy, but I didn't want to sleep anymore, so I forced myself to get up.

I made breakfast and took a shower, simply trying to pass more time before visiting Vincent again. As I ate, I remembered the conversation he had with Margery at the kitchen table. He was hiding something and I was adamant about finding out what it was.

Around noon I went downstairs, only to have my hopes drop the second I saw his door from the distance, seeing that the posted note was still up.

"For fuck's sake, Vincent." – I muttered to myself before shaking my head turning back.

As I returned to my own floor and put the keys in the door, I heard a voice behind me:

"Hey."

I turned around. It was my neighbor from 307. She was standing at her door, unsteadily holding the frame with one hand.

"Do you wanna come in for a cup of coffee?" – she asked with a neutral facial expression.

I stared dumbly, unable to form a sentence.

"Well, don't make me repeat myself." – she said more sternly this time.

"Uh, yes, yeah. I'd love some coffee." – I managed to blurt out.

She smiled and led me inside her apartment which was decorated in a noticeably less fashionable way than my own. It still looked like a cozy place though, despite being a little cluttered.

"Make yourself at home. I'll be right back." – she said and went to make coffee.

I sat, listening to the sounds coming from the kitchen. I was on needles, like waiting for a job interviewer to show up. A few moments later she came back with coffee and sat on the sofa opposite of me.

"We haven't met properly yet." – she said – "I'm Dolores."

"Nathan." – I smiled.

She took a sip of her coffee, while I awkwardly scanned her apartment. There was a picture of a man in uniform standing on one of her shelves, right next to a tiny cross.

"That was my husband, Harold." – she glanced at the picture – "He died 12 years ago. Cancer."

"I'm sorry."

"Don't be. We had time to say our goodbyes, that's what I'm grateful to the lord for. It's hard sometimes without him, but my kids help me out."

I awkwardly took a sip of my own coffee. I didn't know what to say. A moment of silence fell on the room before Dolores continued.

"Planning on staying here long, Nathan?" – she asked.

"You mean in your home or the apartment?" – I asked and we both chuckled.

"Room 304. Very strange place. Very inhospitable."

"What do you mean?" – I stared at my cup.

"Oh don't play dumb. You know exactly what I mean. I'm sure you've noticed some things by now. And I can assure you, none of it is normal."

I put my coffee down and leaned on my knees, staring at Dolores.

"What do you know about my apartment, Dolores?" – I asked.

She exhaled deeply and stared at the coffee table for a moment. I knew what she was about to say would be important, but also unpleasant for her. She said:

"There are things on this earth that simply cannot be explained by logic. Things which are so foul that they are beyond any scientific explanation. I moved here right after this place was built. Vincent from 204... his daughter Susan was the first person to rent the apartment."

"What? Vincent's daughter lived in 304?" – I didn't even try to hide my shock.

"She lived there for only two months before disappearing. Poor Vincent. He hasn't been the same since. I never asked him about it, but now I'm certain it was the apartment. It had something to do with Susan's disappearance."

Dolores looked at her husband's picture. Her facial expression turned to one of painful reminiscence.

"You've seen something there, haven't you?" – I asked.

She continued staring at the picture for a long moment.

"Voices often come from your apartment." – she said, not moving her gaze from her husband's smiling face – "At first I thought there were more people in there. But then someone told me the apartment wasn't even occupied by a new tenant yet. Then one night, I heard my husband calling me from the apartment.

I thought I was dreaming, so I stayed in bed awake, listening. At first there was only silence, but then I heard his voice again. 'Dolly', he called out to me. He was the only one who called me that. You gotta understand that the walls are thin here and you can hear your neighbors clearly. So when I heard Harold's voice I got up and followed it. It became more and more apparent that it was coming from 304. 'I'm in here, Dolly', he kept saying.

I turned the knob and the apartment was unlocked for some reason. I went in, even though my body was screaming at me to run away. I came to this one door inside the apartment which was closed and it was clear to me now that my Harold was in there, right on the other side of the door.

I asked if it was really him, shaking all over. It's been so long since I've seen him and my still sleepy mind couldn't comprehend what it was hearing. What really worried me though, was the fact that I wasn't glad I heard him. I was dreading it. I had seen him die and already came to terms with his death, and then to hear him here in this foul place... it just didn't feel right.

He told me to open the door and I grabbed the knob, almost fully ready to do it. But I couldn't. Something was telling me not to open that door. Harold, or whatever the hell that thing on the other side was, sensed my hesitation, so he asked me again to open the door, telling me that we could finally be together again.

When I willed myself to back away, he became violent, calling me names and telling me the most horrible things, that he never loved me and that he couldn't wait to die to get away from me."

She paused and sniffled, wiping her tears.

"So I ran from there as fast as I could, not looking back and ignoring his taunts. I locked my apartment and went inside my bedroom, hearing the muffled voice of my dead husband. Eventually, it stopped."

She looked at me finally with red eyes and said:

"I never made a step closer to the apartment again. Even though I was friendly with the tenant who lived here right before you came along, I never dared enter 304 again. And then soon after, she disappeared as well."

We stared at each other in silence for a moment before I finally asked:

"Who was that tenant? Do you know her name?"

Dolores nodded.

"Of course." – she smiled – "Her name was Michelle."

CHAPTER 4

Dolores told me everything she knew. She knew the tenant's name was Michelle and that she suddenly became more reclusive before she disappeared, but that was it. She was certain the apartment was directly involved. I asked her if she knew who the landlord was, but of course, she didn't. Seems that no one did and by this point I started to believe firmly that he was somehow directly involved in all this.

I finished my coffee and thanked Dolores, telling her I should probably get going.

"Wait." – she said as I got up.

She approached the shelf which her husband's photo had been on and took the tiny cross. She took my hand and forcefully put the cross in, saying:

"The lord keeps me safe in my own place. But you need much stronger protection in there."

I wasn't an atheist, but I wasn't a strong believer, either. I didn't believe that a wooden cross would somehow protect me from whatever those evil forces in the apartment were, but I wanted to assure Dolores since she was worried.

"I'll put it in my living room. Thank you, Dolores." – I said, putting the cross in my pocket.

"Listen." – she said when I reached the door threshold – "If you hear something coming from that storage room, any voices of anyone who you think is a person you may know… ignore it. I can assure you, whoever is on the other side is not interested in your well-being."

I nodded and she closed the door. I exhaled and took a step towards my room before stopping. Just then, there was the sound of doors opening and closing loudly on the ground floor. A male voice echoed all the way to the third floor, clear enough for me to hear:

"The keys are on you, Margery?" – it was Vincent.

My neighbor was finally back, but I decided to wait a couple more hours, so that it doesn't seem like I'm assaulting him as soon as he came back from fishing. I knew I had every right to do so, but it was in my interest to be on his good side if I wanted to get any information about Susan, Michelle and the landlord.

I returned to my room and ordered some food. After eating and cleaning up, I couldn't wait anymore, so I decided to go downstairs. The more I thought about it, the angrier I got at Vincent. He knew something was wrong with the apartment and even his own daughter went missing while living there and he hid it all from me.

I knocked on his door, trying to stay as calm as possible. A moment later, the door swung open and an elderly lady with a gentle face stood before me.

"Hi!" – she said with a big, warm smile – "You're Nathan, right? Come on in."

Before I could even say anything, she ushered me inside, so I gave her a meager 'thank you' under my breath.

"Vince, our neighbor Nate is here!" – Margery shouted.

"Nathan? Well bring him on inside!" – Vincent shouted back from their living room.

"You go on ahead, the living room is there." – Margery said and went inside the kitchen.

I went to the living room. The apartment looked exactly like in the vision I had in room 204.

"Nathan, good to see you, son." – Vincent shook hands with me and gestured me to sit down – "We just came back home recently."

"Yeah, I saw your note. How was fishing? Catch anything big?" – I asked.

He sat down across from me and then leaned in and whispered:

"My biggest catch to this day is still my wife." – he smiled.

"I HEARD THAT YOU OLD BASTARD!" – Margery's voice came from the kitchen.

"I meant that in a good way!" – Vincent rebutted, but kept smiling.

It was clear that the couple was used to this sort of joking among them and were probably comfortable with it.

"I sometimes forget how you can hear everything in this building. Margery's gonna start cooking soon, you should stay." – Vincent said.

"Sure thing, thanks." – I said.

I really didn't want to stay, especially since I'd eaten prior to that, but wanted to stay on Vincent's good side. We made small talk for a while, him talking about his trip and me about work, leaving out the parts about the door and everything that happened related to it.

Ten minutes later Margery shouted from the foyer:

"Vincent, I need to pick some things up from the store, if you hear any sizzling noise, ignore it." – Margery said.

"Sure, Marge." – he said.

A moment later Margery left the apartment, leaving me alone with Vincent.

"Everything okay in your apartment, by the way?" – he asked casually.

This worked perfectly for me to initiate the topic.

"Uh, yeah. Everything is fine. I was just wondering about a few things."

"Yeah, like what?" – Vincent leaned back.

"Do you know anyone who lived in this building by the name of Michelle?" – I asked hesitantly and locked my eyes with his.

He stared at me for a moment before shaking his head, with a confused look on his face:

"Can't say I do. Like I said, don't talk to other tenants much."

"You sure? The lady on my floor, Dolores, said she saw you talking to one of the previous tenants." – I bluffed, hoping it would work.

Vincent looked uncomfortable, but tried hiding it. He thought for a moment and then snapped his fingers.

"You know what" – he said – "you're right, I did talk to one tenant. But I didn't know she lived in your room."

"Dolores said you guys got to know each other well, like exchanged names, things like that." – I refused to back down.

"Well, I don't remember." – he said angrily – "What's it to you, Nathan?"

"I know you lied to me, Vincent. About knowing the other tenants. About Susan."

"What are you talking about?"

"You told me Susan moved out. Dolores told me she lived in room 304 and disappeared shortly after. What's going on, Vincent?"

He shrugged and said:

"Look, Dolores is an old woman. A little delusional, too. Susan simply moved out and is currently in university."

I nodded, staring at the coffee table. A moment later, I said:

"The other tenants could get suspicious."

Vincent's eye widened:

"What did you just say?"

"That's what you told Margery." – I looked at him – "You were sitting at the kitchen table. You were both pale and tired. You assured her you'd have everyone keep the secret. What secret, Vincent?"

Vincent stared at me for a long moment and then leaned on his knees, shifting his gaze to the coffee table. He exhaled deeply and nodded.

"We moved here right after the place was built. We bought this apartment and wanted to leave it for Susan after we were gone, but she insisted she had her own place for renting in the meantime until left for college. So we indulged and rented 304 for her.

We never met the landlord. The real estate agency handled everything and we never asked any questions. Everything seemed fine at first, but not long after that, Susan simply disappeared. Her apartment was left unlocked and she was gone. No signs of forced entry, no signs of struggle, just gone."

By this point tears were beginning to well up in Vincent's eyes. He continued:

"The apartment was closed down for a short time while the investigation lasted, but after they found no evidence inside, the landlord started renting the place again. I still hope and pray that she will one day come home to us, unharmed. Having no conclusion like this is far worse than knowing you have to bury your own child."

He looked at me with red eyes.

"So yeah. That was the secret. I didn't want people to talk and to ask me and Margery about it, constantly reminding us of our loss, alright? We can't leave this place, but we want to forget."

"Vincent, I'm so sorry…" – I suddenly felt stupid and bad.

"It's alright. You didn't know. And it is a mysterious situation, being in an apartment with a locked storage and a landlord who you never met."

"About that door. Has it always been locked?"

"Always. Never opened since we arrived."

"Are you absolutely sure?"

"I know what you're implying, Nathan. But a door is just that. A door. Susan complained about sounds coming from the storage, so I had it checked out by professionals."

"Mice, right?" – I sarcastically asked.

"Yeah. Mice. Nothing else. Susan was kidnapped by someone and that's a fact, she didn't disappear because of something locked behind a door."

The front door opened and Margery stumbled inside with a grocery bag.

"Nathan, I think you'll love what I'm making" – she said enthusiastically.

Vincent stood up and said:

"I'm afraid Nate can't stay, Marge. Has some work to do, coding or something. Right, Nate?" – he looked at me.

"Yeah. Maybe next time." – I said, hesitantly.

"Oh, that's too bad. I'm making my famous stew, can't you stay a little longer?" – Margery said.

"I'll be sure to try it next time, ma'am." – I smiled – "Thank you for having me, though."

"You stop by again, son." – Vincent smiled and I could tell he meant what he said.

I returned to my apartment, replaying the entire conversation in my mind for a while. I couldn't imagine what Vincent was going through. I pushed the thoughts out of my head and decided I had to mentally prepare for my journey in the storage room tonight.

3:19 am came faster than usually and as always, the door opened. I lazily got up from my chair and ventured inside, through the corridor and into the dilapidated apartment room. Martin was there, as always.

He bowed his head down, but I simply ran past him. I couldn't afford to waste any time. I was ready to rush through the first floor towards the stairs, when I heard a loud 'ding' to my right.

I jerked my head towards the sound and saw one of those old-style elevators with metallic bars which could slide to the side. It was open and the lights inside which contrasted the rest of the rundown building were beckoning me. I hesitated for a moment, but then decided that wherever the elevator was going was probably my desired destination. Besides, if the apartment wanted to kill me, there were plenty of other ways it could have done so by now.

I entered the elevator and observed the buttons. All of them besides the button for floor 3 were missing, so I pressed that one. The elevator door slowly closed with a loud, rusty creak. A moment later, it started ascending, producing all sorts of unnerving metallic and scraping sounds. I thought the elevator would stop at any moment or worse, start dropping, but before I could process that thought properly, it came to a stop and the door opened with another loud ding.

In front of me was a very dark hallway, the elevator light and my torch barely illuminating anything. The floor looked like a metallic platform and not a regular one. I could see between the tiny bars of the floor, but my flashlight only revealed more darkness. I took a careful step forward, testing to see how stable it was. When I was sure it wouldn't collapse under my weight, I went forward, making sure to walk slowly and carefully.

On both sides of the hall were sturdy, rusted doors with numbers on them. This was definitely my floor.

The metal resounded under every step I took and I was afraid that if anyone was nearby, they'd hear me from a mile away. After a grueling minute of going forward through the dark, I started to see something in the distance. A faint light emanating from the left wall ahead.

I hurried up as it became apparent that the light was coming from one of the rooms – from room 304. I felt an irresistible urge to rush inside the room and as I felt myself walking towards it without my own control, I completely gave into that feeling and just went on. Everything would be alright, all I had to do was just reach the room.

And then, just as I was only a few feet away from the room I felt something grab me by the hand and forcefully yank me aside, opposite of 304. I lost balance and fell sideways, scrambling to my feet in a panic. When I stood up, I realized I was in a dilapidated room, with the light from 304 peering in across the hallway through the door.

A young woman stood in front of me.

"Don't go there. That's what it wants you to do." – she said.

It was Michelle.

"It's about time you found me." – Michelle said when she got no response from me.

"It is you!" – I said – "I went through hell and high water to find you here because you called me. What in the hell is going on here?"

"I know. I'm sorry you had to go through that. But you need to stop others from getting hurt by the apartment." – Michelle said.

"Tell me everything." – I said – "What do I need to do?"

She sighed and closed the door, effectively cutting off the light from 304. As soon as she did so though, a pale, neon light flickered to life in the room we were in and I could finally see Michelle clearly. She had heavy bags under her eyes and looked a lot skinnier and paler than the version of her which I saw back when I first entered the apartment. She very much reminded me of the creaking lady. I glanced at the surrounding walls and saw various messages scrawled all over them, just like the ones when I first entered the apartment. Some of them read:

CANT GET OUT

WHO IS THE LANDLORD??

CANT REMEMBER

CREEEEAAAAAAK

Some of the messages had names of who I assumed were tenants of the building and previous tenants of room 304. The entire room, with nothing in it but a small set of chairs next to a table and surrounded by carved walls looked like the residing place If a schizophrenic person. For a moment I questioned my decision to come here.

"Let's sit." – she pointed to the set of rusty chairs around a small, round table and I reluctantly obliged.

She stared me down for a good ten seconds or so with her tired eyes, before saying:

"If you're here, then you're in danger as well. This apartment... there's something very wrong with it."

"Yeah, no shit." – I scoffed, getting impatient and anxious.

"You don't understand. The stuff you saw, they're fucked up alright. But you have no idea to what extent that goes." – she leaned forward as she spoke.

"Then tell me. What is going on? How did you end up here? How do we close the door forever? I need to know everything."

She leaned back into the uncomfortable chair and said:

"The door can't be closed. I tried bolting it shut, but the door just doesn't obey the normal laws of physics."

"Then we need to think of something else." – I said.

Michelle looked down at the old table with a defeated gaze. She sighed and spoke:

"I moved here not long ago. Everything seemed perfect, save for that storage door. It was locked and I didn't mind it at first. But after only a few nights, I started hearing noises coming from inside. And not just regular, normal noises like rats or whatever. Even though I wish now that that's what it was. I swear I heard voices." – she leaned in again and her voice turned into a whisper.

"What kind of voices?"

"My mom. She passed away a few years ago. But she sounded like she was right there in that storage, in trouble, begging me to come save her. But I couldn't get the door open. And then when I called the police, the voices stopped, so they didn't believe me. Then one night, the door just opened. It always opened and closed at the same exact time."

"Yeah. 3:19 and 4:19." – I nodded.

"Exactly. Except when I entered, it wasn't a storage. It was the hallway from the hospital where my mother died. I couldn't believe it at first, it looked like I was back in that hospital, but it was physically impossible for me to be there. But the deeper I went the deeper I wanted to go. I had to find out if my mother was there. The hospital hall stretched for much longer than it should have and then when I finally reached the end I felt myself entering this world.

I was strangely drawn to the room where my mother was hospitalized, which happened to be on the fourth floor. So I followed my instinct and went there. Except when I got there, it wasn't the patient's room. It was room 304, with the door wide open and my mother calling me from inside.

So I rushed inside and then realized it was a trap. The apartment, it wanted me to get to room 304 so that it could trap me here like an animal. Once you get inside room 304 from this side, you're trapped here forever."

"Trapped? Is that why you've been here this whole time?" – I asked, hanging on every word Michelle said – "What does the apartment want? And what the hell is it exactly?"

Michelle shook her head:

"I don't know what it is. Whatever it is, its only purpose is to trap people here and then feed off of their life, until all that's left of them is an empty husk. I've been stuck in here for months and I know I'll never make it out."

"There's gotta be a way to release you from here."

She shook her head again:

"No. I tried everything, believe me. Even my sister tried to save me, since I informed her of everything before going in. But when she came, she didn't make it out of the limbo between our world and this one before 4:19 before the doors closed. Now she haunts this place as a mindless husk, producing a horrible sound of creaking doors."

"Wait." – it all started coming together – "The creaking lady is your sister?"

"You've seen her, haven't you? Poor Daniella… such a horrible, horrible fate." – she looked down, tears forming in her eyes and then back at me – "You have to destroy the place. Burn it to the ground. Release us and everyone else who fell victim to 304. Please."

"But you'll die then, won't you?"

"Please, Nathan. I can feel myself getting weaker every day and losing myself. I can hardly remember my past life and the people I loved. The apartment, it takes everything away from you. That's why I made these reminders on the walls. But every day I forget more and more. I don't want to end up like my sister, Nathan. Please." – she started sobbing.

A moment later she calmed down and I spoke again:

"Michelle, no one seems to know who the landlord is. Do you have any idea who it could be?"

"Not a clue. Whoever he is, he's responsible for all of this, but I don't know why he'd do it. Or maybe there never was a landlord and the room is its own owner. This whole apartment has its own fucking set of rules, I don't know anymore."

I nodded and asked her:

"Vincent from 204, his daughter Susan was the first person to go missing. Have you seen her in here?"

"No. I saw a lot of people here and I spent a long time looking for Susan, but she's nowhere to be found. Maybe Dolores was wrong. She was adamant about it, but maybe the apartment didn't take her."

"Seems too much of a coincidence. I'm sure she's somewhere in here."

"Even if she is, she's probably lost just like Dani and I. You have to burn the apartment nonetheless, Nathan. And don't tell Vincent anything about it. He says he firmly believes the apartment had nothing to do with her disappearance, but if you tell him you'll burn the place, he might try to stop you."

"I will. But I'll have to warn the other tenants. They need to get out." – I said.

"I'm counting on you, Nathan." – she said – "We all are."

Michelle froze in her sitting position. The tear which was sliding down her cheek stopped in place and she retained the horrified expression on her face. I waved my hand in front of her face, but she didn't flinch.

"Do you understand now?" – I turned to the left where the voice came from.

It was Martin, standing in the middle of the room, as calm as always, but this time with a vague smile of satisfaction. I stood up and faced him.

"I do." – I hesitantly said – "Whoever you are, whosoever side you're on, this will all be over soon, Martin."

He approached me and shook my hand, putting his other hand on my shoulder.

"It was a pleasure meeting you, Nathan." - for the first time I saw sorrow in his eyes and I realized that this was the last time I would probably see him.

He smiled widely and when I blinked, Martin was gone and I was back in my room. I looked down and saw a zippo lighter in my hand. I looked at the storage door, which was closed now.

At the foot of the door was a gasoline canister.

EPILOGUE

By this point I had already seen too much in order to be baffled by the sudden appearance of a gas can in my apartment. It was clear, the apartment had to be destroyed. I felt bad for the other tenants, since some of them probably owned the place, but it was too dangerous. Besides, insurance would cover their losses. I was worried about being arrested for arson, but whether it was my sleep-deprived and traumatized mind, I decided to go forward with the plan anyway. I still wasn't sure who Martin was and what his role in all this was, or whether I could even trust him. It didn't matter though, because the apartment had to be destroyed nonetheless.

I bent down and reached for the gas can, when I heard my doorbell ring, almost making me jump out of my skin. Confused, I looked at my watch to see if perhaps it was later than I thought. 4:23 am.

Who could it be at this hour? As I approached the door, a knocking on it resounded. Whoever it was, they were not about to leave. I peered through the peephole and saw an old man's face on the other side of the door. Vincent. Dammit, I can't let him see the gas can. I put the zippo in my pocket and hurriedly picked up the surprisingly heavier than thought can, hauling it to my bedroom. I then rushed to the door, hearing my doorbell ring again.

I unlocked the door and opened it, trying to act surprised that it was Vincent.

"Hey, Nate. How's it going?" – he smiled.

"Vince? It's 4 am, is everything okay?" – I asked, holding the door half-open and ready to close it any moment.

"I was actually gonna ask you the same. What are you doing up at this hour? Sounded downstairs like you're having aerobic exercises."

I didn't know what he meant, but decided to play along, so I said:

"Oh, sorry about that. I uh, I slipped and fell and then just knocked down a lot of things which I had to clean up. Didn't mean to wake you up."

"Nah, it's fine, son. Just wanted to make sure you were okay."

"Yeah, I am. So um…" – I waited for him to say goodbye.

Vincent puckered up his lips and nodded, looking down at his shoes, before looking back at me.

"Can I come in for a few minutes?" – he asked.

I was so caught off guard that I simply opened my mouth, not sure what to say to politely decline.

"Just for a few minutes." – he said when he saw my hesitation – "I know it's really early in the morning, but just wanted to talk to you about something."

I nodded hesitantly and opened the door widely, gesturing him to come in. We sat in the living room and I didn't offer him anything to drink this time, since I wanted him to leave as soon as possible.

"Listen, son." – he started – "About our last conversation. I'm sorry about the way I behaved. It wasn't very polite of me to see you out before Marge served lunch."

"No, it's fine." – I dismissed his statement – "I mean, I should be the one apologizing."

"No, no. You were curious, and it's normal. Hell, I'd have a lot of questions if I were in that situation, too. Susan was like that, too. Curious about everything, never stopping until she completed a task or got her answers. You remind me of her a lot, you know." – he looked at me with sadness in his eyes.

I didn't respond. I was somewhat moved by what he said, but my mind was elsewhere right now. Every now and again I'd glance at the storage door. Vincent looked down and let out a chuckle, shaking his head. He looked at me and continued speaking:

"The truth is, I had stopped thinking about her, since I simply wanted to push it out of my mind and never think about it again. But that's impossible. This apartment is a constant reminder. And then there's you, Nathan. Every time I see you, I remember her. And it makes me sad and happy at the same time. I know it all probably sounds stupid."

I sighed and said:

"Vincent, it's 4 in the morning and you're tired. We can talk about this over a beer tomorrow."

Vincent chuckled again:

"Yeah, I guess we can. I just want you to know that if you need anything, any help at all or whatever, I'm here for you. You understand?" – he shot me a stern look.

"Yeah. I think I do." – I nodded.

"Alright, well I should get going. Margery's baking a pie tomorrow, so stop by any time you like. I tell you, that woman is one hell of a cook." – he stood up.

He took a step towards the exit, but then stopped and glanced at the storage door. He stared the door up and down.

"Something wrong?" – I asked him.

"No. Nothing." – he smiled at me and went to the entrance door.

"I'll be there tomorrow around 6, maybe." – I said.

"Sure thing. I won't be going anywhere, so feel free to stop by any time that works for you." – he smiled again and turned to leave – "Have a good night, Nate."

He waved, facing away from me, which reminded me of our first encounter, that night when I first heard some noises coming from the storage and came to ask me to keep the noises down.

I waved back and watched all the way until he was out of my sight. When he was gone, I waited another few minutes or so at the door. Then I went back inside my apartment and closed the door. I grabbed the gas can and started to pour the liquid all over the apartment. Whoever the landlord was, he could go fuck himself along with this goddamn apartment.

I sparingly poured the liquid all over the floor, walls and furniture, tainting the once pristine apartment with stains and a pungent gasoline smell which permeated the air. I poured extra gasoline on the storage door and the surrounding walls and floor and then dispensed the rest of it around the kitchen and living room, gently putting the can down. It took everything in me not to use this adrenaline to toss it violently on the floor, but I didn't want to arouse suspicion with Vincent downstairs.

Once all that was done, I stood for a moment to observe my masterpiece. The apartment was definitely going to be uninhabitable after this, at least for a while. I could only hope that the fire would spread enough to destroy the entire place beyond repair.

I opened my apartment door just enough to peek out into the hallway and when I was sure no one was there, I stepped outside and went to the fire alarm. I had to warn the residents before I actually started the fire, otherwise they could get hurt. I owed at least that much to Dolores and Vincent. I thought of Michelle and how withered she looked back in that strange world. I thought about her sister and how the apartment enslaved her as nothing more than a tool. I thought about Martin, about Susan and everyone else who probably fell victim to the apartment and with those thoughts I smashed the alarm glass with my elbow as hard as I could.

I pressed the big red button and the alarm blared, causing my ears to throb. I backtracked to my apartment and saw the door to 307 was open. Dolores stood at the threshold, visibly scared.

"Nathan! What's going on?!" – she asked, probably still confused after just waking up.

"You need to get out of here now, Dolores! It's not safe here anymore!" – I shouted over the alarm and still barely heard my own voice.

She looked at me with a look of concern and leaned in to shout into my ear:

"Whatever you plan to do, make sure to finish it! No one can set foot inside that apartment ever again!"

I nodded and gestured her to leave. She didn't even bother closing her apartment door and instead hurriedly made her way to the stairs. She looked at me one last time, before descending.

I didn't have much time before the fire department was informed, so I quickly went back to the entrance of my room. I pulled out the zippo and tested it out. A small flame sparked to life. I remember thinking it would have been a damn shame it if didn't work and I had to go borrow a lighter from a neighbor. I closed the lid of the zippo and carefully knelt down, observing room 304 one last time.

I put my thumb on the lid to open it and then the back of my head suddenly exploded with pain. I stumbled forward, dropping the zippo.

"No, Nathan! I won't let you do this!" – a voice resounded somewhere in the distance and I knew right away without a doubt that it was Vincent.

I tried to turn around, but my vision was blurry and I could hardly move. I felt Vincent grabbing my shoulder and forcefully turning me onto my back.

"I won't let you kill my daughter!" – he shouted, towering above me at the entrance.

My vision started to clear up and I saw him now, a look of utter anger on his face. He was holding a crowbar firmly and breathing heavily.

"Vincent…" – I barely muttered – "You don't understand…"

"Oh I understand. You were trying to burn my apartment down and kill my daughter!"

"What?" – I propped myself on my elbows and started to back away from him slowly.

Vincent closed the door behind him, shutting us both into room 304.

"Yeah, that's right, Nate." – he said as he turned to me – "I'm the mysterious landlord you've been looking for."

"You?! You knew what was going on the whole time, didn't you?!"

"You don't get it, Nate. It was all an accident. It was never supposed to be this way. I never meant to hurt her."

"What are you talking about? You did something to Susan, didn't you?" – I asked, still on my elbows, now in my living room.

"It was an accident! She never even told me about her condition! How the hell was I supposed to know she needed those meds?!"

Suddenly, in addition to the pain in the back of my head I started to feel pain in the front as well. My vision got dark and then Images started flashing before my eyes. I saw Vincent and a young girl standing in the apartment. I felt as if I was actually there, observing the entire scene clearly. Vincent was in his pajamas and the girl looked like she was dressed for a date.

"Dad, what are you doing here?" – the girl asked.

"Do you have any idea what time it is, Susan?" – he angrily said to her.

"We lost track of time, I'm sorry. I didn't mean to stay so long." – Susan replied.

"It's 3 am, Susan! I told you to be home by midnight!"

"I said I was sorry!"

"That's not the point!"

Susan looked down at her shoes timidly.

"You never listen." – Vincent shook his head – "You need to be taught some manners."

He grabbed her by her wrist and she struggled for a moment before breaking free from his grip. This seemed to enrage Vincent more and he backhanded Susan, knocking her down.

"See what you're making me do?!" – Vincent shouted as he opened the storage door.

And that's exactly what it was – a normal storage with normal walls and normal tools inside. He grabbed Susan by her ankle and dragged her inside. He slammed the door shut and locked it, as Susan started banging on the door, pleading with her father to let her out.

"You need to think about your actions and listen to your parents!" – Vincent said as he glanced at his watch – "It's exactly 3:19 am. I will be back in one hour to let you out once you've thought about your actions."

He stormed out of the apartment, as Susan continued to plead.

"Dad, please!" – she pounded on the door – "I need my meds! Let me out! Please!"

Susan's muffled pleads turned into wheezing and then into shallow panting. Eventually, her breathing stopped and everything went silent. Another flash appeared in front of my eyes and when it disappeared, I saw Vincent entering the apartment again.

"4:19, time's up, Sue." – he strode to the storage door and knocked on it loudly with his palm – "You ready to listen now?"

There was no response from the other side.

"Hey! You little brat!" – he slammed the door again – "You hear me?!"

Silence.

"Fuckin' brat!" – he pulled his keys out and forcefully stuck them in the keyhole, turning them aggressively.

"You're going to learn how to-" – Vincent pushed the door open and stopped in his tracks, his eyes widening in horror.

The storage room was gone and instead what stood in front of him was a corridor which stretched into infinite darkness. There were pulsating veins and tendrils stretching across the walls and floor, making the entire place look like a living amalgamation.

"Susan?" – Vincent called out to her.

As a response, the tendrils started to slither slowly towards him and he screamed and shut the door in a panic. Another flash blinded me and I was back in reality, on the floor of my living room with Vincent standing over me. The blaring of the fire alarm returned along with the pain in my skull.

"You did that. You killed her!" – I shouted at Vincent angrily – "You let the apartment take her!"

Vincent shook his head:

"You still don't get it. The apartment didn't kill her. She is the apartment, Nathan. When I locked her in there and she died, her anger and hate for what I did created this abomination which desires to feed on people. I thought about burning the place myself, but then I realized. She is my daughter and I have to keep her happy. So every few months I find new tenants who walk inside the room and never come back. Do you even realize how difficult it is to find oblivious tenants like that guy Martin, who don't run away before being consumed by the apartment? Everyone has some fucking questions all the time. But Martin was good. He never asked a question and then one day he just disappeared and Susan was satiated. The tenants serve as food for Susan. But you Nate... I had different plans for you. I liked you. You could've stayed alive."

He took a few steps towards me, so that he stood inches away from me.

"I'm sorry son, but I can't let you leave." – he said.

It was at this point that the storage door slowly started to open to the darkness inside.

"Vincent, wait!" – I raised my hand up in a stop sign, focusing my gaze on the door.

Vincent ignored me and raised the crowbar above his head with both hands, ready to bring it down on me. I was still transfixed on the door. A pair of eyes appeared in the darkness. A pair of familiar, bloodshot eyes.

Before Vincent managed to bring down the crowbar on my head, the creaking lady- Daniella - jumped and tackled him at an impossible speed, closing the distance between the two of them in the blink of an eye. The creaking was louder than ever now, so loud that the alarm could almost not be heard. She grabbed Vincent's head with both hands and slammed it on the ground over and over, as if he was a ragdoll. When he went limp, she pushed her bony fingers into his eyes. Blood spurted out of Vincent's eye sockets, as he scream and writhed, unable to break free from her.

And then, still holding him by his head with one hand, she dragged him inside the storage room effortlessly, as he screamed. The door slammed shut and Vincent's hysterical screaming got drowned out until it, along with the creaking stopped completely, leaving only the alarm.

I stared at the door for a while, not fully comprehending what just happened. When I finally came to my senses, I crawled towards the entrance, grabbing the lighter which fell out of my hand. This time I didn't hesitate and ignited the floor as fast as possible. As soon as the flame touched the gas-stained carpet, it spread quickly in a wave and the room was engulfed in the brightness of the fire. I bolted out of the building as quickly as I could with my throbbing head. Sirens of the firemen greeted me outside, along with the tenants who stood on the other side of the street and watched in horror as their homes burned up.

Dolores waved to me from the crowd and I approached her.

"You made it." – she said.

"Yeah. It's over." – I stared at the burning window which used to be my apartment.

The flames were spreading onto the adjacent rooms quickly and the firefighters were having trouble containing the damage.

"You did right thing, Nate." – Dolores said – "I'm sure it's what Michelle would have wanted as well."

"I just hope they find peace." - I said.

"My sister is here to pick me up. Come on, we'll give you a ride."

I followed her. I turned around one last time to look at the burning building and saw people in the windows. They stood motionless, staring at me. I could tell from here who they were – Michelle, Martin, Daniella and everyone else who fell victim to the apartment. I can't tell why, but I believe they were grateful and were saying goodbye.

"You coming, Nate?" – Dolores shouted.

"Yeah, I'm coming." – I looked in her direction and then back at the building.

The former tenants were gone, leaving only an empty building with a dancing flame.

SOMETHING TERRIBLE CAME WITH THE RAIN

CHAPTER 1

It was supposed to be an ordinary day. One moment I was getting ready for my shift at work and then the next thing I knew I got a text for an emergency alert. The text read:

Emergency! Heavy rains with possible floods imminent. Do not leave your home under any circumstances, effective immediately. Lock your doors and cover your windows. Avoid making loud noise or using devices that emit light. If your household members have been outside in the rain, do not let them inside. Await further notice from the authorities.

This was weird, to say the least. First off, the weather outside was fine. I was outside just prior to receiving the text and not a single cloud was in the sky. And then the instructions themselves, they didn't make any sense. Don't let your family members inside if they've been out in the rain?

Before I could process that thought properly, I heard drumming of the rain on the roof of my home. I glanced out my window and realized that the previously sunny weather had now turned into a sudden downpour. The drumming I had heard on the roof became louder by the second, until it was the only sound permeating the house.

Despite my skepticism at the instructions of the message, I decided to abide by the rules and pull the blinds over my windows, as well as lock my doors. I returned to my living room in order to send my boss a text that I won't be coming to work, but upon my attempt, I realized the message could not be sent. Not only were the services off, but there was no internet either, so I couldn't check what was going on on the news.

I wanted to turn on the TV, but I remembered what the message said about light-emitting devices, so I did the only thing an internet-deprived person could do at that moment – I took a nap. The rain was loud, but the drumming of it put me to sleep more easily.

I woke up some time later, confused and groggy. The battering of the rain hadn't let up. If anything, it was only more violent now. I glanced at my phone and realized it was 5 pm. Still no service or internet. I got up and went to the kitchen to grab some water. Still half-asleep, I poured water into a glass and brought it to my mouth, however something stopped me before I could take a sip.

In addition to the heavy rain outside, I heard a distinctive sound of footsteps splashing in my backyard. It was brief and sounded like someone just ran from one end to another, but it was definitely there.

I scanned my backyard through my back door, but it was empty. I was sure I heard footsteps, so I decided to open the door and peek outside. As soon as I did so, the already loud thundering of the rain became even louder, almost sounding like a waterfall was next to me.

I stepped forward to the edge of the grass and right away saw fresh footprints across the lawn. They started from one end of the fence and ended all the way across the lawn on the other side. It was as if someone had jumped over the fence, ran across my backyard and jumped again into my neighbor's yard.

"Hello?" – I foolishly called out, looking at my neighbor's fence.

No response came back. Of course it didn't. Maybe it was the neighbor's kid who got caught in the rain and decided to hurry back home. I turned around and went back inside, closing the door behind me and somewhat muffling the noise of the rain. I drank the unfinished glass of water and returned to my living room.

Just as I was about to sit down, I heard another noise. A group of voices coming from the street. I could barely make them out due to the battering of the rain, but they spoke loudly to each other, so I could just barely hear them.

I peeked outside my window and saw a group of armed soldiers standing in the middle of the street, in front of my house. They were talking among each other and from their body language and hand gestures, it was apparent they weren't chatting about everyday mundane activities.

I wanted to know what was going on, so against my better judgment, I opened my front door and stepped onto the porch.

"…report back after a full sweep!" – I came outside just in time to catch one of the soldiers shouting.

As soon as they noticed me, they pointed their guns at me in unison.

"Whoa, don't shoot!" – I raised my hands instinctively – "I just wanted to know what's going on!"

"Sir, you need to go back inside right now!" – the soldier at the front, who was shouting orders earlier said.

And then something happened that I cannot comprehend to this day.

As the soldiers stood there pointing their guns at me, something flew through the street at an impossible speed and grabbed one of the soldiers at the back, taking him along with it and disappearing out of sight. It all happened in a split second and all that remained of the soldier was his gun that fell on the ground with a muffled clatter.

I felt my hands and jaw slowly drop and my eyes widen, as the soldier who was at the front continued barking orders at me. The others seemed oblivious to their squad member's disappearance, until one of them glanced to the side and saw the gun on the ground.

"Hey lieutenant, where's Ramirez?" – he asked.

The whole group turned towards the gun on the ground and started looking around for the soldier and shouting his name. I wanted to tell them what I saw, but I wasn't even sure of what happened myself.

One of the soldiers pointed down the street at something I couldn't see from my porch and when their whole squad looked in that direction, their look of confusion turned into one of palpable fear. They pointed their guns at whatever was there and just as I was about to strain my neck to look at what they were so worried about, I was ordered by the lieutenant once more to get inside, this time a lot more violently.

I would have ignored the order itself, but the demonic, high-pitched scream that suddenly came from down the street is what caused me to run back inside, lock my door and prop it with my back, while my heart pounded like crazy, even though I had no idea what the fuck was going on. Gunshots were mixed in the air along with the animalistic screeches that now sounded like they were right in my ear.

A moment later, both the screaming and the gunshots ceased and the only thing that remained was the drumming of the rain. My heart was pounding fast and my thoughts racing a million miles per hour. What the hell had just happened?

Before I could process that thought entirely, there was a knock on my door.

"Sir, you can open the door, it's safe now." – it was the lieutenant.

Safe from what, I thought to myself. I stood up and stared at the door, holding my breath.

"Sir, open the door." – the soldier said again.

Something didn't seem right in the way he said it, but I couldn't quite put my finger on it.

"Sir, if you don't open the door, I will be forced to break in." – the lieutenant repeated.

There was no intonation in his sentence. It was as if he just read it as a line off a paper.

"Sir, I am warning you-" – his sentence cut off when the sound of gunfire echoed somewhere in the distance.

There was a sound of violent splashing footsteps moving away from my door, which I assumed came from the lieutenant. I glanced through the peephole and sure enough, he was gone. But the sight in front of me is what made my heart drop to the pit of my stomach.

Strewn about the street in front of my house were the mangled and mutilated dead bodies of the soldiers I had just seen, their blood washed away by the pouring rain. I counted the bodies and my suspicions were correct - the entire group had perished.

CHAPTER 2

I felt guilty and stupid for disobeying the alert instructions like that. In my skepticism and lack of understanding, I thought it was a simple rain warning and decided to carelessly move about my property. Now those soldiers were dead and I may have had part of the blame to take. I tried to push that thought out of my head and to figure out what I should do next.

I checked my phone again and there was of course, still no signal. I made sure my windows were covered properly and turned on the TV. I flipped through the channels, but none of them seemed to work. I quickly turned off the TV out of fear that I'll attract more of whatever the hell was out there. I went to the storage room and fetched my dusty old radio. After putting in the batteries, I turned up the volume and started fiddling with the frequencies.

Static, static, static. No, wait. There was something on one of the frequencies, along with static. There were voices in the background, just barely audible. I adjusted the radio wheel until I could hear the voices more clearly.

"Did... from HQ?" – one of the voices said.

"Negative. S... sweeping... until we g-" – the other voice responded.

"You... -na go back aft... this?" – voice 1 asked.

At this point, the voices became a lot clearer.

"Yeah, HQ ordered a retreat and they'll cordon off the city." – voice 2 responded.

"Wait, what about search and rescue?" – voice 1 asked.

"Fuck that. This whole fuckin' town's a mess as it is. HQ said there's not gonna be any more rescue attempts." – voice 2 replied.

"So, 36 got way out of hand, huh?" – voice 1 asked.

"Yup. It's not our problem anymore. Any survivors on your end?" – voice 2 said.

"A couple, but they already saw too much, had to dispose of them."

"Copy that. Once you're do... be su... back... base-"

The voices started to cut off again bit by bit and then they went silent completely, leaving me only with static. What the hell was that all about? What was 36? And what did they mean they had to dispose of the survivors and that there would be no rescue? Something was definitely very wrong here and it was clear that the army knew something that us, the civilians didn't.

One thing was for sure though. I had to get out of town, I couldn't wait for rescue which wouldn't even come. Being out there with hostile soldiers or even worse, those things that wiped out the soldiers didn't put my mind at ease, but I had no other choice.

I went upstairs and packed my bag. I put in a pair of clothes, because I knew I'd probably be drenched from the rain. I also packed a flashlight and some food and water.

I peeked out my bedroom window and saw that the downpour was finally showing signs of subsiding. The streets were completely empty, save for the dead soldiers. From here I could see across from my house that my neighbor's door was left open, allowing the wind and rain to seep inside. I tried not to think about what might have happened there and I had no intention of finding out.

I put on my backpack and approached the stairs. Not three steps down, I heard something coming from the radio. Along with the static, there was the sound of slow wheezing. I quickly went down and grabbed the radio, putting my ear against it to hear the sound better. I tried adjusting the frequency, but no matter how much I did, nothing changed and the static and wheezing remained the same.

Frustrated, I figured the radio was broken and turned it off. But the static and wheezing didn't stop. And then I saw something with the corner of my eye that made my blood run cold.

Mud tracks.

They were all over my carpet, coming in from the kitchen and leading to the corner of my room. I froze in place, listening as the radio static and wheezing permeated the room. After what seemed like forever, I broke out of my trance and looked towards the corner.

The first thing I saw were bony feet caked with mud. As I slowly moved my gaze up I realized I was staring at a crouched, emaciated figure which faced the corner of my room, but I couldn't tell its features due to the dark.

With extremely trembling hands, I pointed my flashlight to the corner and flicked it on. A tiny, completely nude and emaciated humanoid creature that I could only describe as a human-like goblin came into light. Its spine was pronounced against its tight skin on the back so much that I could count the vertebrae. Its limbs looked like they had no meat on them whatsoever and could barely hold its fragile frame. As soon as the flashlight illuminated the creature, it jerked its head towards me with mouth wide open and scared eyes. The radio static and wheezing got much louder and it was just then that I realized – the sound was not coming from my radio.

It was all I could take. I turned around and bolted out of there and into the rain which had now turned into a drizzle, not even bothering to close my front door. I ran down the street, occasionally looking behind me to see if the goblin-creature would come chasing me.

My sprint slowed down to a jog and eventually I stopped and looked back towards my house, leaning on my knees and panting, listening to the sound of rain around me. I breathed a sigh of relief momentarily. And then I heard a blood-curdling scream behind me.

I turned around and saw a young man who was covered in wounds all over, crawling towards me with anger in his eyes and bloodlust I had never seen in anyone before. As he got closer, I realized he was missing both legs in what looked like a terrible accident, leaving only two mangled stumps, but that didn't stop him from closing in on me.

I started running again and it was just then that I realized how much the streets were actually not empty. I saw dead bodies of both civilians and soldiers. I saw crashed vehicles and more corpse-looking people crawling out despite their fatal injuries. I saw amalgamations of creatures I cannot describe in words, roaming about the streets or lying dead along with the soldiers, their dark blood staining the ground beneath them.

I looked back and saw that despite my running speed, the legless man was still close behind me. I turned right and ran across the lawn, climbing over the fence and into a backyard. I stopped and stared at the fence, figuring I was safe. There was no way the crawling man could reach me here. But a second later, the he came crawling over the fence, still screaming at the top of his lungs.

I started backpedaling, but slipped and fell on my back. The legless man lunged at me from a distance that would make an Olympic athlete envious, but before he could fall on top of me, he fell backwards on the grass with a loud bang. I looked to my right and saw an elderly man pointing a shotgun at the attacker.

The legless man got right back up and started crawling again, until the man blasted him one more time. This time, the crawler fell backwards and writhed on the floor with a scream impossible to be made by humans, before completely ceasing all movement and noise and I was left with nothing but the sound of rain again.

And then the old man cocked his shotgun once more. I looked up at him and saw that he had it trained on me and the way his knuckles had turned white, I knew he was ready to shoot me right there.

"Wait, don't shoot! I'm not one of them!" - I raised one hand, still sitting on the ground.

"Prove it." - he said with a rough voice.

"What do you mean 'prove it'? I'm talking to you, aren't I?" - I scoffed.

"That don't mean shit." - he spat on the ground.

"Look, I just left my home minutes ago because of all the crazy shit that's happening. I have no idea what's going on, I swear." - I recited in one breath.

He didn't budge for a while, the expression on his face looking like he was weighing his options. Finally, after a moment of contemplation lowered the gun down and gave me his hand, saying:

"You'll catch a cold out here, son. Let's get you inside."

A young woman in cargo pants with a gun in her hand opened the back door of the old man's house. When she saw us, she stepped aside and let us in, while carefully eyeing me.

"Take your damn shoes off." – the old man said – "Don't want you tracking no mud inside."

"Dad, no. He might need to run out quickly in case they get inside." – the girl said.

"Fine." – the man grunted and proceeded into the living room, leaning his shotgun on the sofa where he sat.

"Make yourself at home." – the girl said – "But don't try anything stupid."

She went past me and inside the living room. Everything about her confidence in verbal and body language told me she was trained for this exact type of situation, but I didn't want to ask her anything yet. I joined them in the living room and sat opposite of the old man.

"Name's Harry." – he said as he lit a cigarette – "And this here is my daughter Alyssa."

I introduced myself as the old man kept staring at me silently. I couldn't decipher any emotions on the old man's face.

"You live close by, don't you?" – Harry asked.

"Yeah. A few blocks away. That creature made me get into your backyard, I didn't mean to trespass." – I said.

"Are you headed to the hospital?" – Alyssa asked.

"No, why?" – I shook my head.

"Some survivors gathering up there. Said so on the news before they stopped broadcasting. They're probably still there, though." – Harry said.

"Harry, do you know anything about what's going on?" – I leaned forward.

"Devil's work, I tell you." – Harry responded nonchalantly – "Ever since they started mining two years ago, I kept tellin' 'em something would go wrong."

"Dad, come on, not this again..." – Alyssa rolled her eyes.

Harry simply ignored her and continued:

"It ain't natural to go digging into the earth. Wasn't meant for no humans. I can bet you they woke somethin' up down there at the quarry."

"So do you know if the military has any plans for a rescue mission?" – I pretended not to know.

I also wanted to know if Alyssa was with the army and hoped I would get my answer this way. Something told me that if she was with military, I'd already be dead.

"Ain't no military coming to save us, son." – Harry said – "Saw them retreating with their armored vehicles and Alyssa here saw them shooting civilians on site."

Alyssa nodded.

"So you're not military?" – I asked her directly.

"Ex." – she responded.

I nodded and then said:

"So I guess our best bet is to go to the hospital." – I finally said.

Alyssa nodded.

"You could go there and wait it out." – Harry said – "Or find the survivors there and use numbers to bust your way outta town."

"Hospital's close by. But there may be some of those monsters roaming around." – Alyssa said.

Just after a few minutes of talking to her, I could see a resemblance to her father, despite her not being as stubborn as Harry. I nodded and we sat in silence for a moment.

"Do you know anything about 36? I heard them talking over the radio about '36 getting out of hand'." – I finally asked.

They both seemed confused, but before they could give a proper response, there was a sound of glass breaking in the kitchen, followed by a gurgling noise. Harry shot up and grabbed his shotgun, while Alyssa pointed her handgun at the doorway. I saw a hatchet leaning on the side of the fireplace, so I grabbed it and got ready for whatever was coming.

A moment later, the gurgling got louder and a man that looked completely charred - as if he was burnt all over – shambled inside. When he saw us, his gurgling turned into a painful scream, which were cut short with Alyssa's bullet to his head.

Another sound of glass breaking, this time behind us and another charred person, a woman, jumped inside, completely ignoring the deep cuts on her body from the broken window. She started crawling towards me and when she grabbed onto my foot, something kickstarted my fight or flight instinct. I raised the hatchet above my head and brought it down with full force on the woman.

The blade struck the top of the woman's skull, making her stop moving completely. I didn't have time to react, as another charred person stumbled in through the window, this one having patches of blazing skin on his body.

I pulled the hatchet out of the woman's skull, but the man managed to grab my hand before I could swing again. A loud bang resounded and the man fell dead from another one of Alyssa's bullets.

More of them kept coming in and the room turned into a cacophony of gunshots and Harry's 'come on you ugly sons of bitches' shouts. I managed to bring down one more charred creature with the hatchet and as I turned around I saw that one of them tackled Alyssa to the ground and thrashed violently, while she tried to free her hand of his grip and shoot him.

I swung the hatchet as hard as I could, embedding it in the attacker's collar bone. He screamed an inhuman scream and fell backwards when I pulled out the blade. He started scooting back with his heels, holding his bleeding shoulder, but by this point adrenaline took over my actions completely, so I had no intention of stopping.

I gripped the hatchet with both hands and brought it down on the creature over and over, first severing one of his arms at the forearm and then finally killing him with a strike to the face.

Just then I realized everything was quiet again. No gunshots, no gurgling, no swearing on Harry's end, just the sound of our panting.

"I owe you." – Alyssa patted me on the shoulder as she stood up – "Bet you're thankful now you didn't have to take off your shoes."

"These goddamn fuckers!" – Harry cursed as he reloaded his shotgun - "You can't stay here any longer, kids. Get to the hospital!"

"Wait, what about you?" – Alyssa interjected.

"I ain't leavin' our home behind."

"Don't be stupid, dad. If you stay here, you'll die!"

"I promised your momma that this would always be our home. I'm not letting these hellspawn take it away from us!"

He could see the disapproval in Alyssa's eyes, so he put his hand on her cheek and said:

"I know you're worried babygirl, but I'll be fine. I have enough food and water to last me here for a month and the basement is the safest place in town right now. But you need to get yourselves outta here. You understand?"

Hesitantly, she nodded and put her already packed backpack on. She and I went to the front door and Harry escorted us there. It was dark already outside, but the rain still wouldn't let up.

"Now remember what we talked about." – he said – "If the rain gets too heavy, you find cover immediately, you hear? That's when the nasty ones come out."

He looked at me and shoved a handgun into my hands:

"You keep my daughter safe, you hear? You keep her safe."

I looked at the gun and nodded. I never used a gun before, but now it seems I would have to if I wanted to survive. Harry and Alyssa hugged tightly for a long moment, with Harry whispering that he loved her, before she broke away hesitantly and turned around.

"Come on, let's go." – she told me and walked down to the pavement.

"Thank you, Harry. For saving my life." – I said and gave him one last look.

For the first time in the short time that I knew him I thought I finally saw an emotion on his face. An emotion which didn't suit him in the slightest. Despair.

I expected Alyssa's mood to change drastically after leaving Harry behind, but she was as focused on surviving now as she was prior to that. The streets were way emptier now than they were when I first ran outside my house. We walked in the middle of the road to avoid getting jumped from the corner, even though we knew it was equally risky exposing ourselves like that.

Whenever we heard an inhuman sound in the distance, Alyssa made us stop until we were sure we weren't in any danger. Walking in the rain gave us some cover, which allowed us to move relatively faster, but we still had to be careful.

"Wait!" – I whispered to Alyssa, pointing down the street – "See that?"

There was a little girl a few hundred yards away from us, standing in the middle of the road, facing away from us. My initial instinct was to go and see if she was okay, but based on everything I'd seen by that point, I knew there was a high probability that this wasn't a little girl in distress at all.

I was right, because as soon as Alyssa saw her, she cursed under her breath and pulled me aside behind a bush.

"What's wrong?" – I asked.

"Whatever you see there, that's not a little girl." – Alyssa peeked behind the bush where we hid – "Saw her, or someone resembling her, a bit earlier. She stood exactly like that and when a guy approached to help her during the chaos, she turned around and she had no fucking eyes or nose. Instead, her entire face was replaced by a big fucking vertical line for a mouth with sharp fucking teeth. The poor guy never stood a chance."

"So what do we do?" – I asked.

"Let's try a different street." – she suggested.

We sneaked through a backyard, ignoring the dead bodies along the way and went through the adjacent street. Halfway through, I heard a pained groan coming from a dark alley to my left. I readied my hatchet, while Alyssa readied her gun. A creature crawled out into the light, barely able to pull its own weight with what was left of its human-looking arm. The thing looked like a swollen blob in its shape, barely recognizable where the head was, which I could only tell from the eye visible under the heavily swollen blisters. Some of the blisters looked volatile, pulsating under the street light, looking like they would pop on the slightest touch.

I tried not to think about whether it used to be human, as it pathetically dragged itself towards us, groaning through the small slit of a mouth, the one visible eye wide open and darting from Alyssa to me intermittently.

"Leave it." – Alyssa said – "It's harmless unless it manages to grab you. I've seen one earlier."

She holstered her gun and urged me to follow her. I gave the amalgamation of the creature one last glance before following my partner.

"What exactly have you seen, Alyssa?" – I asked while walking behind her.

She was silent for a moment before responding:

"I got caught in the downpour while heading home. It was like a warzone. Military killing everything… monsters of all shapes and sizes killing everything… and civilians just trying to escape. I didn't stick around to find out, since the heavy rain brought some really bad monsters."

"Wait, look!" – I pointed to a graffiti on a billboard.

It said '36 WILL SAVE US'.

"You mentioned it before, right?" – Alyssa asked – "What is it?"

"I don't know. Heard the military talking about it over the radio. Whoever or whatever it is, it's responsible for all the crazy shit happening in town."

We walked in silence for the rest of the way until we reached the hospital. It's a good thing too, because the rain started to get heavier by the time we reached the entrance. There were no monsters in front, but when we entered, our hearts dropped at the amount of dead bodies at the front desk, both human and otherwise.

"Shit." – Alyssa cursed quietly and readied her gun.

"This was a bad idea. We should get out of here." – I said.

As if a higher force heard me, it started raining cats and dogs again, so going outside at this point was impossible.

"Let's proceed carefully." – Alyssa said – "Maybe they barricaded themselves somewhere upstairs."

We got past the reception, carefully stepping around the dead bodies. The hospital wasn't big, so we figured we'd check it out quickly enough. The elevator was completely demolished, so that was out of the question. Really though, it looked as if a truck drove into it, bending the door inward all the way to the backside.

We climbed the stairs to the second floor and as soon as we did, the air became heavy. It's hard to explain, but it was as if someone had been keeping all the windows shut for a long time, making the room stuffy.

There were no dead bodies, but the place was chaotic – stretchers and trash bins knocked over, etc.

"Let's split up to check each side separately." – Alyssa said when we reached the end of the corridor – "I'll check the patient rooms on this side, you check that one. Let's meet up here once we're done and if you see anything, scream."

I wasn't exactly happy at the thought of roaming this place alone, but I hesitantly nodded and we split up. All the other rooms were empty, just like the rest of the floor. It didn't make sense, but the only possible outcome was that the survivors probably barricaded themselves on the third floor.

I came back to the meeting point and then I heard Alyssa calling me from around the corner.

"Hey, come check this out!" – she said from one of the rooms.

"Coming!" – I said and followed her voice.

Just when I was about to open the door, I felt a firm grip on my left hand. I jerked my head in that direction and saw Alyssa holding my wrist, shaking her head with a worried look on her face.

"Don't. That's not me." – she whispered with a trembling voice.

My mind couldn't process what I was looking at. I stared at her and then back at the door.

"Hey, you still there?" – Alyssa's voice came from the room again, followed by an approaching set of footsteps.

"Come on!" – the Alyssa still holding my wrist pulled me into one of the adjacent rooms, where we quickly hid inside the locker.

"Quiet now!" – she whispered.

A second later the door opened and through the cracks I saw Alyssa walking in and looking around.

"Dammit, where'd he go?" – she mumbled and turned around to leave the room.

Just then, I felt the grip on my wrist tighten even more. I looked down and in the dark I saw the hand holding it. But it wasn't Alyssa's hand. The fingers which held me were boney and elongated.

I looked to my left and saw not Alyssa, but a bald, old man who looked like his life was way overdue by a hundred years. I felt my blood run cold and when I tried screaming, I was unable to, so I instead burst through the locker, falling on my shoulder painfully.

I got up and ran outside just in time to see Alyssa pointing her gun at me.

"Run!" – I shouted and saw her looking over my shoulder before she bolted out of the room with me.

We ran to the stairs and up on the third floor, making our way past the dozens of bodies of patients, staff members, monsters, etc. A realization raced through my mind that there were no survivors and as we reached a dead end, blocked by a makeshift barricade, we turned around to see if the old man followed us.

A second later he climbed the stairs, striding menacingly towards us. At this point, the lights started flickering and every time they would go off and come back on, the man was much closer. Alyssa started shooting, but it was as if every time she fired a bullet, the lights would go out for a split second and the man would appear in a different spot, always a step closer.

And then he finally reached us, but instead of attacking us, he simply went past us. We followed him with our gaze and the lights went out again, but this time they didn't come back on. There were sounds of loud crashing and objects being thrown, at some moments right next to me.

When the lights finally did come back after almost a whole minute, the barricade behind us was completely ransacked and the way clear. The old man was nowhere to be seen.

I looked around at all the dead bodies of monsters around me and inspected the identical tattoos they all had on their wrists, or whatever extensions of extremities they had. The same tattoo I saw on the old man's wrist when he held me in the locker. A simple, two-digit number.

36.

We didn't have time to think about the monsters branded with the number 36, because a sound came from behind us, from the place where the barricade had previously been. We proceeded carefully, past more dead bodies.

And then something small ran past us in the dark. Alyssa gestured for me to follow her, so I did. There was nothing around the corner, but we still proceeded carefully. Whoever jut ran past us was close by. Another barely audible sound, coming from right behind a wheelchair in front of us.

Alyssa slowly approached it and then kicked the wheelchair aside. A small boy came into visibility. He screamed and ran past us before we could grab him.

"Hey wait! We want to help you!" – I shouted after him but he didn't listen.

He disappeared into one or the rooms and Alyssa and I wasted no time running after him.

"Little boy, where are you?" – Alyssa frantically looked around the room.

A minute after searching, we found him under a patient's bed. I shone my flashlight and saw his terrified face. He was no older than 6 and he looked like he had seen more than enough for the next 20 years.

"It's okay, we won't hurt you." – I knelt down slowly, holding my hand in front of myself.

He was panting and his eyes were wide.

"Hey, what's your name?" – I asked.

He still didn't answer.

"My name's Alyssa." – Alyssa introduced herself behind me – "Where are your parents?"

The kid's eyes widened even more and he started backing away. It took me a moment to realize it was not we who scared him.

A faint, grunting sound came from behind us and as soon as I turned around, I saw another one of those blobby amalgamations, like the one in the alley, tackling Alyssa to the ground. She held it back with her foot, trying to wiggle out of its reach.

I gripped my hatchet firmly and thought for a second about what I should do. Just like the one before, the creature looked very volatile and I didn't know how dangerous getting close could be. But when I saw how dangerously close it was to reaching Alyssa's face with its deformed fingers, I brought down the hatchet on its back with full force.

There was a loud popping sound and I fell back as something warm and slimy hit my face with unimaginable force. I swiped my hand across the goo on my face and spat it out of my mouth.

"Hey, you okay?" – Alyssa helped me up.

"Disgusting!" – I spat out the rest of the slime from my mouth and cleaned myself off.

The monster lay dead sideways on the floor, its back ripped open.

"Just find the damn kid." – I pushed Alyssa away, still disgusted.

I heard her trying to talk to the boy and little by little, he finally came to trust us and let us approach him.

"What's your name?" – Alyssa asked.

"Dewey." – he shyly said, looking at his feet.

"Are your parents close by, Dewey?" – Alyssa asked him.

The kid's face turned red and his eyes glossy. Alyssa hugged him while he cried. A few minutes later when he calmed down, she pulled back and asked him:

"Dewey, how did you get here? Where are the others?"

"My mom and dad and I came here, but there was a fight."

"The monsters killed them?" – Alyssa asked.

Dewey shook his head:

"There was a man in black clothes. He and some other people said 36 is good and other people said 36 is bad and then they got into a fight."

"So the man in black and his men killed everyone, including your parents?" – Alyssa frowned.

Dewey nodded.

"Do you know this man's name?"

"Martin."

"Did they say where they would go?" – I asked.

"Dad said they couldn't leave the city because the soldiers were bad, so they planned to go to the old mine, where 36 was. But when dad said they had to get rid of 36, Martin got angry and that's when he attacked everyone."

"The old mine? Why would they go there?" – Alyssa asked.

"Hey, maybe your father was onto something after all." – I smiled – "What else do you remember, Dewey?"

Dewey thought for a moment.

"Martin told me I could be saved if I went with him. But I didn't want to go. A bad man who was there wanted to hurt me, but Martin said no."

"So they went there. There really might be something there." – I said – "Dewey, how many men were with Martin?"

Dewey counted on his fingers for a moment before responding with a simple 'six'.

"If we take them by surprise, we can take all of them." – I said.

Alyssa looked uncertain, so I said:

"Look, chances are all exits out of town are heavily guarded by military. But if we can get to the bottom of this whole thing, we may be able to undo some of the damage and maybe even survive."

She nodded and looked at the kid.

"Dewey, you'll have to come with us. We'll keep you safe."

By the time we got out, the rain was a mere drizzle again. Since the mine was on the other side of town, we took the closest functioning car we could find, to hell with the noise and monsters. I let Alyssa drive.

Although we saw monsters on the road, most of them didn't seem to care about us. They'd glance at us and then continue roaming mindlessly, as if they knew they couldn't catch us in the car.

"You okay, Alyssa?" – I asked when she got really quiet.

Dewey was sleeping in the back by this point.

"Yeah." – she said – "Just thinking about my dad. You know he used to take me to this park right here every weekend when I was a kid."

"Oh, Harry didn't seem like the gentle type." – I smiled.

"He wasn't." – she smiled back – "We'd do military drills there, while everyone else played."

"You wanted to be a soldier ever since you were a kid?"

"Yeah. And I enjoyed every second of it. You know one time when he wasn't looking during training, I sat on the swing, just for fun, to take a break. Not a minute later, I fell off and hurt myself. He saw me and when he approached me he said: Babygirl, while you're having fun there, your enemies are training hard and you're making it that much easier for them to kill you in combat. There's time for fun, but it's not now, because while you're doing something, you need to do it with complete dedication. It helped me during boot camp… and after mom passed. He said it's what helped keep him alive in war, too. I wonder if this is a little too much for him, though."

"Harry's tough. He could take down a whole horde of those creatures." - I said.

After a moment of silence, I spoke up again:

"You know my father was never around. Always worked hard to provide for us. Whenever I asked to spend time with him, he said I'll thank him one day for always being busy. And then he died and I never thanked him for it. I didn't care about his money, I just wanted him to spend time with me. And I never got that."

"Seems we both got polar opposites." – Alyssa said.

"Yeah. You know this one time he-" – I started coughing.

"You okay?" – she asked.

"Yeah, probably just caught a damn cold from this rain." – I said, clearing my throat.

"Well don't go getting a fever on me now. We're here." – she said.

She pulled over in front of a huge fenced off area which led to the quarry.

"This place is huge." – she said – "Where do we even start?"

"I think I got an idea." – I said, pointing to one of the signs on the fence.

There was an arrow pointing to the right side and it said *SITE 36 THIS WAY.*

CHAPTER 6

"You should probably stay with Dewey while I scout ahead." – I told Alyssa.

"No way." – she disagreed before I even finished my sentence – "You'll need my help taking Martin's men down."

"Listen, I'm just gonna go and che-" – my sentence was abruptly caught off by a sudden cough – "I'm gonna (cough)... scout and (cough)... come back s- (cough)... soon..."

"Hey, you okay?" – Alyssa looked at me suspiciously.

"I'm fine." – I said and cleared my aching throat.

"What's going on?" – Dewey said groggily.

"Sorry to wake you up there, buddy." – I said.

"Listen." – Alyssa softly said – "We're gonna go find the bad men. We need you to stay here, okay?"

Dewey was less than enthused by this, so Alyssa went on to explain why we needed him to stay quietly in the car while we checked out the mine. After a few minutes of convincing, he finally agreed when Alyssa told him that his job is to keep the car safe, deeming it as an extremely important task.

"We'll be back soon, okay?" – I told him and smiled reassuringly.

As soon as we closed the car doors behind us, Alyssa took point and carefully proceeded on the old dirt road leading to the quarry. The place seemed to be deserted, not counting the dozens of dead bodies of both humans and monsters. The rain still wasn't letting up and my guess was it wouldn't for a long, long time. We followed the arrow signs to 36, until we started hearing faint noises in the distance. The cacophony of screams, growls and moans was definitely coming from numerous monsters, but we couldn't see in the dark where they were.

We followed the only remaining path to site 36, with the noise getting louder and louder. We finally reached an opening and it didn't take us long to realize we were at the edge of the quarry itself.

The noise was coming from the direct center and when we looked in that direction, we gasped. Hundreds, no, thousands of monsters were converging atop each other like a huge swarming pile, monsters of all shapes and forms, forming a nightmarish abomination of a mountain. Although a lot of the stray ones looked in our direction, they didn't seem concerned about us, but we tried not to make any sudden moves nevertheless.

"Look, entrance 36." – Alyssa pointed at the distance.

"Looks like we have to go around them." – I said – "I don't think they'll hurt us. But let's be really careful and keep our distance."

I took point this time and just as I predicted, the monsters weren't aggressive, despite making eye contact with us. Still, we proceeded carefully around the horde, keeping as far away as we could from the big pile. The mountain of monsters was a lot bigger and louder than I thought when we got closer to it and it became clear that the monsters were constantly falling and climbing and falling, over and over and over.

Entering the dark mine labeled as 36 felt claustrophobic, but also relieving to leave the army of monsters behind.

"Carefully." – Alyssa whispered, pointing her torch in front of us.

The mine was pretty straightforward and we ran into no trouble, until we heard the voices, that is.

"Wait, you hear that?" – I perked up my ears.

"Bring him forward." – a deep voice echoed through the mine.

"No! Please! I never questioned you father, please!" – another voice pleaded.

Alyssa and I peeked around the corner and saw a group of men standing in an open area, in front of a big tunnel. Two of the men were tightly holding a third one, who was struggling.

"You have sinned, my child. But you can still be saved." – the deep voice said again.

It was a priest. That was definitely Martin.

"Father, please!" – the man pleaded, but before he could say anything more, Martin slid a shiny blade across his throat.

The man fell over with a gurgling sound, clawing at his throat and bleeding to death within seconds.

Martin raised his arms high up and shouted:

"Glory be to 36, savior of our world!"

The men around him did the same.

I counted the men surrounding him. Aside from Martin, there were four other men, all of them armed with assault rifles.

"We can take them." – Alyssa whispered.

I nodded and just as we were about to jump out and start shooting, another voice shouted:

"Father Martin! We found an intruder outside our holy grounds! He's the one from the hospital."

Father Martin looked down at the new prisoner and chuckled, before saying:

"Well now. It would seem you changed your mind about coming here, have you not, Dewey?"

My heart jumped into my throat when I glanced there and realized they had a little boy as a prisoner. Dewey stared at Martin, visibly frightened, but not wanting to show it to the priest.

"Luckily, we have just the job for you in a few days." – Martin continued – "Take him to the Source. Lock him up and keep a close eye on him."

Before I realized what was going on, Alyssa jumped in front of our enemies and started shooting them with an expression of pure anger on her face. Without any time to think, I joined in and in the frenzied shootout we managed to take down all but one of Martin's men, who fled into the dark tunnel ahead. My shoulder got grazed by a bullet in the shootout, but I was not seriously injured.

"Martin, come out you bastard!" - Alyssa took a few steps forward cautiously.

Out of nowhere, he jumped out and shot Alyssa in the leg, while standing behind Dewey, pointing a gun to his head.

"Not a step closer or the child dies!" – Martin said.

I held my gun trained on him, not sure what I should do.

"Shoot him!" – Alyssa shouted.

I would have done it, too. But all of a sudden my vision became blurry and I got dizzy, coughing violently. I felt myself falling to my knees and saw blood coming out of my mouth with each cough. Everything was getting dark.

"Father Martin, are you okay?!" – more men rushed to Martin's side, pointing their guns at Alyssa and me.

"Should we throw them in the pit?" – one of them asked.

"No." – Martin said while standing over me – "They're as good as dead anyway."

The next few hours were blurry. I fell in and out of consciousness and I remember seeing an unfamiliar face – a scientist of some sort. I felt being carried and I remember seeing a bright room.

Some time later, I woke up. It took me a while to adjust, but when I did, I shielded my eyes from the bright ceiling light. I looked around and realized I was in some sort of lab.

A man in a white coat sat on the other side of the room by a PC, typing away. Various vials and incubators of sorts with unfamiliar organs were on the desks around the room.

I shuffled on the bed and started coughing violently.

"Breathe, breathe." – the man in white coat was next to me before I even knew it.

"Who… are you?" – I asked.

"My name is doctor Andrew. I work in this lab."

"Lab?"

An electronic door opened and a woman with a crutch waltzed in.

"Finally awake." – Alyssa smiled.

Her leg was wrapped in a blood-soaked bandage where she had been shot.

"Alyssa, what happened?"

"They took Dewey. I think they plan to sacrifice him. Doctor Andrew saw us on the surveillance cameras and took us into the lab. The government had this whole underground facility set up to study 36."

"Where's the kid now?" – I asked.

"They took him all the way deep into the heart of 36." – Andrew said – "To where the monsters are emerging from."

"Then we need to go save him." - I stood up on wobbly legs, trying to steady myself.

Alyssa sat down with a serious expression on her face. The doc stared at me with concern, too.

"What?" – I asked.

"There's something you should know…" – Alyssa looked down – "Back when you saved me in the hospital… when you killed that volatile creature…"

There was a long pause.

"Well, what is it?!" – my heart was racing and my body trembling.

"I'm afraid you're infected." – Andrew finally spoke up – "The good news is it's not contagious and it doesn't turn you into one of those creatures. It seems to be a new form of bacteria which we've never seen before. So here comes the bad news. Once infected, the bacteria attaches itself to the lungs of the host and-"

"Save the bullshit, doc." – I said quietly – "How long do I have?"

"It's hard to say. Judging by the progress of the bacteria, I'd say… less than a week."

I chuckled, unable to process what I was hearing. After a long pause, I said:

"You said they took Dewey all the way deep, right?"

Alyssa interjected:

"You can't be serious, you can't-"

"I'm the only one who can save him, dammit!" – I tried not to yell too much, since my chest was burning – "You can't do it with that leg of yours, so it has to be me. I have to do this one last thing. Before I die."

CHAPTER 7

Although the lab was enormous and had lots of staff, Andrew was the only one who managed to survive. He explained when the alarm went off, all military personnel went to secure the source on site 36, but perished. Andrew had no choice but to initiate full lockdown.

"So what exactly is 36?" – I asked.

"Well…" – Andrew started – "It all began as an accident. Some miners were going about their business and one day they dug through to this hidden cave system, so to say, which further led down to a huge seemingly bottomless hole. Now at first it was just an interesting tourist attraction, but then people reported hearing voices coming from down there. And then the first accident happened. You remember that little girl that disappeared a few years back?"

"Katie Chandler?" – Alyssa interjected.

"Yeah. The official story was she just went missing during a field trip to the cave with her school. But in reality, she fell down the hole. Well, dragged down is more accurate."

"Wait, the teacher who took the class on the field trip claimed there was no way she fell inside the hole." – I said.

Andrew nodded:

"Yeah. As soon as the incident happened, the teacher was bribed and threatened by the government. The kids' stories of monsters were of course, dismissed. We had our eyes on this place for a while as a precaution, but only after we saw Katie getting dragged down were our suspicions confirmed. After that, the military quarantined the zone. Our lab was set up here and we have been studying the hole ever since. The public was told the area was closed off due to police searching for the missing girl."

"But something went wrong?" – Alyssa asked.

"Monsters occasionally kept emerging from the cave. We tried investigating the hole, but it was impossible. It was as if a completely different world was down there. And then they stopped coming out altogether. But the government wanted to know more about them, so they set up a special machine to draw them out."

"What?!"

"They created a link with the world down there via a machine. Let's call it a portal. But they underestimated the monsters and soon thousands of them poured out of the portal and were set loose on the city."

"So what about the rain?"

"Interestingly enough, as the rain increases, so does the activity in the portal. We still don't know how they are connected, but one thing is for sure; the heaver the rain, the more dangerous they are."

"Doc, on our way here, the creatures outside were merging onto a big pile and they weren't hostile towards us." — I said.

"Yes. The creatures seem to be operating in hive-like mind manner and whatever is controlling them seems to be coming from the source, the portal. We believe they have a queen or something of the like."

"So how do we stop them?"

"Your best bet is to destroy the machine. It's very fragile, so a few bullets should do it."

"But that still leaves the monsters outside." — Alyssa said.

Andrew nodded:

"Yes. And if the machine is destroyed, there may be a number of residual monsters coming out of the hole, the ones that manage to get into our world before the connection is severed. And chances are the government will either nuke the city to prevent it from spreading. But if we close the portal, the monsters may get confused without the connection to their leader. I can then contact HQ and they may conduct a full sweep and rescue mission."

"What are those creatures, anyway?" — I asked.

"Well. We don't know exactly. Our research team believes they were dormant for centuries and those miners woke them up when they dug up their sanctuary. We studied a few specimens, but we still barely know anything about them."

There was a long silence.

"Well, time for me to go." — I stood up.

"Wait, take this." — Andrew went to his desk and returned with a box of pills — "It will suppress the bacteria, but only for a very short time. Take one every hour and no sooner. This strain is highly adaptive and can develop resistance within days."

"Thanks, doc."

My mind was on autopilot and I tried not to think about the fact that my time on this earth was limited. Alyssa stood up with the help of her crutch and opened her mouth to say something, but I could tell she had no idea what to say. There was nothing she could say to ease the situation.

"Don't worry." — I said — "I'll bring him back. And then you need to keep him safe."

"I will. I promise." — she said with glossy eyes.

I coughed painfully and then said to her:

"You know, I planned on asking you out on a date once this was all done. Despite being a stubborn bitch, I think we'd get along."

"If you weren't so ugly, I'd say yes." – she said and we both laughed.

I stared at the ground and then looked her in the eye:

"If I'm not back soon, you'll have to go on alone."

She didn't respond. The doctor escorted me out of the lab. He gave me an assault rifle which belonged to one of the soldiers and told me how to reach the source where the machine was. The lab itself was hidden behind a fake wall which could be raised and lowered, so that explained how the doc stayed safe this whole time.

I stepped outside and turned back to the doc.

"If you make it back, I'll see you on the camera feed and open the passage for you. Good luck." – Andrew said and pushed a button which lowered the fake wall back down, leaving me in the empty mine.

"Hold on, Dewey." – I said to myself and started walking.

I soon reached the area where we first saw father Martin and from there I went inside the dark tunnel ahead. It slowly descended and as it did, the air got colder, until I could see my breath in the air. After I started having a coughing fit, I popped one of the pills and continued, trying to steady my breathing. I felt fatigue taking me over, so I knew I was almost out of time.

When I descended to the bottom, I started seeing lights from torches on the walls. As I continued, the rock walls and floor changed into a metallic corridor. I followed the only path ahead of me, until I heard voices in front. It was a mixture of adult and child voices.

I hurried up and saw in front of me a huge area with a tall ceiling and an enormous hole in the ground. The hole was glowing brightly and looked like it had a sort of whirlpool in it. On the other side of it was a big generator-like machine. This was definitely the place I was looking for.

I arrived just in time to see Martin and his man throw a woman into the hole. Her scream was abruptly cut off when she fell inside the vortex, which became turbulent before calming down again.

"Praise be to 36!" – Martin raised his arms and shouted.

The men around him repeated the phrase three more times.

"Now, Dewey." – Martin turned towards the kid – "Your role is at hand. You will perform a great deed, here."

"Fuck you!" – Dewey spewed at Martin, making him and few other men chuckle.

"Come now." – Martin pushed Dewey towards the hole and stepped back.

Dewey fell near the edge on his hands and knees and stared at the vortex, which started to become violent again. I aimed my gun at the generator. It was far away, but I was confident I could hit it.

Black tentacles started to emerge from the hole and slithered their way towards Dewey, as a deep groan echoed from the hole itself all around the cave. Without any time to think, I pulled the trigger.

The bullet hit the machine with a loud clank and the sound of electrical shocks filled the air. The vortex in the hole disappeared just like that and the tentacles writhed, severed on the ground, purple blood oozing out of them. The deep groan from before turned into a scream of agony and the cave began to shake.

"No! What did you do?!" – Martin shouted.

Multiple screams came from the now dark hole and monsters started to emerge. They wasted no time pulling Martin's men into the hole or slaughtering them on sight. Most of his men had already escaped, some deeper into the cave and others ran past me, ignoring me in their panic.

"Come back, you cowards!" – Martin shouted as screams echoed around him.

"Dewey, come on!" – I shouted in the whole mess and the boy started running towards me.

A thin creature with sharp claws and teeth pursued him on all fours and just as it leapt to grab him, I shot the creature and knocked it backwards. I didn't move again.

"Come on!" – I pushed Dewey forward and we both ran as quickly as our legs and the shaking ground allowed us to.

We ran unsteadily through the tremors and I heard cave-ins behind us. My chest was on fire and I was already out of breath.

"Dewey… run!" – I said between breaths and continued staggering.

And then I felt a powerful force knock the air out of me. I dropped the gun and fell on my side.

"You'll pay for that!" – Martin said as he punched me over and over.

He then put his hands around my throat and started choking me.

"You ruined everything!" – he said, squeezing so hard that my vision got darker by the second – "I'll kill you for what you've done!"

I raised my hands and punched Martin at the forearms as hard as I could, making his grip loosen. I then coughed up some blood in his face and kicked him away from me with the remaining strength.

I turned around on my stomach and started crawling towards the gun on the ground.

"No, you don't!" – Martin said from behind and I felt myself getting dragged back by the feet.

I turned back around to see him holding a big rock above his head. I raised my hands in defense and a loud bang ensued. Martin dropped the rock and a large red stain appeared on his chest. He stared at me in disbelief before finally falling down dead.

"Rot in hell, you piece of shit." – Alyssa said, holding the gun, with Dewey behind her.

"Come on, let's go!" – she said and helped me up as much as she could with her bad leg.

Screams started to fill the air again behind us. We ran back inside the lab and Andrew closed the secret passage just in time for the monsters to slam into the impregnable wall.

I fell on my knees, coughing violently. When I finally stopped, I felt weaker than ever, so much that I could barely stand. I lay on the bed, while Andrew contacted HQ via radio. A few minutes later, he got a response and the military confirmed they would eliminate the remaining monsters and perform a search and rescue immediately.

"You did it!" – Alyssa told me as she held my hand.

But I couldn't respond, since I fell out of consciousness.

I woke up some time later on the same bed. Alyssa and a bunch of doctors were around me.

"Good, he's stable." – one of them said.

"Is he gonna be okay?" – Alyssa asked.

I looked around and saw military people talking to Andrew and more doctors walking around the lab.

"If we had arrived a few minutes late, he would have been dead." – the doctor said – "He can never be rid of the infection. But the bacteria will remain dormant as long as he takes the medication. You'll have to keep a close eye on him. And if there's even the slightest change-"

"I know. I'll take care of him." – she said.

The doctors left and Alyssa sat next to me with a big smile and squeezed my hand.

"Hey, you hear that? You'll be alright!"

I closed my eyes and squeezed back.

There was no news coverage about the incident and all rescued survivors were forced to sign an NDA about the whole deal, under the threat of incarceration and even execution. The official reported story was that there was a virus outbreak, which has since been contained, despite the numerous casualties.

Months later, I live a normal life, albeit with a lower lung capacity. Dewey lives with his aunt now, but Alyssa and I make sure to visit him every week. Everyone else seems to be back to living their old mundane life too, and no one talks about the rain incident.

One thing still bothers me though. Whenever it rains, I always hear something when I'm home. Something that puts me on edge and takes me back to the day when the whole incident started. Something that's always just loud enough for me to hear no matter what I'm doing or where I am in my house.

The unmistakable sound of footsteps splashing in my backyard.

MIRRORVERSE

I glanced at my watch. 3:15 pm. It was almost time to pick up Kevin from school. I leaned against my chair, staring at the spreadsheet on the screen in front of me, with the cacophony of voices, typing and ringing of phones surrounding me from the other cubicles. I still had some work to do, but I figured I'd call it a day. It was Friday and I could wrap it up on Monday instead.

I stood up, giving time to my lower back to adjust to the sudden shift of position. I put my keys in my pocket and turned off the computer, throwing a piece of crumpled up paper from my desk into the trash bin under. I rounded the corner, almost bumping into Katie.

"Whoa, sorry about that." – I stepped aside, smiling.

"Going home already, Jack?" – she asked, clutching the folders to her chest and shooting me a grin.

I took this as a sign that she wanted to strike some small talk and decided to indulge her.

"Yeah, I gotta pick my son up from school. Rachel and I wanted to take him and his friends to laser tag today. You should probably call it a day soon too, you've been working like crazy lately." – I leaned against the cubicle to my left.

"Yeah, I know." – her expression turned sour – "But I can't. Still got to finish a bunch of reports. Should be done by 5pm though."

I shook my head:

"You're a workaholic, you know that?"

She chuckled.

"Alright well, I'll see you Monday then. You have a great weekend, Katie."

"You too, Jack." – she smiled and went her merry way, her heels resounding throughout the office with every step she took.

I wondered for a moment how I managed to almost bump into her, considering the fact that no matter how loud the other employees' voices were, Katie's high heels were ear-splittingly louder, regardless of where she was. You could basically pinpoint where she was at any given time just from that. I went into the bathroom and after relieving myself went to the sink to wash my hands.

As I did so, I glanced at my own reflection and stopped scrubbing out of surprise of what I saw. I looked like I hadn't slept in days. Heavy, dark circles were beneath my eyes and my face looked like I hadn't shaved in weeks, with grey hairs sticking out here and there. My hair was messy and greasy.

Had I really come to work like that? I swiveled my head left and right, inspecting my face, baffled by my own looks. I had shaved that morning and to the touch of the hand, my face was as smooth as a baby's butt, but in the reflection it looked scruffy and unkempt. I leaned in closer, inspecting every detail, amused and perplexed at what I was seeing. I smiled, in order to see how I looked like that and then I froze.

My reflection in the mirror was frozen. I stepped back, bumping into the stall with my back, gasping and blinking violently, trying to make this hallucination go away. But when I opened my eyes again, the reflection was still frozen as it was a few seconds ago. I leaned left and then right, staring in amazement at what was in front of me. It felt like I was looking at my own Skype video while it was frozen during a call. I leaned in again, placing my palm on the cold glass, figuring that this may not have been a mirror after all.

This must be some kind of prank. A camera is somewhere in here, I thought to myself. I looked behind myself in the corners of the bathroom, still leaning against the mirror and as I inspected the bathroom walls, I suddenly felt a strong grip on my wrist. I jerked my head back in the direction of the mirror, only to see my reflection had a furious look on his face. He was holding me by my wrist through the mirror so tightly that his knuckles were becoming white. I struggled to pull away from his grip, but before I could break free, he reached through the mirror with his other hand and grabbed me by the neck, pulling me closer.

I tried screaming for help, but he squeezed too tightly and all that came out was a barely audible gasp. He was pulling me closer by the second and I could now smell the stale sweat and booze on his breath so clearly that it only added to my asphyxiation. His face was merely inches away from mine now and with one final effort, he jerked me towards himself with all his force.

I closed my eyes, bracing myself for a crash with either my reflection's face or the mirror itself, but the impact never came and instead I felt myself falling backwards on my ass. When I opened my eyes, I realized I was on the bathroom floor. I stood up as fast as I could with my back against the stall, my legs shaky, grabbing at my neck which was still throbbing, along with my wrist. I stared at my reflection in the mirror, seeing palpable fear in my own eyes. It no longer had the scruffy look, but resembled that of my real self from this morning.

I stood there for what felt like a very long time and when I saw that my reflection wasn't making any movements different than my own, I dumbly waved my hand in front of it. The reflection mirrored my own movement perfectly, putting me at ease a little bit. Just then, another employee walked inside, shooting me a suspicious glance before heading into one of the stalls. I collected myself, looking at the reflection one more time and tidying up before heading out.

"You okay, Jack?" – Katie asked me with a concerned look on her face.

"Uh, yeah. Yeah." – I nodded.

"Are you already done for the day?" – she asked.

I frowned:

"Um, yeah. We talked about this a few minutes ago, remember? I gotta pick up Kevin from school."

Her look of concern changed to one of confusion now. She opened her mouth as if to say something and then closed it.

"Well, I should get back to work." – she gave me a PR smile and left, her hurried footsteps echoing throughout the office.

I left the office workspace and turned left down the hallway.

"See you Monday, Mark." – I waved to a coworker who had passed by.

"You're... going home?" – he turned around to face me.

"Yeah. You try not to work too hard either, yeah?" – I turned to face him while backpedaling and then continued in the direction I started.

"Um, Jack?" – Mark called my name.

When I looked back at him, he was standing in the middle of the hallway with the same concerned look on his face like Katie.

"Yeah?" – I asked with a fake smile on my face.

"The elevator's this way." – he pointed behind himself with his thumb.

"What are you talking about, that part is under renovation, see the elevator's over-"

I turned around and pointed in the direction I was originally facing and then stopped mid-sentence. At the far end of the hallway from wall to wall was a 'do not cross' tape, marking a clear border between the pristine floor and the one littered with dust and other powdery material.

"I uh..." – I started, staring at the tape and then turning back to Mark and looking behind his shoulder – "Uh yeah, my bad. You're right, the exit is the other way."

"Are you... feeling okay, Jack?" – Mark asked.

"Yeah, yeah. I just, you know, got confused a little bit, is all." – I chuckled and waved my hand in dismissal.

"Alright man, well you take care. I'll see you Monday." – Mark forced a visibly fake smile and disappeared in the office space before I could even utter a 'you too' properly.

I looked back at the renovated area and then at the office door. What was going on today? First the hallucination in the mirror, now forgetting where the elevator was? I had been working here for two years now and there's no way the elevator could just switch places like that. Then again I never went to the other side of this floor, so maybe there were two elevators and the main one was simply not functional? I shrugged those thoughts away and decided I'd take a nap as soon as I got back home. But the strange occurrences didn't stop there.

On my way out of the building, I couldn't find my car at first and it was only after the security guard came to ask what was going on that he was able to point me to my car – all the way on the other side of the parking lot. I thanked him, probably looking like a madman to him and made my way out of there. My son's school was close by, so I drove there, but when I arrived to my destination and parked my car, instead of the school being on my right, it was across the street. At this point I started to worry a little bit. Had I suffered a head injury in the bathroom and now all the information in my mind was jumbled up?

My thoughts were interrupted when I glanced to my right and saw an old lady who was standing on the sidewalk, staring in my direction blankly. I ignored her and took off my seat belt. I got out of the car and the sound of children's playful voices instantly filled the air, along with the occasional adults shouting warnings to the kids. I looked to the right and the old lady was still staring at me with her unrelenting gaze. I nodded to her, to which she didn't respond. What is it with old people, I thought to myself and crossed the street, getting to the front of the school, where children in large numbers were exiting the building and making their way home, some alone and some looking for their parents.

I recognized some of Kevin's classmates and figured Kevin himself would be out any moment. I waited a few minutes with my hands in my pocket, occasionally glancing at my watch. Then one of the adults came out. It was Mrs Steiner, Kevin's teacher. I approached her and when she looked up from her purse and caught my glance, she froze in place, staring at me with a blank expression on her face.

"Mr Conley." – she said – "Is there something I can help you with?"

"Uh, yeah." – I said, surprised that I even needed to explain – "I'm here to pick up Kevin. Is he still inside?"

Her blank expression changed to that of serious concern. She stared at me for a few seconds before saying:

"Are you here to pick up some of Kevin's belongings? Did he leave anything at school?"

"No, what? No, I'm here for Kevin." – at this point I was probably as confused as she was.

"I think you need to leave now, Mr Conley." – she responded after a pause – "And I strongly believe you should get some help."

She took a step forward, but I got in her way.

"What? What are you talking about? Just tell me where Kevin is. Did something happen to him?" – I insisted, furious and scared.

She sighed.

"I know the truth is hard to accept and I am so sorry you had to go through that, but if you come here again, I will be forced to call security."

She tried to leave again, but I grabbed her by the arm, attracting the suspicious glances of some kids and adults nearby. Mrs Steiner jerked her head in my direction. She looked like she was ready to pepper spray me by this moment. I let go of her arm, realizing suddenly that I was being too violent.

"Mrs Steiner, please. Just tell me what happened to Kevin. Was he in an accident? Is he alright?" – I pleaded.

She stared at me for a moment, as if to contemplate what she should do and then she said:

"Mr Conley, I'm sorry but... your son died six months ago."

CHAPTER 2

"Is this a fucking joke?" – I shouted louder than I intended, attracting more glares around me.

Mrs Steiner was clearly shocked, but said nothing.

"Where's Kevin?!" – I demanded – "Kevin! KEVIN!"

I frenetically spun around, looking for my son, completely disregarding the scared kids and parents who were holding their children close to themselves and evacuating the school.

"Mr Conley, please…" – Mrs Steiner interjected, but I ignored her, calling Kevin's name over and over.

"WHERE'S KEVIN?! WHERE'S MY SON?" – I paced back and forth around the schoolyard, while people were avoiding me in a large arch. Two security guards rushed in and before I knew it, I was forcefully being dragged out. Their pleas for me to leave which later turned into threats about calling the police fell on deaf ears, as I kept trying to find Kevin. I ended up being thrown out and when I tried to get back in, they blocked my path.

"Please, I have to find my son!" – I tried to get past the guards, unable to control my panic.

"Sir, I'm warning you, if you don't leave right away, I will be forced to call the authorities!" – he put his palm on my chest, pushing me back.

That finally snapped my full attention to him and with hesitation, I returned to my car. I had to call my wife Amanda. She would assure me that everything was okay, right? She had to. I whipped out my phone, scrolling through my contacts. I dialed her phone number, glancing out the car window in the direction of the guards who hadn't budged from their location. They were still shooting me suspicious looks, probably waiting for me to leave. I waited for Amanda's phone to start ringing, but it never came. I looked at the screen and saw that the call had been disconnected.

I dialed again, but the same thing happened. I slammed the phone on the steering wheel out of frustration and put it back in my pocket. She was home, so I just had to go there. Maybe she already picked Kevin up and this was all an elaborate prank? I remember hoping against hope that that was the case.

I put the keys in the ignition and started up my car. I drove off with screeching tires, probably attracting the glances of even more people along the way. It took everything in my power not to run all red lights on the way home, but I knew in my hot-headed state that being pulled over by the police would only exacerbate the situation. When I finally pulled up in front of my house, I got out of the car so fast that the seatbelt initially pulled me back. I slammed the car door and strode to the entrance, forcefully trying to open the door. It was locked.

I put my keys inside, but they didn't fit for some reason. I rang the bell and then knocked three times loudly, shouting:

"Amanda? Are you home?!"

The sound of key turning was heard on the other end and the door opened. But it wasn't Amanda. In front of me stood my neighbor Nick.

"Jack, everything okay?" – he asked worriedly, holding the door with one hand.

As soon as I glanced behind my neighbor inside his home, I realized what a huge error I've made. I was looking at my neighbor's home and not my own.

"Oh, I'm so sorry, Nick. I uh…"

"Drinking already, Jack?" – he smiled and tried to shrug it off as a joke.

I chuckled nervously:

"Yeah, sorry about the disturbance. Hope I didn't interrupt anything."

"Don't worry about it, buddy. Take it easy, will ya?"

"Yeah, you too." – I smiled and turned around to cross the street, where my home actually was.

I approached the door and tried to open it. Locked. I pulled out my keys and hesitantly put them in and sure enough, they fit like a glove. I pushed the door gently, revealing the dim interior. What I saw inside was my home and yet it wasn't. The foyer floor had my shoes scattered all over the floor. Amanda always made sure the foyer was tidy and the shoes organized, so this looked like she had been away for a while. There was dirt on the floor, indicating that whoever had gone in hadn't bothered to wipe their shoes first. The living room had barely any sunlight gleaming through. I shut the door, further decreasing the natural light inside.

"Amanda? Kevin?" – I shouted and held my breath, waiting for a response or any noise.

None came.

I went inside the living room and again was faced with the feeling of surrealism at what I saw. Everything was exactly how I had left it this morning, but some things were off. There were discarded booze bottles on the table and under it, some flipped over, the contents spilled and dried on the carpet. There were grease-stained papers and bags from fast food all over the place. What the fuck happened here?

Amanda is crazy about keeping the place as clean as an operating room, so to have her leave it like this indicated that something was very wrong here. I approached the table and saw a flipped over photo next to the half-eaten burger. I picked it up and inspected it. It was a picture of Kevin. I stared at it and suppressed the tears welling up in my eyes. I was confused by everything and scared. Scared for myself and for my wife and son. I was afraid I'd never get to see them and hear their voices again.

Just then I heard a vibration in front of me and moving the food papers away I saw a cellphone. It was my own cellphone, no doubt about it. I unlocked it, revealing dozens of missed calls and messages. Most of the messages were people asking me where I was and if I was alright. As I scrolled through, I saw that some messages were from Amanda. The first thing that struck me as odd and confirmed my suspicions was the fact that she was in my contacts simply under the name 'Amanda', rather than 'Wife'.

I read her messages as fast as I could:

Jack, are you okay?

Hey, call me back when you get this

Why aren't you answering? I'm starting to worry.

There were missed calls from her as well. I called her number and waited for the phone to ring. After just one ring she picked up.

"Jack? Is that you?!" – her voice resounded on the other end.

"Amanda, yeah it's me. Where are you?"

"Where am I? Where are you? Do you know how long you've been gone? Your disappearance was filed to the police, they're looking for you."

"What? Amanda, listen I don't know what's going on, but... where's Kevin? I went to pick him up from school and then everything just got jumbled up... Mrs Steiner said he's dead... Amanda, what's going on here? Where's our son?"

I heard Amanda sigh over the phone.

"Jack, I think you should get help. Listen, I have to go. It's best we-"

"Amanda, please. Can we please just talk about this? I don't know what's going on and I feel like I'm losing my mind. I can't remember anything. Please..."

There was silence over the phone and then she said:

"I'll be there in 20 minutes. But I don't have much time."

"Thank you."

I hung up and stared at nothing for a while. Would I finally get some answers when she arrived? In the meantime, I decided I should check the rest of the house. I went up the stairs and into the bedroom. It was almost as messy as the living room, with bottles of liquor on the nightstand and on the floor. Dirty clothes were piled up in the corner of the room and the bed sheets were hanging off the side of the bed. The curtains were draped over the windows, dimming the room entirely. The whole room reeked of booze and sweat. I noticed that all of Amanda's belongings had been removed from the room and only mine remained. Before I exited, I noticed some meds on the night table next to the half-emptied liquor bottle. Antidepressants and sleeping pills.

I left the room and closed the door, immediately eliminating the odor coming from inside. I went down the hallway and slowly approached the door on the right. I grabbed the knob and hesitated. I took a deep breath and pushed the door open, revealing the interior of the room.

Kevin's room was exactly how I remembered it. Everything was in place and tidy, contrasting the rest of the house's abominable mess. His bed was made and school books rested upon the desk facing the window. Sunlight gleamed inside, like a sanctuary of light from the darkness in the house. The TV screen reflected dust from sunlight and on the floor below was his console with a single game neatly resting atop it. I looked around, absorbing my surroundings, inexplicable sadness suddenly overcoming me.

Where are you, Kevin? What happened to you? Tears welled up on my eyes again and I turned around before I could allow myself to start crying and closed the door firmly. If I could, I'd build a wall over the door just so I wouldn't have to look at it again and be painfully reminded of my loss.

Before I could process that thought clearly, I heard the doorbell ring. I ran down the stairs as fast as I could and opened the door, letting in a gust of fresh air.

"Hello, Jack." – Amanda looked like hell.

Her hair was unkempt and she had heavy bags under her eyes. Her skin was pale and she looked like she had lost a lot of weight.

"Amanda." – I said dumbly, staring at her.

I hadn't even thought about how I should behave when she arrives. Do I hug her? Do I act friendly? According to what I knew we seemed to be living apart, so I had to test the waters first.

"Can I come in?" – she asked.

"Yeah, yeah. Sure." – I snapped back to reality and stepped aside, letting her in.

She took off her shoes, glancing at the dirty foyer along the way and then went straight to the living room. I knew she was probably disgusted by the mess in front of her.

"Sorry about the mess." – I said – "I uh…"

"It's alright." – she said, standing uncomfortably in the middle of the room.

I cleared the table and sat on the couch, telling her to feel free to do the same. She sat opposite me and looked around at the room once more.

"Amanda, I have a lot of questions." – I swallowed and leaned in, jumping into the topic right away.

"Likewise. You just disappeared a week ago. Where did you go?" – she looked at me judgmentally.

"I have no idea what you're talking about. Listen, I was at work just now and I know it doesn't make sense, but I was supposed to pick up Kevin from school and we had plans for the weekend for him and his friends. I finished work earlier and all of a sudden everything got confusing. Mrs Steiner said he died when I went to pick him up and I just, I don't…"

"Laser tag."

"What?"

"We were gonna take him and his friends to laser tag." – Amanda smiled.

"Yes! That's it! I went to pick him up and everything else was just a mess. Nothing is where I remember it to be and people look at me strangely, I don't get it…"

"Jack, that was six months ago. That was the day Kevin died."

I stared, dumbfounded. I had somehow traveled 6 months into the future and completely forgot about everything during that time. Amanda continued:

"Jack, this is clearly a coping mechanism. You suppressed everything from that day on to deal with Kevin's death. I understand it, but you need help. You can't run from this."

"How… how did he die?"

She stared at me and her expression turned from judgmental to hateful.

"You killed him, Jack." – she said through her teeth.

CHAPTER 3

The next few days were a blur. I spent the majority of my days drinking and sleeping. I kept replaying the conversation with Amanda in my mind over and over.

"You killed Kevin, Jack."

"No, that can't be true. You're lying!"

"It's true, Jack. You were speeding and the car breaks didn't work and... you survived unscathed, but Kevin... there was barely anything left of him." – she started crying.

"No! NO!" – I grabbed my head, pacing around, feeling like my heart was going to explode.

"It was an accident, Jack. You didn't mean to kill him. But I never forgave you."

I exhaled sharply, wiping my tears.

"So you decided to leave me?" – I asked.

"I had to get away. The house brought too many painful memories for me and you were in your own world as well, drinking yourself unconscious daily and... I had to get away from all of it."

I wish I could say that Amanda and I had a reconciliation and that she forgave me, but by the time she left, we were both heavy-hearted and tired from crying. I had no strength to ask her to stay, even though I wanted her to be with me through such a difficult time. I saw the resentment in her eyes and knew better than to ask.

I hated myself for ruining our family and I hated myself for not remembering my child's death. I knew it was probably poetic justice for me to go through this pain for the second time, but I begged god to take it away. The pain was so excruciating and exhausting that I even contemplated ending my life with pills.

And then three days after my meetup with Amanda I woke up at 3pm with a hangover and went into the bathroom to clear myself up. I looked in the mirror and saw what an empty husk I've become. My hair was messy, my beard unkempt and scruffy, the bags under my bloodshot eyes adding to my age. I didn't care about it though.

I bent down to wash my face and when I stood up, I sobered up immediately at what I saw. In front of me was my own reflection, and yet it wasn't my own. The person in front of me looked clean and tidy, with perfectly shaved face, healthier skin tone and neat hair. Suddenly I remembered what transpired at my work bathroom a few days ago. I had been grieving and completely misplaced it from my mind. I stared at my reflection and its lack or blemishes and my anger boiled. I was angrier than I had ever been before in my life. It was this reckless son of a bitch who took everything from me and I hated him for that. I wanted nothing more than to reach into the mirror and bash his head on the sink over and over until only a bloody, unrecognizable pulp remained. This urge was so irresistible that I felt myself unwillingly raising my hand and diving it into the mirror, grabbing the wrist of the other Jack with force I never knew I had.

My reflection suddenly looked scared for his life and it fed into my sadistic satisfaction of wanting to hurt him. I reached with my other hand as well and grabbed him by the neck, squeezing tightly. I started pulling him towards me, with the intention of dragging him over to my side and brutally murdering him. I yanked him with all my might and just before he uncontrollably crashed into me, I felt myself stumbling backwards.

I stood up, looking at my reflection, ready to grab him once more, but he was gone. Just my own, dirty reflection remained. I sighed, leaving the bathroom and heading into the bedroom, stumbling on my bed face-first.

"Honey? Is everything okay?" – I heard a voice which put all my senses on edge.

Had I imagined that?

"Honey?" – the voice repeated.

A familiar, soothing voice. It was Amanda. I rushed downstairs, practically jumping down the last five steps and sure enough, there she was. But not the Amanda I saw a few days ago, but my Amanda as I knew her before - beautiful, happy, perfect.

"Jack, what happened to you?" – she looked at me with confusion – "Is this a costume or something? You're Jack the Hobo now?" – she chuckled.

I stared at her in bafflement. My brain couldn't process what I was seeing.

"Jack?" – she shot me a suspicious glance.

"Uh, yeah?" – I asked.

"Are you gonna pick Kevin up, or not? He's almost done in school."

I opened my mouth dumbly and then closed it, muttering a weak 'what?'.

"Your son. Kevin. You're supposed to pick him up. He has laser tag today, remember?" – she repeated in a slower tone.

"Right. Right." – I ran for my keys, feeling a surge of ecstasy overwhelming me – "I'm supposed to pick up Kevin, that's right!"

"Jack wait-" – Amanda started but I was already in the car.

The urge to run the red lights was even stronger than last time, but I resisted it. Especially since I knew I was responsible for Kevin's death by driving. The school was not where I remembered it to be though. It wasn't across the street this time, either. It was all the way on the other end of the street. This raised some suspicions with me, but I ignored them. I didn't care. Kevin was alive, that's all that mattered. I ran to the school and didn't even need to look – there he was, just how I remembered him the day he left for school when I last saw him. He smiled widely when he saw me and ran to me. I embraced him tightly, telling him how much I've missed him and that I'll never let him go. When I finally let him go, holding back tears of joy, he simply wrinkled his nose and said:

"Dad, you stink."

I laughed, kissing him on the forehead and pretty soon he and I were on the way to the car. As I let him in and closed the door, I heard a voice behind me.

"Don't do it."

I turned around and it was the same old lady I saw a few days ago in the same spot, the one who was staring at me from the pavement.

"He's not your son, Jack." – she shook her head – "You know that well. You're taking someone else's son. Don't do it."

I scoffed. I was caught by surprise so suddenly that it took me a moment to respond:

"Listen lady, I don't know who you think you are, but you need to mind your own business, alright? Now if you'll excuse me-"

"You're not in your own world. Your son is alive and there's still time to save him, you just-"

"Alright that's enough!" – I yelled and rushed inside the car, ignoring Kevin's worried gaze as we sped out of there.

"Are you okay, dad?" – Kevin asked.

I looked in the rearview mirror and saw that the old lady still staring at me.

"Yeah, I'm fine, buddy. You ready to kick some ass in laser tag?" – I asked, much to his enthusiasm.

A few minutes later we pulled up in front of the house and Amanda was standing in front of the entrance, smiling.

"There you are!" – she said – "Did your dad drive recklessly?"

Kevin looked at me and I shook my head, winking at him.

"Alright, let's get you inside. Lunch is ready." – Amanda said.

I stared at them, the two people who meant everything to me in the world and I suddenly got the instinctive urge to turn around. As I did, there she was, across the street. The old lady from school. She stood there, our gazes meeting. She shook her head slowly. I sighed and looked back at Amanda taking off Kevin's backpack as he was telling her about something that happened at school. I could just live with my family, even if it was fake and no one would ever know the difference. I glanced at the old lady again.

"Hey, Amanda? Do you think you could take Kevin to laser tag? I have something to take care of."

"What? Now? But this was your idea. I thought you wanted to do this." – she said.

"I know. And I do. I'll be there later, I promise."

I approached Amanda and put my hands on her face, kissing her gently. I knelt down and ruffled Kevin's hair, saying:

"You listen to your mom now, alright?"

As opened the car door, I looked at them one more time.

"You promised, dad. Don't be late! And we're getting pizza later!" – Kevin said, smiling widely.

"Yeah, otherwise we'll have to go on without you!" – Amanda smiled along with him, ushering him inside.

I smiled back bitterly and watched until the door closed behind. I looked at the old lady. She was still staring at me. I did a U-turn and stopped the car in front of her.

"Get in." – I said to the old lady after rolling the window down.

She got in, smiling for the first time since I saw her.

"I knew you'd make the right call, Jack." – she said.

"Who are you really? How do you know me?" – I asked, putting my cup of coffee on the table.

The café we were in had a plethora of young people in it, filling the interior with their voices, allowing the old lady and me to talk in peace.

"I know everything about you Jack. I know what you've been through lately. The strange events that took place in the mirrors..."

"You know about that?"

"Yes. And that's why I'm here. What was done has to be undone. You probably figured it out by now. Most of it, anyway."

I shook my head, confused. I glanced at the other tables to make sure no one was eavesdropping. Even though the topic of our conversation would most likely just have people dismiss us as lunatics even if they heard something, I still felt like a student who was cheating on an exam and afraid of being caught.

"All I know is strange things started happening a few days ago and I feel like I'm losing my mind. Nothing is where it was supposed to me. I went to pick my son up and the school was across the street. I went home and it was my neighbor's house. It's like..." – I trailed off.

"Like you've entered a mirror." – she finished my sentence, blank expression on her face.

"Yeah. And then my son was dead and my wife and I were divorced... what's going on here exactly?"

She leaned back in her chair, never breaking eye contact.

"You switched places with the Jack from a different Mirrorverse."

"Mirrorverse? You mean Multiverse?"

"No, I mean Mirrorverse. That's what the scientists call it. Similar to the multiverse, there are... worlds out there. Millions and millions of infinite worlds, all the same and all different. You've seen them."

I stared at her, expecting her to continue.

"Jack, being able to travel from one world to another is an extremely rare gift. But for some reason you seem to have it. You're able to see into those worlds and even enter them. But going in and out is not good."

"Why? Why is it not good?" – I was sitting on the edge of my seat, probably wide-eyed while she looked like she was talking about something nonchalant like recipes for cooking.

She continued:

"It creates an imbalance. It creates distortions and paradoxes in other worlds. We can't allow that to happen. The Mirrorverse where Kevin is dead... Jack got his son killed in an accident. It may have happened a million other times to a million other Kevins, but none of them would have the impact on balance like that specific one. He is the starting point of everything."

I took a sip of my coffee, giving fluid to my dry throat. She inhaled and continued:

"It may have happened to a million other Jacks, but they would simply mourn Kevin's death and move on. Some of them would stay in an unhappy marriage, some would get divorced and most of them would commit suicide or die from alcohol and drug abuse. But not this Jack. He couldn't come to terms with what he did. So one day, he accidentally saw you in the mirror, a version of himself which still had a happy family and he was overtaken by anger. He hated himself so he tried to kill you and inadvertently switched places with you and then realized Kevin was alive in your world."

"So he wants a world where Kevin is still alive and Amanda is with him? He wants to have a happy family again?" – for a moment, I felt pity and understanding for my impostor.

She shook her head:

"Not exactly. He's lost his mind. He believes his son was taken from him. He can't cope with the fact that he lost his own son and he hates himself for it so much, that he wants to punish every version of himself in every world."

"How?"

"By killing Kevin in all the worlds."

"What?!" – my shout attracted a few glances for a moment.

"He wants to punish all the Jacks in all the worlds by taking the most precious thing away from them."

"But we switched worlds days ago. Oh god, if he picked up Kevin then-"

"Your son is still alive. But we don't have much time, Jack."

I felt a surge of panic coursing through my entire body like electricity. I had to go and save Kevin, now!

"Don't worry. He's still okay. And we still have time to save him." – she reassured me after noticing my fear – "And I know exactly where to find him."

The panic I felt before started to abate, and I leaned in my chair, scratching my beard, looking at the old lady. All these things just seemed so far-fetched. Different worlds in mirrors which you can travel through? Having millions of doppelgangers out there? This all seemed like a movie script and I never even stopped to ask myself if I was maybe losing my mind. Maybe this lady was just as crazy as I was and was feeding into my illusion. Everything she said made sense, but somehow it was still hard to believe.

"Who are you, lady?" – I asked.

She shrugged:

"Just a guardian. I try to keep a balance in all the Mirrorverses. That is and always was my duty."

"So why can't you do something about this? Can't you just return us all to our own worlds or something?"

She shook her head:

"No Jack. I can't meddle in these affairs. I can offer assistance, but you must be the one to restore balance."

"And what happens to the Jack I switched places with today? For all we know there could be hundreds or thousands of others who did the same. The first Jack may have started an infinite loop." – I said.

"It all begins and ends with Jack who took your life away. Once you do what must be done, everything will return to normal and balance will be restored. He can't be allowed to cause any more damage. He has to be stopped."

"What is it that I must do? How do I stop him?" – I turned my palms towards her in an asking manner, getting impatient.

She leaned in so that we were so close to each other I could see every pore in her face, her unrelenting gaze locked with mine.

"You must kill him, Jack." – she whispered - "It is the only way."

I sat in the car, holding a mirror in my lap. The old lady was next to me. The sunny day slowly turned into a grey one, bringing with it the droplets or rain which resounded on the roof of my car.

"I don't understand what I'm supposed to do here." – I shook my head, looking at the lady.

I felt like a teenager in a driving test and she was the instructor, but unlike my actual instructor, she was very patient.

"Stare directly in the mirror." – she said – "What do you see?"

I stared at my dumbfounded face, shaking my head once more.

"Myself?" – I said, unsure.

"Good. Now, try to remember what the first Jack looked like. Remember what he did to you and how he took your life away and once you start feeling an overwhelming emotion, either sadness, anger, hate or such, reach into the mirror. Try it."

I glanced at the mirror and then felt her hand on my shoulder.

"Remember." – she said – "No matter what happens, you MUST kill him. Otherwise this was all for nothing."

I stared at the mirror once more, trying to remember the Jack in the work bathroom mirror. He looked back then very much like I did now – messy hair, unkempt beard, pale face, but more so, and I distinctly remember smelling booze on his breath. The anger I felt earlier towards him was gone and was instead replaced by profound empathizing sadness which a father who lost his child could understand. I saw my own reflection changing, hair and beard slightly growing and bags under the eyes becoming heaver. Without further thinking, I slowly and gently reached into the mirror. I felt the cold glass touching my knuckles as the mirror stopped my hand from going through. I dropped the mirror back onto my lap and shook my head in frustration.

"I don't think this is gonna wo-"

When I looked to my right, the old lady was gone. I looked around and saw her nowhere in the streets. A few people were walking by with umbrellas, but that was it. I then realized I was on the other side of the street, or rather the street was inverted. I knew immediately I was back in my own world. I started the car and slowly drove off. The lady said they would be at the corner of this one street that sold video games at exactly 5:12. I felt my jacket to see if my gun was still there, very careful not to somehow lose it along the way. I had to sneak into the house while Amanda and Kevin were gone to retrieve it and I did not feel content by having to use it, let alone kill someone, but in the end, my son's life was at stake.

Knots started twisting in my stomach, anxiety like before a big test or presentation and with each mile I got closer it only got worse. I tried to keep Kevin's face in my mind's eye in order to prevent myself from chickening out in case I really had to pull the trigger. I arrived at my destination soon and parked the car further away to avoid suspicion from the other Jack. It was 5:05. The street was empty and the sounds of occasional cars driving across the wet roads were heard in the adjacent streets. The video game store at the corner was the one where I would regularly take Kevin to buy him games, so I kept a close eye on it.

5:12. Two people emerged from the shop, an adult man and a child. Jack and Kevin. It was surreal seeing myself with my son there, as if I was watching a hyper-realistic movie. Kevin had a smile on his face and was pointing to the game in his hands, telling Jack something. My doppelganger listened closely, saying something in return, smiling equally. He looked a lot healthier and cleaner than last time. Seeing them together like that, this impostor with my son made anger surge through me and all feelings of anxiety were gone. This was my time to shine. I stepped forward on the pavement towards them. They hadn't seen me yet.

"Jack!" – I called out to my copy and saw his smile drop when he realized who he was looking at.

Kevin seemed perplexed as well, looking at the both of us, wildly swiveling his head left and right. Without a word, Jack picked up Kevin and started running.

"Stop!" – I shouted, sprinting after them.

They ran around the corner and disappeared in the crowd of people in front. I pushed my way through the herd, much to the cursing and frustration of them. Jack was running straight towards a police officer, so he turned inside a nearby building. He could've just told the cop there was a crazy man with a gun after him, but I guess he panicked. Also, he did not know I had a gun on me. I followed closely and when I went inside, they were gone. The light above the elevator was on though and it showed they were going to the top floor.

I was already exhausted from running, but decided I had no choice but to run 10 floors up. I climbed the stairs as fast as I could, making sure along the way the elevator wasn't stopping or changing directions. When I finally arrived, I saw them exiting the door the leads to the roof. Thank god for slow elevators, I thought to myself and followed them. I felt the cold air and droplets on my face once more and immediately looked for my son. Jack and Kevin stood at the edge of the roof, Kevin scared and Jack wide-eyed, panicking.

"You can't have him!" – he shouted, holding my son's hand firmly.

"Dad, no!" - Kevin cried, looking at the evil Jack.

"It's okay Kevin, everything's gonna be okay!" – I shouted over the sudden wind which became strong.

I slowly stepped closer.

"Stay back!" – he shouted, pulling Kevin closer and taking one step towards the edge.

"This has to end, Jack!" – I said, taking another step closer.

"You don't understand!" – he shouted back – "You can't understand what I've been through!"

"I do understand, Jack. I know what happened and I felt the same pain you did when you lost Kevin. The breaks didn't work and the car crashed. It wasn't your fault, Jack."

He looked down and then at Kevin. He looked like he was on the verge of tears.

"I'm sorry, I..." – he started.

"It's okay. It's not too late. But you have to stop this. Kevin did nothing wrong. You need to let him go."

Jack looked at Kevin and then knelt down in front of him. He hugged him and said:

"I'm sorry. I didn't mean for all this to happen. You mean the world to me and I let you down."

He let go and stood up. Kevin stepped back and they shared a moment of exchanged glances. Then, a loud bang echoed on the roof. Jack looked down at his chest and saw a red stain which increased by the second and then he glanced at me.

I lowered my gun, my hands shaking so hard that I could barely hold it. Jack looked at Kevin before he simply collapsed on his back, eyes still open. Kevin screamed and I rushed to embrace him. I comforted him as I watched Jack's body fade before me and I wondered if this outcome was really necessary.

The rest of the day was a blur. I was just happy to have Kevin back and knew that despite the trauma he had just been through, he would be okay. Amanda insisted he had a bad dream and that seeing two Jacks was not possible. I agreed with her and comforted my son. That night I put Kevin to sleep in his room. I tucked him in and he looked at me and said:

"Dad, I once had a similar dream to the one today."

I smiled.

"Oh yeah? Was it scary?"

"I don't know. You were fighting with your twin and I woke up before it ended."

"Well, don't worry. If my evil twin does come, I'll kick his ass."

Just then, Amanda came to the door.

"Jack, there's someone at the door." – she said – "It's for you."

It was 10 pm already, so I wondered who it could be, but I had some idea. When I opened the door, sure enough, the old lady was there. I wasn't really glad to see her, but at the same time I was really grateful for what she did for me.

"Got 5 minutes for a walk, Jack?" – she asked.

I nodded. I closed the door behind me and followed her down the street.

"Well, you did it Jack." – she said – "You got your life back."

"Yeah. But, was killing him really necessary?" – I asked.

"I'm afraid so. Payment was required."

"Payment? What do you mean?"

She stopped and turned towards me.

"Jack, I haven't been fully honest with you. When the Jack you killed started messing with the Mirrorverse, he did some irreversible damage. Payment was required. Balance had to be restored. The Jack who took your son didn't start a killing spree and it never was his intention, I lied about that. He simply wanted a life where he would have his son back."

"But you said-"

"I know. If I had told you the truth you never would have done what needed to be done." – she paced around – "This was the only way. But that's not all, Jack."

I stared at her in silence, the feeling of dread forming at the pit of my stomach once more. She continued:

"When you killed Jack today, you started an unstoppable cycle. In exactly six months, a Jack from one of the Mirrorverses will enter your world… and kill you."

I widened my eyes, opening my mouth, ready to interject, but she interrupted.

"You can't stop it, Jack. I'm sorry. A life was traded for a life and I know how miserable you would've been without your son. So I did you a favor and traded your life for Kevin's. Don't you think that's fair?"

I didn't even know how to start processing this. I opened my mouth dumbly once more and then closed it, swallowing spit through my dry throat. I looked down at my shoes and listened as she continued:

"I suggest you spend your remaining time with your family. Don't travel through mirrors anymore, for I fear the damage could be even greater this time. Live the rest of your life to the fullest. And Jack?"

I looked up at her to see her smiling.

"Thank you." – she said as she turned around and disappeared in thin air.

TALES OF A

SECURITY GUARD

NIGHT GUARD

CHAPTER 1

When I first saw the ad, I didn't think twice.

Earn up to 80$ per night with our simple job as a night guard. No prior experience required.

The ad said and I submitted my resume as fast as I could, fearing it could disappear or be taken by someone else at any moment. Not two hours after submitting my application, I got a response on my email that I've been hired and can start working from tonight.

It struck me as odd that there was no job interview and that I needed to start working right away, but hey, maybe they urgently needed someone. I've been jobless for over a year now, so I naively ignored any red flags and was just happy to have a job.

I went to the given address at 8 pm and it turned out to be an office building.

"Hello?" – I called out when I entered, but no one responded.

The hall I was in was engulfed in darkness and the only source of light was coming through the pane of glass on the door which had the name SECURITY on it. I knocked on the door, but there was no response.

I decided to open it and sure enough, it was empty. On the desk was a note, left clear as day for me to read. It said:

To the new night guard,

Your shift starts at 8:04 pm and ends at 4:04 am. When you arrive to the building and relieve the other guard of your duty, you can stay in the security room as long as you want, but you have to use the elevator to get to the top floor once at any time during the shift. Once up there, you have to proceed to the end of the attic and flip the switch on the wall. That's it.

If the other guard is not in the security room at the time of your arrival, make a report in the notebook and we will inform his family.

As for your duty:

It's very likely that when you push the top floor button (25), the elevator will go past that floor and you may see that it stopped on floor 33. If this happens, do not try pushing any of the buttons, since it will not work.

Go forward through the hallway. Note that the flashlight may not do much to illuminate the area, but still bring it with you (there's a spare in the drawer).

Some people report hearing or seeing office employees working at their desks, coming from any of the adjacent rooms. You may see them doing something like typing on a computer which isn't turned on, or typing one word over and over on the screen. Ignore them at all cost. It is currently unknown if the employees are real or a manifestation of the mind, but ignoring them should keep you safe.

Turn left when you reach the end of the hallway. You may sometimes see a man standing in the middle, blocking your way. He will do you no harm, so long as you maintain eye contact with him. You have to get past him, so put your hand on the wall to your right (or left) and slide it across as you go through to avoid stumbling and losing eye contact with the man.

He will keep following you with his gaze and try to distract you. Reports indicate he may point behind you with a look of fear on his face to try to get you to look away. You may also hear loud crashing sounds or voices right next to you, but ignore them.

Once you reach the end of the hall and round the corner (and not a moment sooner!), you're safe from the individual. When you reach the exit which leads to the staircase, proceed down. Make sure to note what floor you are on and if any of the floors start repeating on your way down, immediately go back up to floor 33 and then start descending again.

If you see any of the other stair doors open, proceed carefully, especially focusing on the ceiling (or underside of the stairs). You may start to hear footsteps coinciding with your own behind you. Don't stop to listen and don't turn around, just proceed as you normally would. If you feel that the footsteps are getting closer, go faster, but try not to arouse suspicion.

If you hear a high-pitched scream coming from above (it usually sounds like a mountain lion), run down to floor 25 as fast as you can and pray you are faster than the thing chasing you .

If you are forced to continue going down despite the floors repeating, enter the closest floor. You will find yourself back in the hallway of floor 33, so simply repeat the steps from before.

Once you reach floor 25, you are in the clear. First, call the elevator and jam the door to keep it open. Press the floor 1 button and go back to the switch. After flipping the switch, the lights will go out. At this point, you will start to hear screams all around you, similarly to the one described before. Run to the elevator as fast as you can and enter it, while unjamming the door.

If you did everything right, you should have at least five extra seconds to close the elevator before the entities of the building reach you.

You should be back on the first floor of the security room once the elevator stops. You may spend the rest of the shift however you desire, so long as you don't leave the property between 8:04 pm and 4:04 am. Note that leaving the building at any given moment between the mentioned times will put you back on floor 33. Also note that not flipping the switch before 4:04 am will result in you not being able to leave the building.

Thank you for performing your duties!

Management

It's 1:24 am right now and the elevator doors just opened on their own.

CHAPTER 2

I barely made through the building and it was mentally agonizing beyond words.

At 2 am I entered the elevator, which had been opened for almost an hour prior to that. I took the note with me and followed all the rules written there. The elevator stopped on floor 33 despite my hopes. There was the sound of typing to my left and when I peeked through the shattered glass I saw a guy in formal attire sitting by an old PC layered with dust (which wasn't even turned on) and typing away vigorously. He'd even glance over his shoulder and call out to his imaginary (or invisible) coworkers, saying things like: 'Cindy, do you have that report ready?' or 'The client said we should meet at 2 pm.'

I tried not to look at him as I tip-toed through the hallway and turned left. A tall man in a coat stood in front of me and he was staring right at me. I knew I had to maintain eye contact with him, so I slowly went past him. The entire time he tried to distract me by pretending he was about to hit me and hoping I would flinch, pointing to things behind me in a very convincing manner with a look of horror on his face, etc. I swear at one point someone even screamed 'watch out' right in my ear.

Luckily I made it unscathed and going down the stairs to floor 25 was uneventful. I made it to the end of hallway on 25, flipped the switch and rushed back to the elevator as blood-curdling screams echoed all around me. The elevator doors closed just in time for me to hear something heavy slam into it with full force. Luckily, the elevator started descending and the screams slowly faded.

It stopped on floor 1, but the door wouldn't open. I pressed the open button in vain and then... the elevator started moving down. I slammed the number 1 button over and over, but the elevator failed to respond. It went down for an impossible amount of time, descending by my estimation at least 15-20 floor down. And then it finally stopped and the doors opened. In front of me was some kind of a waiting room, with a sofa and lamp table next to it. There was a door opposite of the elevator.

I pressed the buttons over and over, but there was no response. It was clear the elevator wanted me to step out on this floor. Sure enough, as soon as I did, the doors closed again and the elevator went back up. I cursed, frustrated and scared shitless.

I inspected the room and just then realized there was a hastily written note on the lamp table. I picked it up. Here's what it said:

If you're reading this, that means you fell for their trap, just like me. The good news is you made it through the first task on floor 25. The bad news is there is no job and you aren't gonna get paid. Whoever these guys are, they're running some fucking experiments on us like some lab rats. We need to get the fuck out and get to the police.

Read this next part carefully, because your life will depend on it. When you go through the door on your left, you'll find yourself in a mansion of some sorts. You need to make it to the third floor, but it won't be easy. Follow these rules:

FLOOR 1

Go through the hallway, but whatever you do, don't fucking look in the mirror to your left. You may see with your peripheral vision the reflection not mimicking your own movement or just facing and staring at you, but DO NOT look at it. Close your eyes if you have to.

Once you're past the mirror, turn left and go straight. You may hear the toilet flush in the bathroom to your right at this point. If this happens, hide immediately. There's a closet close by. Hide inside and don't make a sound until the old man comes out of the bathroom and is gone. Wait at least one full minute before going out.

Once you're in the clear, climb the stairs in the main hall to the second floor.

FLOOR 2

Turn right and take the second door to the left (blue door). I have no idea what will happen if you take the other doors or turn left. Once through the blue door, you'll find yourself in a big room full of mannequins. Dozens of mannequins will be on both sides. You may hear giggling, and some of them change the direction of their gazes and their positions or poses when you don't look, but I think they won't harm you if you don't disturb them.

If any of the mannequins' heads drop to the floor and roll in front of you, run as fast as you can and close the door behind you once you're out. You should be close to the stairs again now. Follow the hall how to winds and don't worry about any voices you hear from the adjacent rooms, even if they beg you to come help them. If you hear or see any of the doors opening, hide again. The old man might seem someone you can overpower easily, but don't even fucking think about it. Once he's gone, climb the stairs.

FLOOR 3

Remember that man from floor 33 who you had to keep eye contact with? He might be here again, but he's gonna be more aggressive this time. You're gonna hear someone scream something like 'I got you now!' right behind you, but ignore it! You will also start feel a stinging and burning sensation in your eyes. Do your best not to blink. If you have to blink, try not to keep your eyes closed for more than a second. Maintain eye contact with him and go through the hall until you can turn left (left from the original position! That means your right as you're facing the man backwards).

If you see a woman in patient's gowns standing in front of the elevator, facing away from you, just stand next to her and wait for the elevator. If she asks you to come inside the elevator with her, politely decline. If she doesn't say anything, you can step inside with her, but don't talk to her, just stare in front of yourself.

Once you're in the elevator, you'll see that there are no buttons inside. The elevator will start going up on its own. When the elevator stops, wait until the woman steps out and stay inside until the elevator starts moving again. If she asks you if you'll come with her, politely decline again. Once the door closes, the elevator should go up a few more floors. Now if the woman was not there at all, but then you took the elevator and she enters when the doors open, exit immediately. I don't know where you will be and I have no idea what you need to do there, so you're on your own. Hope you don't run into her.

I came back to give you this warning, compiled from my own and other peoples' experiences, so chances are I either made it out or I'm dead somewhere else along the way.

If you manage to get out, expose these fuckers and don't let anyone else get fucked over.

Good luck,

Guard who came before you.

You've gotta be fucking kidding me, was my first thought. Ten minutes later though, I was in the clear and managed to get to the elevator by following every rule the guard laid out. I was lucky though. Aside from the old man in the bathroom, no one else bothered me. I heard a giggle and a set of footsteps in the mannequin room, but neither the staring man nor the patient woman were present, so I managed to safely take the elevator, my heart thumping the entire time so fast I thought it was going to burst out of my chest.

The elevator started going up and I prayed I would be back at the reception. My hope was short-lived, because when the elevator stopped and the doors opened, I was in an advanced security room with a bunch of camera feeds across the entire wall.

On the desk on top of the keyboard was another note.

I sat at the desk in front of the camera screens, because I felt like I really needed some respite after the ordeal from before. I was so tired and scared. On the one hand I felt really vulnerable without a weapon, but on the other hand I was glad I didn't have anything that I could potentially use to end myself. I tried not to think that suicide could prevent a far worse fate.

I glanced at the camera feed. It seemed to be covering some sort of run-down hospital. No one was on any of the cameras, except for one. That patient lady from before was peeking around the corner of one of the cameras, as if she was waiting for someone to give them a jump-scare. I looked down at the note in front of me. It said:

Still alive? Good.

You're gonna need to follow an even stricter set of rules in order to get past this area, especially making sure you do things according to specific times. First off, no matter when you enter the room, the alarm clock on the desk is going to say 3:19 am.

I glanced at the small clock in front of me. 3:19 am and it just turned into 3:20. I continued reading.

You need to follow these rules according to the times and DO NOT be late nor early anywhere, this is the most important part.

First off, take a look at all the cameras and see if the staring man is anywhere on them. If he is, you'll see him staring directly at the camera. Turn off the camera and then turn it back on again. The man should be gone. If he's not, repeat until he is.

Take some time to rest and prepare. At exactly 3:35 am, go out and conduct a patrol around the building as if you were on regular guard duty. You need to check every room on floors 1 and 2 and you need to be back in the security room by 4:00 am.

While you're patrolling, you may see a doctor in one of the rooms. He usually just appears out of nowhere, the room is empty the one moment and then you turn around and he's there, performing surgery on a mangled corpse. If you see him, back away slowly and try to exit the room without being noticed. If he calls after you, don't ignore him. He'll ask you to assist him by giving him surgical tools from the tray, so just do what he asks. Try not to give him the wrong tools, otherwise you might be the one he's going to dissect on that table next.

You probably saw the woman peeking behind the corner on the camera by now. Don't worry, she'll be gone during your patrol.

Once you are done with your patrol, get back to the camera room. You may sometimes see another guard sitting by the desk when you return. You can talk to him normally like you would to a friend or coworker. Do not try to talk to him about your current predicament. At 4:15 he'll say he needs to conduct a patrol and as soon as he leaves the room, lock the door behind him.

From 4:15 to 4:30 you may hear knocking on the door and rattling of the knob, but you'll see no one on the camera covering the outside of the security room. Ignore the knocking and rattling, no matter how incessant it becomes. Even if you hear desperate cries for help in the voices of women or children or the guard from before, don't open the door. They can't get inside if you don't let them in, so you should be safe.

4:30 – 4:40 you have a break, so take a moment to recuperate. Do not take a nap!

From 4:40 am you should focus on the cameras. You will start to feel really sleepy. No matter what you do, you must not fall asleep. As you get sleepier, you will also start to notice movement in your peripheral vision or start to feel like someone is in the room with you, standing right over your shoulder and breathing. Just focus on the cameras, no matter how vivid the presence becomes.

At 5:00 am, if you hear raspy breathing coming from the ceiling, DO NOT LOOK UP! Close your eyes and count to 10. You will feel cold fingers touching you and the raspy breathing will be in your ear, but whatever you do, keep your eyes closed until it all stops completely. Continue focusing on the cameras until 5:29, but do not leave the security room under any circumstances.

At exactly 5:29 am, get ready to move quickly. As soon as the clock ticks 5:30 am (and not a second sooner!), unlock and open the door and run for it. Just run straight into the elevator at the end of the hallway and ignore the growling behind you. Don't look behind, because you need every second here. The elevator door will be open and it will automatically close and take you out of there once you're in.

I'll be waiting on the other side. Good luck, brother.

Guard who came before you.

I placed down the note and exhaled sharply. It was 3:24 am. I glanced at the cameras. The staring man was on one of the cameras. I restarted in and sure enough, in less than a second while the camera was off he just disappeared.

At 3:35 am I went outside, conducting my patrol carefully, but still doing my best to hurry up. I glanced at my watch every minute or so.

As I finished the last room and was about to exit, I heard someone humming behind me. I turned around and saw a surgeon in blood-stained clothes dissecting a corpse on the table which was not previously there. I froze, but the doc was transfixed on the 'surgery', humming more violently as he sawed through one of the corpse's arms.

Seeing this broke me out of my trance and I slowly backed away, reaching for the door. As I turned around to face the exit, I stopped dead in my tracks.

"Ah-ah!" – the doc exclaimed and I turned around, heart ready to explode.

"Almost forgot to take care of this." – the doc grabbed a scalpel and continued cutting the corpse, paying no attention to me.

I silently exhaled in relief and left the place slowly. As soon as I was at a safe distance, I sprinted back to the security room. The room was empty, no guard in there like the note mentioned.

I locked the door and continued following the agonizing rules on the list until 5:29 am, ignoring anything else in the room until then. As soon as the clock ticked 5:30, I heard a growl behind me. I opened the door and ran faster than I ever knew was possible, while the growl behind me turned into something that sounded like demonic barking. It kept getting closer and closer.

I ran into the elevator, practically ramming the backside with my shoulder. I turned around just in time to see a pair of red eyes staring at me from the hallway before the elevator door closed.

The elevator started going up and stopped shortly after. When it opened, I found myself in an empty white room with an electronic door on the other side. The only two things that contrasted the white walls and floor were a monitor mounted on one of the walls and the silhouette of a person in a dark uniform. He had the sign which said 'SECURITY' on the back.

"I finally found you!" – I smiled and stepped out of the elevator.

The guard looked at me with a confused expression, so I tried to explain who I was and thanked him for leaving the instructions behind for me. He shook his head:

"What are you talking about?" – he asked.

"You said in your note that you'd be waiting on the other side." – I said.

"What note? Look bro, I'm just trying to find my way out of here. Been trying to find a way to open this door for ages." – he looked even more confused by this point.

"Look man, I've been following these notes you left, because you said you'd be here, so just cut the bullshit." – I took out the note and presented it to him.

He inspected it with a serious look on his face and then looked at me and said:

"Afraid you got the wrong guy, bro. This isn't my handwriting."

"Well if it wasn't you, who was it then?" - I angrily remarked.

Just then, the monitor on the wall turned on and a message flashed across the screen.

CHAPTER 4

WELCOME, NEW RECRUITS.

The message on the monitor displayed before disappearing. A new message replaced it and the guard and I had to get closer to read what the wall of text said.

You've done well so far. You're not far from reaching your goal, but know that your tasks will get harder from here on out and you will have to work as a team to survive.

The door will open in 1 minute. You will see a guardhouse to your left. Enter it and read the note.

As soon as we were done reading, the monitor turned off and the electronic door opened with a loud hum. A cold gust of air hit me in the face instantly and as we stepped through the door, I realized we were outside in some sort of park.

"What the fuck?" – the other guard said – "Hey maybe we can just run for it. I mean, fuck their rules, right?"

I shook my head:

"Gotta be a catch. They wouldn't just let us leave. This probably isn't even real. Let's check the guardhouse, first."

We went inside the guardhouse, which had a desk and chair inside. The note was on top of the desk next to a clock which read 00:05. The note said:

Out of all the rules there are three main rules you need to strictly follow at all times. The first rule is never, EVER go off trail. If you do, getting lost will be the least of your troubles.

Never stay together for too long, because it attracts them more easily to you. That is the second rule.

Ending with the first two rules, the third rule is, whenever the guards reunite, they should use code phrases (example: guard 1 asks 'where does the cat go?' and guard 2 answers 'to the alley'. Note that the code must be recited exactly how the code is agreed upon, word by word.)

Moving on to the rest of the rules, one guard should stay in the guardhouse, while the other patrols around the park (patrols take about 10 minutes). For the guard patrolling:

Under no circumstances is the guard allowed to leave the trail when patrolling (see rule 1). Turn left at the crossroads and you will come back full circle back at the guardhouse. If you happen to hear the other guard's voice coming from the trees, calling for help, ignore it. You will hear his voice on a loop, usually repeating the same phrase with the same intonation over and over. Pay attention to the sounds of animal life, too. If the park suddenly gets quiet, finish your patrol normally, but do not look behind or glance at the trees. During your patrol, every 5 minutes or so, loudly shout a simple word like 'hello' into the air. If your voice doesn't echo, run back to the guardhouse immediately.

Should you, see a hiker in the middle of the trail, keep the flashlight pointed at his face at all times. He will ask you to move it away, stating it's too bright, but don't listen to him. He will also tell you he understands your situation and will tell you to follow him since he knows a way out. Decline his offer. After this, he should leave. Do not take the light off him until he steps off the trail. For the guard in the guardhouse:

To stay safe, keep the door and window firmly shut at all times, save for when the patrolling guard comes back. It may get annoyingly hot inside, but do not open anything. You may take off your jacket or shirt to alleviate the discomfort.

Do not pay attention to any tapping on the windows. If you hear or see droplets falling on the desk in front of you, slowly stand up and leave the guardhouse. Stay outside for 2-3 minutes and the droplets should be gone when you go back inside. If they are still there, exit again and wait for another 2-3 minutes. When the patrolling guard returns, ask him the code question while avoiding eye contact. If he doesn't respond or responds incorrectly, exit the guardhouse while avoiding eye contact and then return inside. The fake guard will be gone.

If you survive until 1:00 am, both guards should proceed together to the end of the trail and turn right at the crossroads (do not do this before 1:00 am). At this point, the forest life will be completely quiet and the only sound surrounding you will be occasional hurried footsteps coming off the trail. They can only approach you in the dark, so do your best to train your flashlights on them, even if you can't see them clearly. Guards should divide to cover both sides with light.

End your task by reaching the end of the trail with a gate. That is your exit point (make sure to take this note with you, you will need it).

"Dammit." – the other guard said and we sat in silence for a moment.

I scratched my cheek and said:

"Alright, I'll take the first patrol. What should be our code?"

He thought for a moment and then said:

"Shit man, I dunno. How about this? I'll ask 'What should these fuckers do?' And you can say 'let us go'."

"You got it. What's your name, by the way?" – I asked.

The guard said his name was Sam and I introduced myself, as well. I left for the patrol with the flashlight and stuck strictly to the trail. Nothing major happened, no sounds off the trail, etc, but I did run into the hiker mentioned in the note. He seemed friendly and all, but I followed the rules and kept the beam pointed in his face, declining everything he asked.

Eventually he left and I finished my patrol and returned to the guardhouse. After we confirmed the codes, Sam left for his own patrol. I followed the set of rules until he came back, confirming the code with him. By the time I finished my third patrol, it was 01:03 am and it was time to go.

We quietly walked the trail, focusing on our footsteps and the deafening silence around us. And then the footsteps off the trails started.

It sounded like someone was frantically running from one tree to another, stopping for a few seconds in between. This recurred over and over as Sam and I did our best to focus our beams on the source of the sound, but no matter how quick our reactions were, we never seemed to be able to catch whoever ran there. I caught a glimpse of a nude, emaciated man or woman here and there, but they always seemed to be just out of reach, either hiding behind a tree the moment I shone my light or disappearing into the dark altogether.

Finally, Sam and I reached the end of the trail and entered a fenced area with a gate on the other side. There was a pedestal in the middle and an object on top of it. When we approached it, it became clear it was a gun, with a note under it.

Sam took the note and read it aloud:

"Read the first letter of each paragraph of the previous note."

We both looked at the note and read the letters silently together. And then as the realization hit us, we scrambled for the gun. After a moment of wrestling, the gun was in my hand and I held it pointed at Sam.

"Don't do this, man. I have a wife and young daughter, please." – he begged.

I held my finger on the trigger, intermittently looking at him and the gate. I had to get out of here. I've had enough of this bullshit. I looked at Sam's pleading face one more time. A moment later I lowered and then dropped the gun on the ground and said:

"I'm not gonna play their game. I won't become a killer for their entertainment. We can find a different way out, I'm sure."

I went towards the gate to inspect it and then heard Sam's voice behind me:

"I'm sorry, man."

I turned around and saw him pointing the gun at me.

"What are you doing, Sam?"

"You read the note, man. One must die. There's no other way."

"Put the gun down, dammit. We can both make it out of here alive. We just gotta work together." - I didn't believe my own words, but I'd be damned if I'd murder another human being for these sick bastards' entertainment.

"I'm sorry. I have to get back to my family." - Sam said.

"Sam, no!"

He pulled the trigger, but the bang never came. Instead, there was a click and Sam dropped the gun, holding his hand in pain.

"What the fuck, something just pricked me!" – Sam shouted.

He and I stared at each other and then all of a sudden, Sam's eyes rolled behind his eyelids and he fell to the ground, convulsing and frothing at the mouth. I ran over to help him, but I didn't know what to do. He stopped moving completely a moment later and his eyes closed, as his breathing stopped along with the movement. I shook him and called his name, but it was too late. He was already dead.

Just then, the gate started to open.

CHAPTER 5

I knew I couldn't afford to waste any more time, so I went through the gate, leaving Sam's body behind. I listened as the gate closed and the ground beneath my feet started moving. Then the lights came on and I realized I was in a big elevator which started descending. Part of me had somehow come to terms with the fact that I was probably going to die here, but for some reason when you're in a situation where your life is at stake and you desperately want to get out by any means necessary, your body defies your wish to give up and pushes you to fight on.

The elevator stopped and the gated door opened, revealing a damp, dark room in front of me. There was a little cart next to the door on the other side. A folder lay on top of the cart. A circular logo with the name 'THE COMPANY' was on the front. Below was the motto 'Your safety is our success'.

When I opened the folder, I saw Sam's face. It was his file. In it I saw everything about him, including age, family and even behavioral patterns observed by these freaks. And then the next page was my file. They knew everything about me. Not just my age, nationality, etc., but also my ways of thinking and everything I have been through during the test so far. They even had predictions about my behavior before I even did something. They knew my every move. The last page underneath my file was a note. Here's what it said:

Congratulations on surviving this far!

You have only one last task to complete before you earn your reward, which is to reach the elevator on the other side of this area. The list of rules for the final part is as follows:

Once you are through this door, proceed straight through the corridor. Do not look, get close or touch the glass on the left and right side, despite the irresistible urge. Don't stop for longer than two seconds at a time. During the entire time, you will hear whispers coming from the other side of the glass. If the whispers suddenly stop, run as fast as you can do the door.

Once you reach the door, you will find yourself outside on a wide bridge. There will be one person aimlessly wandering there. He may look weak and drunk, but don't underestimate him. Only move when he is not looking at you and when he faces you, stand as still as you can. If you see him stop all movement suddenly and go silent, he may have sensed you. The best thing to do is to stand still and not breathe. He may approach and inspect you, but do not move a muscle until you see him calmed down and facing away.

Do not even think about making a break for the door when you're close to it and him being a distance away. If he sees you, he will catch you no matter how close to the door you are.

Close the door behind you and you will find yourself in a dormitory. You will see pebbles on a wooden plate next to you. Put them in your pocket and make sure to always have at least one ready in your hand. Proceed through the next area as quietly as possible, especially if you hear footsteps and sniffing close by (be especially aware of creaking floorboards). If you assume you may have attracted its attention, toss the pebbles at a distance to distract it (do not run while it is distracted). Do not go for the exit yet, as the creature is standing in your way.

Look for room 109. By this point the creature will most likely be aware of your presence, so get inside the room and lock it as fast as possible. You will see that there is nowhere to hide, since the room is empty. That's not a problem, since the creature is blind. Run to any corner of the room and stay there as quietly as you can. Try to remain calm as the creature screams and rams the door.

Once it is inside, it will inspect the room and sniff the air. You'll be safe as long as you make no sound. After a minute or so, the creature will leave and you will be able to get to the next exit safely. Exit the dormitory through the back door and close it. When you turn left you will see-

The rest of the note was unintelligible, save for a few words and the signature 'The Company' below. I narrowed my eyes, scanning the page over and over, but no matter how many times I read it, the text remained the same. I cursed loudly and put the page in my pocket, inhaling and exhaling deeply. Final stretch. No matter what happens after this, it would be over and I knew it.

I opened the door and as soon as I did, the whispers came from both sides. It sounded unnatural, as if whoever was on the other side of the glass was mocking me with their friends behind my back and trying to be quiet, but failing. I proceeded for a whole minute before the whispers suddenly stopped. And then loud slamming on both sides of the glass started. Handprints started to appear on the glass. First one, then two, then ten, a hundred, a thousand, all within the span of ten seconds or so.

I sprinted across the corridor and rammed the door with my shoulder. I turned around to close it, but the corridor was calm again. No sounds and no handprints. I took no chances as I closed the door behind me.

I turned back and faced the sight before me. I was on a wide metallic bridge in the middle of nowhere. There were street lights on it, illuminating the entirety of the area. A very frail-looking person stood in the middle of the bridge, hunched forward and looking like he could barely hold his weight on his own legs. I couldn't see below the bridge, because It was too dark, but I was definitely somewhere that looked like outside.

Slowly, I started to cross the bridge, making sure to stop whenever the person on the bridge looked in my direction. He seemed completely oblivious to my presence when I stood still, since he cut in front of me a few times without even looking in my direction. It wasn't until I was close enough that I could hear the wheezing sounds coming from the person, as if he had difficulty breathing. Could he really overpower me?

Nevertheless, I carefully crossed the bridge and closed the door. As soon as I entered the dorm, I took the pebbles and perked up my ears. No sounds yet.

Hastily, I found room 109 and as soon as my hand touched the doorknob, a blood-curdling scream echoed throughout the hallway. I quickly entered and locked the door and then rushed into the corner, standing as still as possible, doing my best to steady my breathing.

The door started to rattle violently as whatever was on the other end rammed it over and over. I could see with my peripheral vision that the door was about to give way and soon enough, it fell straight from the hinges. A naked, skinny-looking creature with no eyes and a sharp row of teeth burst inside, jerking its head in all directions, looking for me. It then started to intermittently sniff the air and stop to listen.

I had to clasp my hands over my mouth to stop myself from whimpering. Soon enough, the creature left the room. I waited for a whole minute before peeking out into the corner, still scared shitless. No one was there and I proceeded to find the exit. After opening the back door, I found myself in another hallway. I turned left and braced myself, ready to face whatever was there. In front of me at the end of the hall was an elevator. But between me and elevator stood none other than the staring man.

Our eyes locked and I knew what I had to do. I heard screams in my ears and felt things brushing against me from behind and touching my neck and face, but I didn't take my eyes off him. I hurried up to the elevator, and it opened on its own. I entered and continued staring at the man and just before the door closed, something unexpected happened.

The man nodded and looked away.

The elevator started ascending this time. I had no idea where it was going to take me, but before I could process that thought properly, it opened again. In front of me was a room engulfed in darkness and only a small beam of light shone in the distance ahead. Hesitantly, I stepped out of the elevator and started walking towards the light. And then more lights turned on from the ceiling, blinding me for a moment and illuminating the entire room.

"Excellent work." – a voice in front of me said.

It didn't take me long to realize that I was in some sort of control room and the voice was coming in front of me, from the place where the beam of light had previously been. There was a big rotating chair there and whoever was talking was facing away from me, so I couldn't see them.

"You have successfully completed your assignment." – the voice said again.

"Who the hell are you? What do you want from me?!" – I shouted.

The chair swung around and a man in a suit revealed to be sitting in it.

"To congratulate you." – he said – "I usually don't like to go out on the field, but this is a special opportunity."

Anger started to boil in me when I saw how nonchalant he was about this whole situation. I started to stride towards him, but then heard the distinctive sound of a gun being cocked behind my head.

"It's okay, Sam." – the man said.

I turned around to look at my assailant. It was Sam, the security guard, alive and well.

"Sam?" – I asked – "I watched you die. What the hell is this?"

"Sam is an amazing actor. I'm starting to think he should've gone for a different career." – the man in the chair said.

"You were in on this the whole time? I don't believe this." – I asked and then faced the man in the chair again – "Well your test is complete, right? Time to kill me?"

The man threw his head back in laughter and said:

"Kill you? Don't be silly. This was necessary for evaluation. We have to go through a very strict hiring process, because we hire only the most suitable candidates. I know the test was stressful, but you passed with flying colors! Forget that whole 80$ per shift thing. The money we'll be paying you will cover all your debts, medical bills and then some."

I let out a chuckle at the absurdity of the situation and said:

"Hiring process? This was what, some kind of job orientation the entire time?"

"Well... yes. What our company deals with here is not ordinary guard duty, as you saw back there. And this is why we need to make sure our candidates don't do something to endanger themselves... or others."

"So all those things back there? They weren't real?" - I asked.

"Oh they're as real as they come. And you were in actual danger the whole time. We have intervention always ready, but sometimes... accidents do happen. This is the process candidates are subjected to. And out of 43 applicants, you were the only one to make it to the end!"

"So you want me to work for you?" – I looked at Sam, who had a neutral expression on his face and then back at the man – "What if I refuse?"

"Then you get a slightly higher compensation than was mentioned in the ad and you go home and look for another job." - the man shrugged.

"I could go to the police and rat you out." - I replied.

"You could. You could tell them everything. But you'd find that the police found no trace of anything you mentioned. No ghosts, no monsters. Not even an ad listed by any company you mentioned. In fact the company itself is not registered anywhere. There's nothing, except an old abandoned building."

He motioned for someone on the side to come. A woman approached me with a paper and pen. She handed them to me. At just one glance I realized it was a contract for the company as a security guard and the compensation was shocking, to say the least. The amount they paid would cover all my bills and I could finally move out of the shithole I live in now. The man continued:

"You could walk away and go to the police. Or you could work for us. Help the world and the fragile residents by keeping them safe from the horrors you witnessed. Because their safety is our success." - he smiled.

I frantically clicked the pen over and over, looking at the man's smug face and then at Sam. He nodded subtly to me as I looked at the contract once more. So much money...

Before I could change my mind, I signed the contract and handed it back to the lady. The man smiled widely and then stood up and shook my hand as he said:

"Welcome to The Company."

SECURITY GUARD

UPDATE 1

I've been a security guard in my company for over two years now, but the work my company does is not your typical run-of-the-mill. To put it simply, my company accepts jobs which no other security company will. That includes high-risk assignments which often result in deaths of the staff members or abandoning their posts.

Let me take it from the top.

When I started working here, they had a very long one on one with me to explain all the potential dangers I would be facing. They also made me sign an NDA and a bunch of other papers which stated that if something were to happen to me, the company would not be held responsible.

They explained that the job is risky, but also paid well. I had been jobless for a while and jumped at the opportunity regardless of the risks. Unlike most other companies though, they made me read through the entire NDA aloud and made sure I was aware of all the rules. Some of the things I read there made me think initially that this was all a joke. But then I saw that my superior was dead serious.

My job would basically be to provide support to the guards at other posts via comms and patrol the perimeter I was stationed at. Now our HQ was located in an office building compound which had multiple companies renting the adjacent buildings. I would mostly work nights with the occasional mornings. The rules were as follows:

I was to do a full sweep of the compound and all offices, save for building 4, the call center office. I was not to approach building 4 under any circumstances, no matter what I heard from the outside. Even if I saw someone inside from the windows, I was not to engage. When I asked for more details, they refused to answer me, stating that I should simply obey their orders if I value my life.

Now, people have a normal 9 to 5 job in that building and nothing seems to be wrong during the day. When I do ask the employees about it during my morning shifts though, they all seem to either not know anything or abruptly find an excuse to end the conversation.

For building 6, the designer company, the rules were even stranger. Here's what the chief told me:

"In building 6, you may sometimes run into someone. A woman, to be precise. She's going to try to start a conversation with you. It is imperative that you ignore her presence at all costs. She will try to talk to you, taunt you, but she will never get in your way. An extremely important rule to remember and I cannot stress this enough, is that if you see her in the building don't run or exit the building before finishing your sweep. Trust me, she'll know. Do the sweep as you normally would, check every room and then quietly exit, ignoring her all the way. She will become increasingly agitated and violent, might even try to startle you, tell you there's something behind you in a very convincing manner. Just ignore her. If you don't... well, you don't wanna know what happened to the last guard."

I've since encountered the woman once and it was a grueling and agonizing experience I would rather not talk about.

Another rule I had to remember was not opening the gate between the hours of 22-07. The chief said that under no circumstances am I to open the gate, even if the next guard comes 5 minutes earlier to relieve me of duty, the gate was to remain closed.

That brings me to the experience I had once. It was about 6 months after I started working and the sun was almost already up. I heard knocking on the gate and when I went out, I saw through the gate the silhouette of my coworker.

"Hey, mind opening the gate?" – he asked.

As I approached and put my keys into the keyhole, my phone started ringing. I answered it without even looking at the caller, but when I heard the voice, my blood froze.

It was my coworker.

"Hey, I'm gonna be late 30 minutes today, sorry man!"

I hung up and just then realized it was 6:50 am. I stared at the silhouette on the other side of the gate, who suddenly started banging on the door, demanding to be let in, stating he had lost his cellphone and he was the real coworker. I retreated to the guardhouse and waited for what seemed like forever until the banging stopped. In reality, it only lasted until 7 am. Those were all the rules I had to follow on my own post and most of the time it's uneventful, however I've heard stories from other coworkers.

*

Since I'm in contact with guards at other posts, one of them told me this story. He worked as a guard in a residential building and one night an old man who lived there called him to come to his apartment. He didn't explain what was wrong, just told him to go there, so he did. When he reached the apartment, the wife of the old man was crying, stating that her husband was dead. The guard tried convincing her that her man was very much alive and had in fact brought him there, but when he turned around, the old man was gone.

It was then that he saw the old man's dead body in his chair near his sobbing wife. He quit the same night.

*

Another creepy thing that happened was on a farmstead which our company has guards posted on. A guy by the name of Jeff who worked there told me about his own experience which made him run away from his post in the middle of the night.

So apparently, the farm was empty at that time since it needed some more stuff built first, but his duty was to basically patrol circles around the farm and make sure there were no squatters or vandals. So one night, as he's walking around he hears someone calling his name in a playful tone. He dismisses it as his imagination at first, but when it recurs, he asks who's there and demands they show up with their hands in the air.

Now I haven't seen this so I can't guarantee anything, but Jeff swears it's true. He says all of a sudden, out of the crops a man just stands up. The top of the crops reach to his waist, which was technically impossible, because the crops themselves were taller than Jeff, and he's a pretty tall guy.

But the man grins at Jeff and continues calling his name playfully, as if he's still hiding from him. Needless to say Jeff didn't stick around to see what the fuck that guy wanted. When he reported it to HQ, they said there were sightings of that man in the past, always calling the names of the guards, but never really doing anything harmful.

*

The final thing I'll share with you here is my experience when I was stationed at a hospital for one month. It was a private clinic of some sorts and my job was to basically monitor the camera feed. Camera 3 was off though and when I asked why, they told me to keep it that way and never turn it on. They also said that from time to time I may see a person on the feed which covered the outside of the security office and that he would just be standing there, facing the door. I was to remain in my office when that happened and not glance at the door. He would usually disappear after 30 minutes or so. Patrolling was strictly forbidden between the hours of 3am - 6am.

Money is one of the reasons why I haven't quit so far and the dangers aren't that bad once you get used to them and you know what you're doing. And plus getting stationed at different posts keeps the job adventurous and dynamic.

If any of you lack any special talents or qualifications like me, this job is perfect for you.

So a lot of you were asking to hear more about my job and the duties that come along with it. I'll be sharing in this post more about the stories I have and what I heard from the other guards. I know you particularly wanted to know about the woman in building 6, so I'll be sharing my experience with that first.

This happened about a year ago, but I still dread going back to the building every time during my patrol. I was doing a sweep of the building, using my flashlight to illuminate my path. As I was done checking one of the offices, as I turned around, my heart nearly popped out of my chest at what the beam of my flashlight landed on. It was a woman in her late twenties, with unkempt hair and raggedy clothes. She was just standing there, staring at me, not even flinching at the light in her face.

I was about to talk to her, thinking she was squatter, completely forgetting about the rule since I had never once encountered her by then. And then when I remembered the rules, that I was supposed to ignore her, my heart starting to thump fast. I lowered my flashlight to my waist, pretending I was looking at something on the wall to prevent her from seeing my beam bouncing up and down from my trembling hands. I remembered that I had to do a full sweep before leaving if she was here and I was only done with one floor, so at the thought of this I cursed in my mind.

"Hey, I'm sorry, I think I fell asleep in one of the offices and stayed after closing." - she said, but I ignored her.

I pretended to look around some more, but knew I could only do it for so long before she got suspicious. So I decided to test my luck and just went for the door. As soon as I was inches close to her, she just stepped aside and let me move along. I strode to the next office, but heard her following me right behind.

"Hey, can you please let me out? My children must be worried sick." - she repeated.

The next fifteen minutes or so, she was breathing down my neck, constantly trying to grab my attention. As I entered one of the offices, she pointed to the corner opposite of where my beam was and said:

"Hey, who's that over there?"

I fought the urge to look there, knowing she was lying, but half scared that someone would just jump me right around the corner. As I progressed with my sweep, she became increasingly irritated, throwing stuff in my direction (not at me mind you, but trying to startle me but throwing them in front of my face, etc.), suddenly jumping in my walking path with a loud scream before moving aside again, clasping her hands over her mouth and pointing behind me with wide eyes which screamed utter fear, even saying things like "I know you can see me, I know you know I'm here, I can see how scared you are".

I ignored all her provocations as much as I could and by the time I was back on the first floor, more than ready to get out, she was saying things like "Are you sure you checked all the rooms?", giggling along the way. I put the key in the keyhole and everything went quiet. I didn't wait to see if she was gone, but instead just went out as calmly as I could and locked the door behind me. I couldn't sleep for a few weeks after that.

*

A few months ago I was stationed at an office building. At first it seemed like a common job, but I knew there was a catch before I even signed up. Sure enough, I was right. My partner and I were stationed on floor 43, which was undergoing renovations. Our job was to simply stand in front of a door. The door had a card reader and we were given access, but were strictly forbidden from entering.

People in hazmat suits would be coming in and out all day long from 8 am - 4 pm. We were to let them in and out as they pleased, keeping track of the number of people who came and went. Now the catch was, after 16:00 we were ordered not to let anyone in or out. That meant even if someone knocked on the door at 16:01 we were to ignore them entirely. There would always be at least three people who'd try to leave the room after 16:00, always asking politely and then becoming increasingly desperate, saying they simply lost track of time and pleading with us, saying that their family was waiting for them home.

We always ignored their crying and pleading, no matter how desperate it was, until it turned into whimpers and then finally stopped. Now I've only seen the room from the door and from what I could see, it was just a normal room undergoing renovation like the rest of the floor, so whatever was in there must have been deeper inside or hidden in plain site. As for the numbers we tracked - the number of people who got out by the end of the day was always lower than the number of people who went in.

*

One story a guard named Chris told me was about his time in an old mansion guarding a big mirror. He and his coworker were in the security room, patrolling every hour, especially making sure that the mirror was covered with the sheet. They were to under no circumstances look at the mirror. They had a camera feed of the mirror which was on the bottom floor under the stairs, but it was turned so that the reflective side faced away from the camera.

This one night, Chris' coworker goes for a patrol and as he enters the mirror room, suddenly the sheet just slides off. Now the guy who told me this said it was technically impossible for the sheet to just come off, because it was fastened tightly, but somehow it did and his partner just finds himself staring at the mirror. Chris locks the security room, as per the instructions from HQ and calls the intervention team. Meanwhile he glances back at the camera feed, only to find his coworker still staring blankly in the mirror. He thought the camera was frozen, but the timer was moving, so his partner was just very still. He tried radioing him, but there was no response. After about a minute or so, all of a sudden his partner pulls out his gun, puts it in his mouth and blows his brains out.

Chris was transferred the next day since a special team was sent to secure the mirror and his services there were no longer needed.

*

One position that everyone is massively trying to apply for is the surveillance office in a small town close to my own. Why they want the position is what I'll get to in a bit. So basically, the camera feed on the monitors in HQ over there cover various private households. One of the households is said to have a man in a suit show up at the doorstep from time to time. Now usually, guards need to go out to the address and make sure everything is okay or apprehend the intruder, but for this specific individual, HQ left a very unique guide.

Here are the instructions left by HQ:

If the security official notices an individual in business attire on Camera 12 during his shift, the steps below must be followed when confronting the individual:

1. Approach the individual and wait for him to turn around. He will continue to smile for the entirety of the conversation, but should his expression change, disengage and run to safety as quickly as possible. Be advised that while firearms are not prohibited, they are highly ineffective against the individual. Do not turn or look away from the individual once he has turned around, unless you need to evacuate.

2. The individual will after turning around inquire "Lovely night, isn't it?". If the individual has not asked this question, follow the previous step and evacuate.

3. If the individual has inquired the aforementioned question, respond with "Yes it is. What can I do for you?" or "Indeed it is. How can I help you?". A combination of both works as well. If the individual ceases to smile during this interaction, proceed to evacuate immediately.

4. If done correctly, the individual will now ask "Can you sing me a song?". If he says anything else, evacuate.

5. From here, you are to sing the pre-taught song to the individual, while ignoring his taunts and distractions. If so much as one word, pause, tone or stress are missed, evacuate. If the individual stops smiling during the song, evacuate.

6. If done correctly, the individual will say "Splendid! Thank you for the beautiful song!". If he says anything aside from that, evacuate.

7. If step 6 was done correctly, close your eyes for at least 10 seconds and then open them. On the front steps where the individual stood will now be a briefcase, containing a large sum of money, while the individual himself will be gone and the household safe.

8. On the way back, the security official may encounter people of various ages in dire need of help (most common occurrences include starving women with newborn babies, lost children, an attractive young woman hitchhiking, etc.) They are to be ignored and not offered assistance under any circumstances.

9. Return to post and turn off camera 12

Note: The company does not claim the reward from the individual, therefore the security official is free to keep it.

The high risk- high reward position makes it attractive to many people, but most of them never live to tell the tale. I was also told that the candidates go through rigorous training, focusing primarily on sprinting. The candidates also need to pass the test which simulates the encounter with the businessman no less than 5 times with 95% or higher score. They are forced to remember the song perfectly, going through a computerized scanner which detects any notes which were off. I don't know what the song is, but I was told it's a simple tune which sounds like something taught in preschool.

Anyway, this is as far as I'll go on this post, but I have some more stories to share in my future updates. In the meantime stay safe and try to stay away from these kinds of things. They sound attractive due to pay or rush some people thrive on, but a tiny mistake can cost you your life. Or worse.

Here are some more stories about places that I was stationed at and the ones I heard from other guards in the company. A lot of these guards are dead now and I reckon the same could happen to me at any moment on my shift, so in case there's a lack of updates, most likely something happened to me.

*

So one memorable experience I have had (and not in a good way) was when I was stationed at a local park with another guard. The park wasn't too big – had a playground, running track which wound in a circle around the park itself and a tennis court. Everywhere else around were thick trees, so following the running track gave a very convincing impression of being in a forest, away from civilization.

My coworker and I were to start our shift in the park at 7pm and would end it at 7am. There was a tiny guardhouse near the entrance which we would spend most of our shift in and every 2 hours we would go patrolling around the park, very strictly following the running track where the path was illuminated. We were given a heavy duty flashlight and a backup torch in case the main one runs out of power. HQ issued an order that if we found any burnt out light on our path, we were to retreat to the guardhouse immediately and let maintenance know about it in the morning. Under no circumstances were we to step into the dark patch of the track.

This one night, I was doing my rounds around the park when all of a sudden I hear my partner's voice. He simply shouted "Hey, help me!" from a distance. I couldn't tell where it was coming from, so I called out to him, moving my beam across the trees beyond the path. Now, the light we were given is able to penetrate darkness so well that you could see at least 100 meters in front of you. But when I illuminated the area my partner's voice was coming from, there was nothing. Moreover, the voice seemed to change the positions it was coming from.

He yelled again "Hey, help me!". I called him once more, asking him to tell me where he was, but there was no response. I didn't dare wander into the darkness, especially with no signs of him anywhere, heavy-duty light or not. Then my partner yelled for help again and I realized something which made the hairs at the back of my neck stand straight.

His cries for help were on a loop. Always saying the same thing, same intonation, same length of pauses. I even looked at my watch and sure enough, I was right. Call for help, 8 seconds pause. Call for help, 8 seconds pause. I then realized how suddenly quiet everything was. Usually the park was somewhat loud at night – crickets, owls, etc. Now it was so silent I could hear my own heart thumping. I turned around very slowly and walked out of there, doing my best not to sprint as my partner's looping cries for help persisted almost halfway until I was back at the guardhouse.

When I finally got back, my suspicion was confirmed and my partner was there, visibly confused at what I had just told him. We called HQ to report suspicious activity and in no less than 5 minutes a vehicle pulled up at the entrance. An intervention unit emerged, which was essentially an armored and heavily armed team sent in case of emergencies. I was questioned by the team leader for the next hour, while the others went to the scene where I had heard the voice of my coworker.

My partner and I were escorted out of the place and the following morning we were told that the park contract was voided by the company and we no longer needed to go there. I don't know anything else though, because right after that I returned to my original post back at HQ.

*

I spoke to a former intervention unit member who had worked for the company for over 5 years. He said that some of the shit he had seen was unimaginable and he was willing to share some with me.

For instance, this one time they got a call from a residential building they were securing that there were strange noises coming from one of the rooms. The team arrived on the scene and questioned the guard who reported the incident. Apparently, his job was to make sure no one entered room 416. He explained that the room itself was unoccupied, but that noises would be heard constantly between 2am and 3am. Usually those noises would include child-like giggling, loud footsteps, bouncing of something on the floor, etc. The residents learned to ignore the noises, but this one old lady, Mrs. Rogers managed to get in, which he saw on the camera feed.

Now the intervention unit was told not to go in after anyone after 20 minutes had passed, but they still had time, so they rushed to the room. The guy who was telling me this said that as they approached the room they heard voices, like a group of people trying to talk in a hushed tone. He explained that it sounded like kids in school when they're trying to whisper, but were unintentionally loud enough for others to hear.

As soon as they touched the doorknob, the voices stopped in unison. Not like the conversation was over, like literally as if someone pressed a mute button in the middle of a sentence. They burst inside the empty room which looked like no one stepped inside for years, weapons raised.

No one was there. And as they're standing there, completely silent, they hear a barely audible, wheezing sound from above. They all look up and as they do, they freeze. The guy who told me this said that what he saw still keeps him up at night sometimes.

Mrs. Rogers was standing on the ceiling like a spider on all fours, craning her head so much they thought her neck was broken and she was looking directly at the unit upside down, wide-eyed. Spit was occasionally dropping from her mouth to the floor as she was wheezing. Her fingers had somehow mutated into long claws. Then without any warning, Mrs. Rogers had managed to jump down on one of the team members in the blink of an eye and gunshots ensued. He said that by the time they were done shooting, two more members were down and Mrs. Rogers had hundreds of bullet holes in her body and head and was no longer moving.

He encountered similar scenarios after that, but never came so close to dying again. The building residents were evacuated from the building indefinitely the next day and the official story given was that there was toxic fungi located within the building.

*

The final story I'll share here is going to be the one I was told by another guard who went missing later on. He was stationed at a private school and it had a set of very strict rules they had to follow.

First off, there were ten guards in total in each shift and each of them were assigned to a classroom. Their job was to count all the students after the classes were over. Should any of the students go missing, they were to call HQ immediately.

Now comes the weird part. One day, the guard who told me this story counts all the kids in class and the final number doesn't add up. Instead of 32 students he has 33. He counts a few times to make sure and when the number is confirmed as 33, he tells the teacher to start calling on them by name and separating them from the group one by one. The teacher does so, calling each and every student, but when they're done, there are no surpluses. The list showed 32 and 32 were called on and yet 33 students were in the classroom. They couldn't tell who the extra student was even when the guard was watching them like a hawk to make sure none of them would sneak to the group of called on kids while they weren't looking. Baffled and unsure what to do, the guy tells the teacher to keep an eye on them while he contacts HQ. Already feeling silly for contacting the higher-ups over an extra student rather than a missing one, he expected HQ to scold him for calling about something like that.

But when he says he has an extra student who just popped up, chuckling at the absurdity of the situation, the person on the other end of the line suddenly goes silent. She asks him to repeat what he said and when he does, the woman tells him to get the teacher out of there, lock the classroom immediately and radio everyone else to do the same at once. He does so and only minutes later the intervention unit arrives, escorting the guards out of there. He said he has no idea what happened next, but when he returned to the school the next day for his shift, everything seemed to be normal.

*

No one really knows what the company is dealing with here. Not even intervention was told what these encounters are, since it seems to be a very strict need-to-know basis. One thing's for sure though.

When I hear some of these stories from other guards, I realize how lucky I got to run into some of these creatures and live to tell the tale.

I want to start off by clarifying one thing before I start. The company I work for is NOT the SCP. I know there are a lot of similarities between the encounters which I described and some of the SCP files, but my company has nothing to do with that. We are just as I stated before, a standalone security company that provides technical security, surveillance and physical protection services to clients.

*

I'm going to start this post with a story that still runs chills down my spine. While I was stationed at an office complex similar to the one in HQ where I am now, I had a number of strange experiences. Our job was mostly staying in the guardhouse and conducting mandatory patrols around the complex at the start and at the end of the shift, him taking one side while I took the other.

A few months back, I came to my shift as usual with my partner. So on that day we finished our initial patrol and returned to the guardhouse. We usually talk to pass the time, but this time he seemed unapproachable and quiet, so I figured I should leave him alone and continued to read my book for the time being.

Our shift was almost over when we decided to do our final sweep, so we split up to do our rounds. After I was done, I came back, but my partner wasn't there. I figured he wasn't done with his sweep yet, so I shrugged it off and continued passing the time. When he wasn't back in over 30 minutes though, I radioed him. No response. He was nowhere on the cameras, either. Figuring he may be in trouble, I went out to search for him, frustrated that he wasn't back and it was almost the end of our shift. As I'm patrolling, I see him in the distance across the parking lot, turned away from me and looking at something. I called out his name and he turned around. I waved to him, telling him to get back and he waved back to me. I took it as a signal that he understood what I said and returned to the guardhouse. The guys from the next shift were already there and I went home, telling them my partner would do the debriefing. Not two hours later, I got a phone call from the same guys.

They told me my partner never showed up, so they went looking for him, thinking something may have been wrong. Sure enough, soon after they started the search, he was found dead. I was shocked, to say the least. I asked them when he had died and how, since I had seen him literally minutes before they arrived. They told me that it wasn't possible for me to see him then. I asked why and the answer they gave me chilled me to the bone.

Apparently he died about 10 hours ago. The camera recordings confirmed it. He was seen wandering off camera into the garage and then never seen coming out. One of the guys discovered his body there, no visible wounds or marks on him. HQ recovered his body, but shared no details about the cause of his death.

So that begs the question. If he died 10 hours ago, who the fuck did I see in that parking lot? And moreover, who in fuck's name was with me in the guardhouse for 10 hours between patrols?

*

In that same place, in addition to our patrol around the complex we also had to check inside buildings and make sure everything was alright. So one time on my shift I'm in one of the office buildings doing my sweep on the second floor and I move to the stairs to get to the next floor. I climb up and as I do, I see that the sign on the wall says second floor again. I dismiss it, thinking I must have been on the first floor prior to this and just got confused. I move up one floor and again, the sign says second floor. I stare at the sign in bafflement and decide to try the door. Locked. I climb up one more floor and again, I'm on the second floor. I knew by this point something was wrong. I mean the building itself has only three floors and I had already climbed at least four.

I decided to descend the stairs as fast as I could, but every time I passed by the floor sign, it said second floor. I ran until I was exhausted, trying doors along the way, all of which were locked. I leaned over the railing to look down the stairs and saw the staircase going down infinitely into a black abyss, same for above. I radioed my partner, but there was no response. No signal on the phone, either. I decided to sit down and think about everything, already half-accepting my impending demise.

It must have been hours there that I sat and ran down the stairs intermittently when I suddenly heard the sound of door opening below. I was so relieved to actually hear something besides my own footsteps that I didn't even think about the potential dangers it might entail. I rushed down and to my relief, saw the sign for floor one, the door open as I had left it when I entered the building. I bolted out of there and straight to the guardhouse, barging in through the door.

My coworker was reading the newspaper, only shooting me a glance before returning to his reading. When I accused him for not answering his radio, he looked confused, stating he never got any call from me. I asked him why he hadn't looked for me when I hadn't returned in hours and again, he looked confused. He glanced at his watch and then at me and simply said:

"You've been gone for five minutes."

HQ issued a rule after that. The office building was off limits for all personnel after 8 pm.

*

One time during my shift, as I was finishing my patrol, I heard my coworker's voice in the distance. He sounded like he was in distress, so I followed the sound, calling out his name. As I approached the source of the voice, it became obvious that my coworker was in the looping building, begging me to help him. I drew my gun and told him to hold on, ready to risk my life for my partner and just as I was about to enter... I heard his voice behind me, calling my name.

I turned around and sure enough, there he was. I looked back at the building and the cries from the person in the building stopped completely. The coworker confirmed it wasn't him who was in the building and as I turned back to the source of the voice, I could only mutter to myself "you sneaky son of a bitch".

*

One thing that happened to one of the other guys during one of the shifts still puts me on edge. The guy named Chris was in the guardhouse with his partner and the partner decided to go for a patrol earlier. Chris continued reading his book as the partner left the place. One minute later he heard the door shut behind him and the thud of his footsteps of his partner inside.

"Forget something, huh?" – he asked, not looking up from his book.

The partner put his hand on Chris' shoulder and Chris raises his head, ready to turn around.

And as he does, he sees his coworker pass next to the window outside. Chris froze, staring at the window, at the reflection of the figure standing behind him. He says he felt the grip on his shoulder tightening. Bracing himself as well as he could, he swiftly turned around drawing his gun and pointing it at... nothing.

No one was there. I checked the recordings of the camera feed in the guardhouse and sure enough, no one was there with him. I could see Chris on the camera sitting up, visibly becoming tense and turning around with his gun drawn before looking around and finally holstering the weapon. He looked like a crazy person from this angle.

I never figured what that was, or the other occurrences in the complex, but HQ issued new orders shortly after. The guards who were on the shift were to stay together at all times, even patrolling in pairs and communicating via code sentences every 30 minutes to ensure their partner wasn't an impostor.

*

Chris told me of another incident he had during one of his shifts. He said that he saw someone suspicious on camera in front of one of the offices way after working hours, so he went to investigate. Halfway through, the partner radioed him and said he lost the person out of sight. It was strange though, because apparently he only turned around for one second and the guy on the camera was gone. However he said he thought he noticed movement on the camera which overlooked the windows of the office from the outside. He said it was on the second floor.

Chris decided to investigate it. As he's doing his sweep on the second floor, his partner radios him again halfway into his patrol and asks him if he found anyone. Chris says no, asking him if he sees anything on camera. The partner first says no and then he pauses mid-sentence. Chris asks him to confirm what he said and the partner tells Chris he should come back to the guardhouse. Chris wanted to finish the sweep, but the partner insisted he come back to the guardhouse at once. Frustrated, he returned and asked him what was wrong.

"You really didn't see anyone in there?" – the partner asked.

When Chris said no, the partner called him over to look at one of the camera feeds. He rewinds the footage to where he can see Chris in the window with the flashlight and tells him to pay close attention. Chris wasn't alone there.

When his beam flashed across the window, it caught a silhouette staring at the camera. The next few seconds of the recording were spent by him talking to his partner on the radio and in addition to the window silhouette there was now a person standing directly behind to him. As Chris moved through the room, more and more people became visible in the room, all staring directly at him, while he was completely oblivious to their presence. After that he saw himself exiting the building, while the people in the building were disappearing or more like, blending in with the darkness.

Overall, I've worked in various fucked up places, but this one seems to be the most dangerous and aggressive one, with even HQ not being able to predict some of the things. There are more stories to share, but I'll post them another time. If any of you know of anyone who has similar experiences to mine as a security guard, chances are we work for the same company.

I know a lot of you guys have been eager to see an update, but I've been too busy with work to update more frequently. I'll try to update more often. Anyway, here I am with some more stories from my company.

The first story I'm going to tell you is about a big office building our company has a contract with. I never personally worked there, but some of the guys I know did. One of the guards told me about the place in more detail. Apparently, it's a normal office building where people work a regular 9-5 job, but our guards need to be there 24-7. From around 8 am until 6 pm until all employees leave, it's pretty leisure. However the guards and the employees have one very strict rule to follow.

The building has no doors, including the one at the entrance. So at first glance, it looks really strange to see all these offices, bathrooms, etc, with naked door frames. After the employees leave, guards are to conduct patrols every hour until the end of the shift. They have to make sure all the door frames have no doors on them and should they spot an actual door anywhere on the premise, they are to make sure it isn't closed.

If the door was open or at least left slightly ajar, the guards would need to put one of those door holders on the ground, to prevent the door from closing. The guards would carry a bunch of door holders on patrols just for this purpose. If the door was closed however, they were ordered not to go near it under any circumstances.

They also had a map of the building and had to memorize where each room was, making sure that the layout of the rooms was exactly how it was on the map, including the direction the office desks and furniture were facing, etc.

Now, the guard who told me this shared his own experience with me. He said that everything was calm for the first few months and then during one of his night shift patrols, he ran into a door on the second floor which was slightly ajar. He could see an office space behind the door and following the instructions, he pulled out his door holder and went to put it in front of the door.

However as he did so, he apparently stumbled forward and actually pushed the door, which shut with a loud click. He swears he couldn't have just fallen like that, so he firmly believes something or someone somehow made him fall. When he saw that he accidentally shut the door, the guy panicked and decided to push everything under the rug by quickly opening the door, hoping no one would notice. But he says that when he opened it, that office was no longer there. He was instead looking at the bathroom.

He thought he was in the wrong place at first, because there was no way the bathroom would be there. So when he double checked, sure enough he was right. The office space he initially saw was supposed to be there. So he closed the door and opened it again. This time he was staring at the kitchen. Fascinated by the whole thing, he kept closing and opening the door over and over, seeing all the different rooms from the building.

He said he would have gone on some more, but his partner radioed him to ask him how far in he was with his sweep. The guy ended up closing and opening the door for a few more minutes until he finally saw that same office again. He placed the door holder on the floor and bolted back to the security room. He reported the appearance of the door to HQ, leaving out the details about closing and opening it.

Everything was fine that night, but the following morning he was called by his boss, who asked him what the fuck he was thinking closing the door like that. The guard was confused about how his boss knew about it. The boss told him that apparently, some of the rooms had shifted around and now the entire office building was completely jumbled up.

No one was harmed and nothing really happened other than that, save for the only inconvenience being the workers having to go from the third floor all the way to the ground floor to use the bathrooms. He continued working there, but never saw another door there again.

*

One specific story which stands out for me is from a guard who was stationed as security in a residential house between 9 pm and 4 am. The owners, a married couple lived there and they would leave the house every night at 8 pm and the guard who was appointed was told by the owners that the duties are fairly simple. HQ briefed the guard before he started working by giving him a list of rules to follow. Here's the transcript of the written rules:

Duty starts at 9 pm, however make sure to be there at least 1 hour earlier. Before leaving your home for duty, take a sharp object and leave it inside your home near the exit (for instance on the shoe stand). Any sharp object will do, however the sharper the better (preferably something that can easily puncture skin). If you can't make it at least 30 min before 9 pm to the house where you perform your duty, inform HQ and skip your shift.

Do not attempt to enter the house at or after 9 pm under any circumstances. Once inside and owners leave, follow these rules carefully:

9 pm – 10 pm: You can move freely throughout the house, with the exception of entering the basement.

10 pm – 11 pm: Stay in the living room during the entire hour. Do not leave the room under any circumstances. Do not leave the house, either. If you need to use the bathroom, use a bottle or any other means.

11 pm – 11:23 pm: You will hear someone knocking on the window. Avoid looking at it. The knocking may become relentless and loud, but do not look at it. You may turn on the TV for distraction.

11:23 pm – 00 am: The knocking will have stopped by now, but you now may hear children crying upstairs. Ignore it. No children reside in the house.

00 am - 00:25 am: You may move freely around the first floor of the house, although it is advised you stay in the living room / kitchen area and prepare for the next step.

00:25 am – 00:30 am: Below the sink in the kitchen is a bucket full of fresh meat. Take it to the basement. You do not need to enter the basement, you can simply leave the bucket near the door inside, but make sure to close and lock the door again. A very important thing to note here: make sure you do not spill or drop any blood or meat from the bucket on the floor anywhere outside the basement, since it can accurately smell blood up to a mile away. If you happen to spill any blood, do not bother cleaning. Simply follow the next step.

00:30 am – 1 am: You may hear growling noises coming from the basement, but do not bother investigating. If you have previously spilled any blood around the house, do not bother cleaning up and instead sit on the couch. Turn on the TV and turn up the volume to the max. Clasp your ears with your hands and keep your eyes firmly shut. Face the ground and stay in this position until 1 am. If there is a pause on the TV for more than a few seconds, try to produce any loud sound of your own by screaming or speaking loudly to drown out any unnatural noises you may hear.

1 am – 2 am: You may freely move throughout the entire house again (basement excluded). This is the time to use for bathroom breaks. Do not attempt to leave the house. You should also use this time to memorize the room layouts (furniture, specifically). During this hour, you may hear a voice coming from the bedroom on the second floor. If you do, investigate. If there is a man in the room, lock the door and return to the living room immediately. Do not attempt to talk to the man. If the room is empty, you may continue to move freely.

2 am – 3:33 am: Nothing major will happen during this hour. Ignore any ringing of the phone. Do not pick it up no matter how much it rings

3:33 am – 3:55 am : Now is the time to take stock of all the furniture in the house. If you see any extra furnishing, do not sit on it or touch it in any way. You will start to feel extremely sleepy by this point. Whatever you do, you must not fall asleep. It is recommended you spend this time in the kitchen and leave the sink water running, so you can splash your face whenever your eyelids become too heavy.

3:55 am – 4 am: The owners will have returned by now. Before leaving, make sure to say aloud the sentence "My duty is finished.". Not that if you do not do it, upon entering to your home, you will find that you are back in the house of the owners. Should this be the case, then you only have one option – take the sharp object you left close to the door and inflict mild damage to yourself (minor stab in the forearm or hand, etc). If the house doesn't change to your own home, repeat the previous step until it does.

He quit after just one night.

*

The last story I'll share today is about a place I was supposed to work in, but luckily said no. This was apparently a big lodge deep inside a forest and HQ had a ton of people waiting in line to work there. There were no duties there. No guarding, no paranormal rules, nothing.

So when I asked what's the catch, they said the guards can never leave the place until another one takes over. When I laughed, the chief stared at me. He went on to explain that there have been cases of people wanting to quit in the middle of their shifts, but whenever they try to, something happens which prevents them from leaving. Either a huge storm, an accident, injury, suddenly coming down with a fever severe enough to stop them from moving, etc. One guy even tried calling his friend to pick him up, but the friend ended up getting lost in the woods. Another guy tried leaving despite the thick snowstorm, but as he trekked through the snow, he ended up right back at the house. He claims there was no way he could have been back there since he only went straight, and yet there he was.

HQ has all these guards in line ready to take over, in case someone fails to show up for their shift own and the guard who was previously there is stranded. They still don't know how the lodge works or why anyone has to be there, but all they do know is that one person always has to be there. The even stranger thing – no one in HQ knows how and when they signed a contract for this place. Whoever the client is, he is sending payments to the company every month and is impossible to track down.

That's it for now. I'll update you guys again in a few days, since there's a bunch of more stories to share.

One of the guards told me that he worked in a residential building. The building itself was normal, but in the basement of the building was a big, round hole. No one knew how it got there and the residents said they just woke up to find it there one day. The old lady who discovered it almost fell inside when she went to retrieve her bicycle.

Various survey and research teams were sent to investigate the hole, but oddly enough, no equipment could determine where the bottom was. Electronics would stop working at a certain depth, throwing something inside produced no sound of impact, chemical lights got swallowed by the darkness, etc. They sent one crew member down there, but after about 10 minutes of descending, he stopped responding. They pulled him out as fast as they could, but he was gone. All that was left of him was the pile of clothes he was wearing, still attached to the safety gear and ropes.

The company was appointed to stand guard in front of the basement and not let anyone in. The guard who worked there, Andy, told me the job was pretty leisure most nights, except that he was bored. Then one night, he heard something coming from inside the basement. It sounded like someone calling his name. At first he thought it was his imagination, but the more he listened, the more he became convinced it was his sister.

Despite getting instructions from HQ not to go near the hole, mostly due to the possibility of slipping and falling, Andy opened the door. Sure enough, there it was. His sister's voice, calling him, right from the hole, clear as a day. He asked her how she got there and if she was okay and she perkily said that everything was fine. She asked Andy to come down there so they could talk. She talked in such a nonchalant way that Andy became suspicious of the whole situation.

She asked him again to come down. Andy refused, telling her that he would call help, to which his sister became increasingly agitated and angry. She demanded that he come down there and help her. Andy didn't budge and his sister said that he would let her die there, just like he let their father die. Andy froze to this and his sister uttered a single sentence which made Andy run out of there.

"Andy, life is nothing but a pile of shit." – those were his father's last words before he killed himself in front of Andy.

Andy bolted out of the building, listening to his sister calling after him and begging him to come down. Andy called HQ, telling them he was never going back. He was assigned to a different post and never had a problem again. The really weird thing about this whole experience was that no one but Andy knew what his father's last words were. He never told anyone that he watched him turn the gun on himself and just stuck to the story that he found him dead.

But the weirdest of all things was the fact that his sister had died in a tragic car accident four years before he ever saw the hole.

The basement was locked tightly afterwards and guards continued working there, but they all reported the same thing. Voices of their loved ones calling from the hole and always asking the one, same thing – to come down.

*

The intervention guy whose story I shared in one of the earlier updates told me another one recently, which chilled me to the bone. He and his unit were stationed at a long-since abandoned hotel. They'd get to do whatever they wanted in the hotel, but at exactly 4:25 am they had to assemble at the reception desk.

Their job was to sweep the entire area for any suspicious activity. The guy who told me this said HQ never told them who or what they were looking for, but they were ordered to shoot on sight upon seeing anyone besides the unit members in the hotel.

They had been sweeping the hotel four nights in a row at exactly 4:30 am until 5 am, but never found traces of anyone. And then on the fifth night, as they checked the second floor, the commander of the unit ordered them to stop and be quiet. There was a sound of muffled giggling coming from somewhere on the floor. Strangely though, as they listened, the giggling was always the same intonation and length of pause. Giggle. Five seconds pause. Giggle. Five seconds pause. He described it as an adult trying to impersonate a child's giggle.

Carefully, the unit followed the sound to one of the rooms and as they stood in front of the door, the giggling became louder and more frequent. The unit burst inside the room and pointed their guns at the source of the sound.

Facing the window was a tall person. Except it wasn't a person. Here's how the guy who told me this described the creature. A very round face, which contrasted its impossibly thin body. It had extremely long arms and legs and it was so inhumanely tall that it had to hunch over and bend its knees in order to avoid touching the ceiling. It giggled again, and it still sounded muffled, just as it did behind a closed door.

The unit stood there, with their guns pointed at this thing, as the creature giggled once more, before going silent. And then it slowly started to turn around and locked eyes with the unit. The creature apparently had a grinning, toothy, round face with large, unblinking eyes and this took the unit aback so much that they froze.

It giggled again, but this time it was deeper and more guttural, albeit still muffled. Just then the creature started running towards the unit, all the while giggling, louder and faster than ever. Everyone fired at will, practically emptying their clips into the thing. Luckily, the Giggler, as he was later dubbed by the intervention unit, never managed to reach them and fell backwards as soon as the force of the bullets connected with it. As it lay there on the ground, it apparently kept giggling some more, but the sound became slower and more quiet, until it completely stopped, leaving the creature dead, with its grinning face never changing.

The commander informed HQ about this, who told them that their mission was complete and they no longer needed to stay in the hotel. The intervention guy concluded that two of the unit members committed suicide within two months after the mission. In their farewell notes, they said they could no longer stand to listen to the giggling at night.

Recently, I was transferred to the operators' room in HQ. Essentially, I'd sit in a room with a lady who served as backup for various guards who found themselves in situations they couldn't resolve. Most of the situations were your run-of-the-mill cases, where guards had drunks trespassing or being unsure if they should investigate certain sounds, etc.

There was only one call that I witnessed which stood out for me. It was late night and we got a call from a guard who was stationed at a private farm. Whenever a call came through, I'd put on the extra pair of headset which would allow me to hear the conversation. Here's the transcript of the conversation.

Operator: This is HQ, what's your situation?

Guard: Uh, yeah. This is Mark from the Spencer farm. There's a guy standing in front of the barn. I can see him on the camera.

O: ...Alright?...

G: He's been standing there for two hours now. I first thought the camera was frozen, but when I zoomed in just now, I could see his fingers are moving. He's tapping them nervously on his thigh. And wait... his head seems to be twitching slightly.

O: Is he armed?

G: I can't see from here, he's facing away from the camera, but I don't see anything in his hands.

O: He's standing on private property, you need to warn him to leave right away.

G: Yeah. Yeah, I'll do that right away.

O: Stay on the call while you do so and tell me if you need backup.

Five minutes later, we heard the guard's voice over the call again.

G: Sir? Sir! Sir, can you hear me?

There was a moment of silence.

O: What's going on over there?

G: He isn't responding. He's just standing and twitching there. His twitching is getting more and more violent. I think something's wrong with him.

O: Get him off the property.

G: Sir? I'm going to have to ask you to-

There was a loud scream coming from the guard. The operator pressed him to respond what was wrong, but the guard kept screaming and panting on the line, followed by the sound of frantic footsteps. There was a sound of door violently shutting and shuffling, before the guard quieted down and tried to calm his breathing as much as he could.

O: Mark, I need you to talk to me. What's going on?

The guard' voice came through in a whisper.

G: Can't talk. He's right outside.

By this point I had already called the intervention unit, who said they would arrive on the scene in 10 minutes.

O: Mark, can you get somewhere safe? Backup will be there in 10 minutes, but I need you to hide. Can you do that?

G: I-I'm inside the locker. He's standing just outside the security room. Something's wrong with his face.

O: What do you mean?

G: It's all wrong. It's like, it's sideways. His head is normal and all, but the eyes, nose and mouth are all flipped sideways. I think... I think he's calling my name... Oh god, he's coming inside.

There was a sound of door slowly opening and then a set of slow and deliberate footsteps. Mark's breathing became stifled as he tried to steady it, probably clasping a hand over his mouth. And then a voice came through, a raspy voice, which sounded as if the person on the other end had something stuck in their throat:

"M-MAA-AR-K" – it said.

Mark's breathing suddenly became more violent and then he started screaming and begging for his life. The call ended and the operator and I stared at each other in disbelief.

The intervention team arrived on the scene soon. There was no trace of Mark or the man that attacked him. The camera feed showed Mark approaching the man, who then turned around to face the guard, and then Mark running back to the security room. From there the man followed Mark to the security room, taking slow, unsteady steps, twitching along the way. He opened the locker where Mark had hid himself. Then the camera feed cut out.

On the frames where the man was facing the camera, I could see his face clearly. It was exactly as Mark had described it – as if the man's face was rotated to the left by 90 degrees. A pair of eyes staring blankly sideways on top of one another and a mouth which looked like a smile, but was instead just a crooked slit. Mark was never found again.

*

My next story is going to be from another intervention unit member. He was stationed at some experimental facility and didn't wanna share any details about its location or nature of the experiment, because as he said, more than his job would be at stake. He spent about five months there with his unit and never saw any action. The regular security guards like me were taking care of the mundane problems like trespassers, etc.

However his unit regularly had drills in case of any emergency scenarios. He said the drills were not the typical military kind, but that there were some rules they needed to know, which pertained to not getting into any kind of physical contact with civilians. Their main objective in the worst case scenario was to seal off all exit points.

Sure enough, one day an alarm sounds in the facility and he and his team get ready to start their mission. As they made their way through the facility, they ran into various dead scientists and other staff members. And then they ran into a survivor. A researcher, all bloody and scared. He raised his hands and begged them not to shoot, while the unit just kept barking orders at him to keep his distance. The researcher kept saying that he's 'not infected', whatever that meant. And as he stood there, eyeing everyone, all of a sudden he snarled, showing rows of sharp teeth which were not there a second ago. And then he lunged forward, tackling one unit member and sinking his teeth into his face.

The guy told me they started shooting long before he even lunged, but it was as if the researcher didn't even react to the bullets. He was riddled with holes and bled, but just kept biting and biting, until he finally just fell over. He tried to jump again, but died a second later. The unit members emptied their clips into the now dead scientist and proceeded to leave the facility, leaving their one dead team member behind.

Once they secured the facility and locked every exit point, locking the potential survivors inside, they contacted HQ and a bunch of armored vehicles with military personnel and hazmat suits showed up. The unit was dismissed from the facility and warned not to talk about any sensitive details related to the experiment, names of staff members, etc. No matter how much I pressed him, he refused to tell me more.

*

The final story in this post which I'm going to share is from a guard named Tom, who worked in an office building. Before he got sent to work, HQ gave him a one-week training. He was strictly forbidden from talking or making any kind of vocal sounds while working in the office. Communication with his partner by talking was forbidden too, so they used hand signals.

Upon arriving on his first day, Tom saw people doing their everyday jobs at their desks, typing away, but never ever talking. They wouldn't even look at him, but would instead stare at their screens all day. Tom followed HQ's instructions and conducted his duties, not talking to anyone. But one day he brought his cell to work because he was bored.

As he made his way through the office, someone started calling him and the song which was set as his caller tone blared in the office. He quickly turned it off, but then realized something terrible.

All eyes in the office were fixed on him. The people had stopped typing and working and just stared at Tom with an expressionless face. Tom mumbled 'shit' to himself and everyone in the office unanimously said 'SHIT' in a synchronized tone.

Tom slowly made his way out and as he went through the hall, he saw through the glass the people were still staring at him. Not only them though, but everyone else in the office stared at Tom as well. He locked himself in the security room along with the partner and eventually the people returned to their normal, talkless work.

The next day Tom was fired for bringing his phone to work and potentially putting himself and his partner in danger. He said it's a good thing too, because he planned on quitting.

SPECIAL THANKS TO YOU, THE READER. YOUR SUPPORT IS WHAT MADE THIS BOOK INTO A REALITY!

Made in the USA
Middletown, DE
12 November 2019